THE SOLDIER AND THE ANGEL

JODI PAYNE

BA TORTUGA

The Solider and the Angel
Copyright © 2020 by Jodi Payne & BA Tortuga

Cover illustration by AJ Corza
http://www.seeingstatic.com/
Cover content is for illustrative purposes only and any person depicted on the cover is a model.

ISBN: 978-1-951011-32-1

Print edition published by Tygerseye Publishing, LLC, June 2020
Printed in the USA

CONTENTS

As always,
to our wives

1

Gabriel never had a bad day.

He had some weird days, days that wiped him out, days he saved a horrible person or couldn't save a good one, a day here and there that he'd like not to repeat, thankyouverymuch—but never a bad one. Nope. There wasn't any such thing as a bad day if you made it home from Afghanistan.

Today had been like a nine out of ten though, man. They'd had winners on the bus: babies on the way, kids that were more scared than hurt, a little old lady with a busted hip that said she was a princess, a homeless guy named Augustus that could recite Shakespeare backward and was going to get a bed and three squares for a night or two. He'd take more todays if he had a say.

He fought his way through the crowd at Mike's, just trying to get to the bar because, goddammit, he was going to toast this day with a beer. The biker bar was always a madhouse on Saturday nights, but as the weather got warmer even more fools came out, and tonight he wasn't sure there was enough room for him anywhere.

Fortunately, his six-foot-four frame made him easy to spot.

"Angel!" Darla shouted to get his attention.

He waved to the bartender, and she pointed at a bottle of beer crowd-surfing its way over to him. He grinned and blew her a kiss, grateful for friends who always had his back.

She waved back at him, all smiles and boobs. Lord, that woman could work her butt off.

He grabbed the beer, giving the guy who handed it over a high five, before taking a deep swig. *Oh, hoppy goodness. Hell, yes.* All he needed now were his two favorite people on earth. He pulled out his phone, texting Sammy and Tommy. One of them would answer. *Mikes or club?*

Mike's. I'm half into a grenache already. Where are you?

Into a what? He swore sometimes Tommy just said shit to confuse him. *Tell me ur not in this swarm*

Lounge

Thank fuck. Omw

He finished his beer before he stomped down the stairs and, with thick fingers, punched in the code for Mike's little private lounge. It was a sweet setup—couches and a few tables, quiet and peaceful, a place where men and women of their persuasion could chill out.

He closed the door behind him, and all the noise stopped. "Ah. Better."

"That was quick." Tommy was his usual vision all in leather, sitting in a deep chair, his boy curled against one leg. "I guess angels really can fly."

"Ha!" He laughed, the sound echoing off the ceiling tile and making him wince. *Shit. Inside voice.* "You look comfy."

Little Sammy smiled up at him, the look warm and

happy. Someone was in a fine mood—new haircut, old jeans, loose button-down that was two sizes too big. In a fine mood and had been busy too.

His fingers twitched. He wanted a hug. Sammy gave the best hugs. Then—talking about friends that always had your back—Tommy leaned over and whispered to Sammy, and the boy slowly got to his feet.

"Angel." Sammy launched into his arms, hugging him tight. He grabbed the boy by his hips, because if Sammy was moving that slow, his back was probably well-striped. He wanted to see. Tommy did the best work, and Sammy was built like a tiny brick shithouse.

How about that? An ancient princess, a beer, a hug from Sammy, and everything was right in his stupid little world. Right on. "Hey, Sammy. You feeling good?"

"So good." Sammy looked up at him, and there was zero question his friend was on cloud nine. "You need anything? Water?"

"Yeah, water would be great. You wanna show off your stripes?"

Tommy jumped in. "Only if you want to, sweetheart."

"Oh. Yeah. Only if you want to." *Please let Sammy want to. Thank you. Amen.*

Sammy blushed but nodded to him. It was still so new for Little Sammy, but he was blooming, working and happy, and making Tommy more relaxed in his own skin than Gabe had ever seen.

Sammy got him a bottle of water along with one for Tommy. Then Sam carefully removed the loose, soft shirt, turning so Gabe could see Tommy's work.

Oh, yeah. Tommy was so good with a flogger. The boy's skin was flushed red, and the lines from the flogger's falls were consistently deep and evenly laid out. It was Tommy's favorite instrument, and it totally showed. "Looks like someone was a good boy." He smiled. "Very pretty, Tommy."

Tommy gave him a nod. "My boy's inspirational, as you might imagine."

"Looking good, Sammy." Really good. He patted a spot on the boy's arm, well away from any marks.

"Thank you." Sammy returned to Tommy, leaning hard against Tommy's leather-clad legs. Tommy rested one hand on Sammy's nape, the act possessive, the "mine" clear to anyone who looked.

Tommy and Sammy met after Sammy's brother, James—Tommy's sub and lover—was murdered by a jealous bartender who worked at Tommy's BDSM club. They'd come a damn long way since that day. Sammy had seemed little more than a hotheaded cowboy then, and Tommy had always spent his time deep in the tradition and formality of the lifestyle. Apart from their shared grief over James, it seemed like the two had little in common.

Gabe would have bet money it wouldn't work out, and he was happy to be wrong. Mostly. He'd take Little Sammy off Tommy's hands in a heartbeat.

Heh. Who was he kidding? He loved them together. And he'd found a real friend in Sammy.

"Sit, craning my neck is uncomfortable." Tommy laughed and pointed to a chair nearby.

"Yeah, yeah, yeah." He plopped down and sprawled, nodding to a married couple and their boy held between them while they played a game of cards.

"So how's things? Work good?" He asked about work because it was polite and all, and work was important to Tommy, but he was always in over his head once Tommy—and Sammy too, for that matter—started talking. He tended to hear art and money and research and donor and *blahblahblah* and he tried, but after a while he'd kind of tune out.

"...reception for the photography exhibit, and I'm trying to find a list of donors that would be willing to..."

Whoa. Yeah. He'd ask about football next.

Sammy grinned at him, eyes twinkling and wicked, like he knew.

"That's about it I guess. You?"

"Same old, same old with me. It was good day today, though. Met a guy who could recite Hamlet backward." He hadn't read it since...a long-ass time ago, but it sounded like Hamlet.

Tommy laughed. "That's a talent."

"He was funny. Sick, though. Bad flu, I think." He'd had better stories as a field medic, but he liked being an EMT. He was good at it, he met tons of people, and no one was shooting at him.

"I don't know how you don't catch every bug in the city."

"Masks, gloves, don't touch your eyes." He grinned. "I did in the beginning actually, but I'm pretty sturdy. Aaron's still getting sick every other week, but he's a baby."

"You're just old." Sammy was a turd. Adorable, but a turd.

"Didn't you bring something to hit him with, Tommy? You know, nipple clamps are great for occasions like this too."

"Actually, I like it when he says that. It makes me feel younger."

Gabe snorted. "If the pair of you got any younger, you'd be in diapers."

"Hey, I'm over thirty." Tommy pretended to be offended. Or he thought that was pretending.

"Yeah, by the seat of your Pampers."

Tommy's jaw dropped, he made a little tick mark in the air, and they all started laughing. Sammy most of all.

Tommy sipped the water Sammy brought him and caught his eye. "So, have you heard about Clint's new bartender yet?"

"He already hired someone?" He was still working up to going back to the club. He would. He probably could now that things were settling down.

"It's a bar, Angel. How long did you think he'd be able to go without?" Tommy picked up the buzzing cell phone on the arm of the chair and looked at it. "Stephanie is calling me."

Nothing like a call from your mother-in-law while hanging out at Mike's.

Sam lifted his head, that frown immediate. "Answer. What if it's Daddy?"

He caught the look between them, and Tommy answered. "Hello, Steph—yes, he's right here, is everything all right?...Oh...bad?...Oh...of course, Momma, hold on." Tommy held the phone out to Sammy, looking very much like he'd gotten bad news. "Sam."

"Is it Daddy?" Sam reached up and took the phone.

Tommy shook his head no. "Talk to your mother."

After James was murdered, Sammy's dad had a stroke. But Gabe thought the man was recovering well. If it wasn't Sammy's dad, then it had to be...*shit*. Sammy's big brother, Bowie, the Ranger, was deployed overseas. *Fuck*. He leaned forward in his seat, watching Sammy closely.

"Hey, Momma. What's...oh. Oh, damn. How bad?...Okay. Germany. Right. Well, let me talk to Thomas, and I'll call you back. Love you....Yeah, yeah. I love you. Bye." Sam hung up and shook his head. "It finally happened. Bowie lost to a bomb."

Gabe sighed. Lost to a bomb. Bowie was a specialist. That could be some ugly shit. "How bad?"

Tommy slid off the chair to the floor beside Sammy. "What can we do?"

"He was lucky. He knew it was going bad. He was running. He's got some damage to his left leg. They think they can save it." Sam grabbed Thomas's hand. "He's in a hospital in Germany. How do you feel about going over to see him?"

"I'll do anything you want, sweetheart. You tell me where and when, and I'll get the tickets." The look that passed between them was so intense; Tommy just took it on for Sammy without any thought at all.

It was hard not to be envious of that. Not of them, but of that look. That kind of connection. He cleared his throat and stood up. "I'll get you guys a car, sneak you out the back. It's a zoo up there."

"Thank you, Gabe." Tommy nodded to him. "Can you water the plants? We'll text you when we know when we're leaving."

That request was not in any way, shape, or form meant to rub salt in a wound, but fuck if it didn't anyway. What was wrong with him?

"Of course, man. Whatever you guys need, you know that. Hang here, I'll text you when your car is outside."

Tommy was getting Sammy up, putting that shirt back on the boy. "I'm real sorry, Sammy. You tell him thank you for me." He gave Sammy's shoulder a squeeze.

"He'll be fine. I swear. I know he will." Sammy sighed. "I guess this means he'll be going home."

For a lifer like Bowie, that might be harder to deal with than whatever happened with the leg. "He's a tough nut. I've got faith." That was about all Gabe was going to say. In his experience, the words "bomb" and "fine" didn't cross paths that often. He headed upstairs to get some air and call an Uber.

2

Bowie sat in the barn. A year. A motherfucking year. Rehab. Wheelchairs. Surgeries. Pain. Now he was home.

Fucking go him.

He had an arm crutch he didn't use nine times out of ten, his pension, and a freedom beard that was prodigious.

"Bowie? Bowie, where are you?"

Hiding. I'm fucking hiding because y'all won't leave me alone. "I'm in the barn, Momma. I'm fine. Just relaxing."

"In the barn?"

No, I'm in the storm cellar swimming with the water moccasins. For fuck's sake. "Yep. I'm fixin' to call Sammy. See how he's doing."

Her shadow appeared at the barn door, wavering a little bit.

Go on. Please. Just go. Leave me alone. Leave me alone.

He waited, almost praying that she'd go.

"Okay...I'm fixin' to run to the Walmart. You want anything?"

"No, ma'am." *Go away!*

"Okay, honey. Love you."

She disappeared, and he grabbed his phone and dialed his baby brother. He needed a fight, and Sam was guaranteed to give it to him.

"Hey, Bowie. How goes?"

"Fine. You? You busy?"

"Nah, just answering emails."

Ah, an opening. "Lazy asshole."

"I miss you too, dipshit. Did you call for a reason?"

"I'm fixin' to hang myself from the ceiling fan, Sammy. This is hell on earth." It was humid and hot, boring and quiet. There was nothing to do, Momma and Daddy watched a shit-ton of television, and no one had anything important for him to do.

"Uh-huh. 'You gotta hold down the fort, Sammy. Momma and Daddy need you, baby boy. You have responsibilities, you're the only one left at home...' Tell me that again? I might feel sorry for you this time."

"Fuck off. You got out, didn't you? I...I can't do this, man. I can't." He looked at his leg and shook his head. "Three more feet. Three more feet was all I needed."

"Uh-huh. And those three more feet saved Sergeant Neill. You saved her."

"Go me." *Fuck.* What the fuck did it matter? He saved her. Now he was tore up and shiftless.

"Listen, I know. Thomas and I made it three days and that was plenty. You want to come up for a visit, maybe?"

The offer was like a breath of fresh air. "Please. Please, man. I hate it here. I need out. This is hell."

"Drama queen."

"Fuck you."

"Uh, no. And you can't have Thomas either."

He snorted, grinning. "Impossible. He's already got a rod up his ass."

"Come up here and say that to my face." Sammy laughed, though.

"You're serious? Tommy won't mind?" Contrary to popular belief, he liked Tommy. Hell, he liked Sammy. The kid had grown up good.

James had too. But it had only taken a single crazy motherfucker to steal James from all of them.

"I'm serious. Thomas likes you. It'll be good. We'll hang out."

"Okay. Give me a few days to get a ticket. I'll text." He already felt like he could breathe better.

"Sure, man. Break it to Momma easy, she's just worried, you know?"

"I will." He'd tell her Sammy needed him. Bad.

"See you soon, butthead."

"Love you too, man." He hung up, feeling lighter. He might not have much more to do in New York, but he'd be somewhere new. Somewhere not here.

Somewhere else.

He couldn't help himself. He needed out.

3

"Whoever thought up this medicine ball shit was a goddamn sadist." Gabe caught the heavy ball from Thomas, did a sit up, and tossed it back.

"Ninety-one, Ninety-two…"

"I mean, seriously. This is hard." Almost as hard as going to the gym after a night shift.

"Getting old is a bitch, hm?" Tommy grinned at him. "Ninety-four…"

"Shut up."

"Ninety-five…did Sam tell you Bowie's visiting?"

"No shit?" He caught the fucking ball again. "How long's he been here?"

"Just got here yesterday. He stayed with us last night. Ninety-eight. Fuck, that one hurt." Tommy huffed out a breath.

"Why the hell are we doing this shit again?" Last night, huh? Must be time to take everyone out for pizza.

"Because I'll be damned if my boy is going to have better abs than I do. All right, that's an even hundred, I'm done."

Tommy dropped the ball on the mat like it had offended him.

"Tommy, I adore you, but Sammy's got washboard abs. Like rocks."

Tommy stood up and lifted up his shirt, showing off a very respectable six-pack. Not Sammy's caliber, but totally legit. "Fifteen months I've been working on this."

He applauded, honestly impressed. He was beefy rather than strong, not cut, but he worked for his figure.

Tommy dropped his shirt and offered him a hand up. "Bowie is getting around rather well. It's impressive given there was a point when they couldn't promise he'd regain enough sensation to walk."

"Yeah? That's good. How long is he staying?" He and Bowie had shared a single, fairly wild night once, and he wouldn't be opposed to repeating it.

"Mmm." Tommy hummed and glanced at him, then opened up a water bottle and took a long drink before answering. "Nobody seems to have an answer to that question."

Oh. Staying with them indefinitely. That was what the medicine ball was about. And the extra miles on the treadmill. One night and Bowie was already cramping Tommy's style. "You ready to hit the showers? Get some breakfast, maybe?"

"Yes. That would be nice."

"How's Sammy handling having Bowie there?" If he knew Sam O'Reilly, the boy would have cleaned hysterically for the last three days.

"You know how my boy is. It's very important to him that Bowie is...comfortable. He was anxious about his brother arriving; he's anxious now that Bowie is here. I'm hoping he'll settle some once Bowie does because I certainly can't...

well. I'm not going to work with Sam with his brother in the apartment."

"No. No, I can't imagine. How used to regular scenes is Sam?"

"Certainly every weekend, but it's not unusual for a session on a weeknight. The trouble is, they're not planned. Sam is very accustomed to getting what he needs when he needs it. As am I." Tommy opened a tall locker and undressed, trading clothing for a towel.

"Damn. Damn, that's got to be stressful. Holler if there's anything I can do. I have a guest room. Not a sofa."

Tommy smiled at him. "We have a guest room now as well; we dismantled the playroom a year ago. But thank you. My guess is, Sam won't move family out." Tommy disappeared behind a shower curtain. "But I wouldn't object to you taking Bowie sightseeing or something."

Sightseeing. Oh, he could handle that. "Sure, Tommy. No problem."

He started the water, the heat pounding down on him. He was going to have to get to bed after breakfast. His late shift was getting to him.

They showered and changed, and Tommy put on a suit for work. "You think we should take Bowie to the club or to Mike's this weekend?"

"Mike's." Bowie could handle the bar, and he could keep the Ranger occupied so his friends could go get some personal time in the lounge.

"We'll plan on that, then. Would you like to meet for dinner first?"

"You know it. I love to eat."

"Good. We'll talk details in a day or two. Speaking of eating, are you ready for some breakfast?" Tommy shouldered a big gym bag and grinned at him.

"You bet. You used up all my reserves, man."

Tommy laughed and headed out into the gorgeous morning. "So, Gabe, Sam and I have been together for over a year now."

"Congrats. Are you buying rings?"

"It's not something we've ever discussed, no."

He rolled his eyes. Tommy took him completely seriously. Go figure.

"I recall we had a short conversation not long after Sam and I got serious about finding you a sub."

"Yep. We did already have that talk. Thanks."

"Gabe."

"You know, Tommy, I'm okay."

"Really? Are you a Dom?"

"What the hell is that supposed to mean?" Was he a Dom? Of course. Why was Tommy picking on him? The guy must be hangry.

"Because a Dom has a sub. A Dom doesn't go years without one. A former Dom might. Are you retired?"

"If I am, it's no one's business except for possibly a sub if I was working with one." Which he wasn't. Gabe wasn't interested in some sweet little boy. Even Sammy, who he loved beyond reason was just dear. He wasn't looking for dear, but bratty wasn't his turn-on either. "I work a lot, Tommy."

"All right. I know you work. But don't tell me it's not my business. What kind of friend would I be if I didn't ask? If I didn't want to help you find what you need? As I recall, the lifestyle wasn't just a hobby for you. Where's your outlet? It's my job as a friend to make sure you're healthy, Gabe."

His cheeks were on fire; he could feel it. "I've gotten off, man."

Mostly with his own hand, but he had a couple of fuck buddies at Mike's.

Tommy smiled at him. "Oh, Gabe. I see now. You're more in line with what Sam and I are doing. You're not separating the two. A sub and a lover I mean. You're looking for twenty-four seven. I thought you were more like Clint, I thought you could perhaps find a sub without finding a lover in them."

"Shit, I don't have time for two relationships." And, he had to be honest, he wasn't half as formal as Tommy, much less Clint.

"That I understand. Though I hate to tell you, you can have your hands full with just one person too." Tommy laughed. "Trust me on that."

"Well, I'm not going through every O'Reilly known to man." Hell, he'd only sampled the oldest one. Nibbled a little.

"Your loss. They're delicious." Tommy winked and opened the door to the little diner-style breakfast place. "I don't think Bowie is an option on the menu, though. Not for me anyway. I'd like to keep the O'Reilly I have."

"I can see that, and your current cowboy seems unlikely to share. He's a little possessive."

"I can relate." They both got a good laugh out of that one.

They got good seats for people-watching, right by the window. He loved that. The city got colorful in the summer; people turned in all the black and gray and put on colorful tank tops and shorts and stuff. Made people-watching way more interesting.

"What's Bowie doing today?"

"Honestly? I think Sam was going to get him out to the park and try to talk. Figure out where Bowie's head is."

"Ah, so they're going to walk in circles, grunt at each other, and eat ice cream." Then Sam would go home and jitter about enough to drive Tommy insane.

He thought the whole thing would be hilarious.

Tommy sighed and didn't seem to find it funny. "Yeah. I'd guess that's about right. And then I'll get home, and he'll be all wound up and worried, and the best I'll be able to do for him is give him a hug."

They ordered breakfast. Tommy asked for a garden omelet, and Gabe ordered pretty much everything else on the menu.

"Well, if I can help, holler. You know I get along with Bowie just fine."

"Thank you. I appreciate that. If Sam's wound up, he will be too."

Hell, he could handle Bowie a little wound up. Could be a good time.

"So, how are you, man? I know you like your routine." Tommy was a creature of habit. Gabe's world didn't allow for that. He was a creature of constant change. Didn't that make him grin.

Everything about Tommy relaxed. *Boom.* He could see it plain as day. "Yes. I do. I've never been so at ease, Gabe. Sam is good for me. And he's happy too. It's nice to be able to say that and know it's true with everything I am."

"Good. I'm fucking happy for you." And he could mean it, too. Jealous? Sure, but happy.

It was all good, right? He was a busy guy. He had friends at Mike's and work and at the club. People seemed to like him around. What more did he need? He was fine.

Anyway, he knew the just-right guy that fit into the tiny niche that really turned his crank would be a bitch to find. The one he had years ago left him for the same reason they'd gotten along in the first place. That was a kick in the pants, huh?

Tommy was right; sometimes the right guy was work anyway. He didn't need complicated. He just needed a TV and a beer.

4

The great thing about his baby brother was that Sam got him. They went to a movie, they sat at a coffee shop and played checkers, they went back to the apartment and watched another movie. No one had to say a word.

Bowie approved.

Hell, Sam even let him have the remote.

No one bitched about his beard, no one wanted him to have any feelings, no one bitched at him when he growled at the TV.

It had been the best day he'd had in more than a year.

"Strawberry."

Then a bowl of ice cream landed in his lap and some squeezy chocolate syrup on the coffee table, and the day got even better.

He grunted his thanks, and they started watching some weird-assed found footage movie and staring at the tube.

Oh, the ice cream was good—not some shit-assed strawberry-flavored ice milk.

"Better?" A huge spoonful of ice cream disappeared into Sam's mouth.

"Perfect. You miss Blue Bell?"

"God, yes. Tell me you ate like a thousand quarts of the blackberry cobbler." Sam grinned over. "Or the cookies and cream?"

"You know it. And? I went to Braums down in Greenville. Every fucking week."

"I hate you a little bit."

Bowie leaned into the cushions and grinned. "Excellent."

The apartment door opened, and Tommy came in, suit jacket over his arm and a briefcase in one hand. "Hello, gentlemen."

"Hey, Mister!" Sammy jumped up like someone pinched him. "How goes it?"

"Fine, boy." Tommy swept an arm around Sam's back and gave his brother the kind of kiss you don't give someone in public.

He buried his head in his ice cream. That was gross. Sam was his brother. Not kissable.

They didn't keep it short or anything. Tommy did finally let Sam breathe, but they were still way too close together. "Did you two have a good day?"

"We watched movies, ate. Good things." Sam leaned hard against Tommy, like he was soaking the man right up.

"Good. Did you make a dinner plan?" Tommy lifted some of Sam's hair with a finger and pulled on it gently. "Something other than pizza?"

"Bowie's going to make hamburger steaks, he said, but I was thinking we could go out..."

"Sure. I'm in. Let me change my clothes. It's warm out. What do you guys want to eat?" Tommy disappeared down the hall.

"You have a preference?" Sam asked, and Bowie laughed.

"I love food. All sorts. Take me somewhere y'all love." He picked up the ice cream bowls and went to wash them.

Tommy came out in khakis and a polo, and Bowie hid a grin. It was hard to believe Sam with someone that dressed like that, even if Tommy was a solid guy.

"Well, there's the Italian place. They have a nice patio in the back, we could eat outside. What do you think, sweetheart?"

"Sounds yummy. I love their lasagna. Or I did, once I finally got to try it…"

"I am never going to live that down, am I? The worst first date imaginable. You know, it was really all Bowie's fault for calling in the middle of dinner." Tommy grinned at him. "You almost tanked this relationship before it got off the ground."

"That would have been a shame." Tommy was good for Sam, damn good, and he thought Sam was pretty fucking good for Tommy.

Tommy gave him a nod. "Instead, I gained a big brother. You know, I've never had a big brother that liked me."

"No? Some people are stupid. Do we have to drink wine at supper?" He never could figure out wine.

"Yes. I absolutely require that everyone drink wine. Unless they're picking up the check." Tommy had one of the best poker faces he'd ever seen.

"Oh, fucking A. Pour my ass a beer and bring my wallet."

Tommy looked at Sam, then grinned at him and cracked the hell up. They laughed themselves into the elevator and were all still giggling when they hit the street.

"I have done well for myself with in-laws."

"O'Reillys are spectacular animals, Tommy, my man."

"You are." Tommy smiled and took Sam's hand. Brave, but sweet.

He had his arm crutch, because they'd gone some today and he was feeling his leg, so he figured that was what folks would notice.

Tommy finally let Sam go and walked behind, letting Sam hang with him on the sidewalk as they walked. He knew what that was about, that they were letting him set the pace.

He fucking hated this, but he hated the wheelchair more. He'd get stronger, and the crutch would be a cane, then nothing. *Dammit.*

"I was thinking we should go to Mike's Saturday night. What do you think? Angel said he'd meet us for dinner beforehand, I'm fairly sure he's interested in that burger place."

"Works for me. I'm always up for a burger and a beer." And Angel was...had been, damn fine to know.

"Great. Oh, hey. Angel asked how long you were staying. Do you know?"

Man, usually it took more than a day before people were ready for him to go. "I didn't get a flight out of town, but I will this evening. I'm thinking either Sunday or Monday."

He thought he'd go to San Francisco or LA. Maybe Atlanta. Somewhere new.

"I'm not rushing you, Bowie. But Angel and I talked about taking you sightseeing, and his schedule is erratic, so he wanted to make sure you two could find a day. Oh—here we are." Tommy jumped ahead of him and opened the door to the restaurant, letting out the smell of garlic and warm bread.

"Oh, that smells damn fine." Bowie inhaled deep. Nothing that smelled that good could be bad.

"I'm telling you, man. The lasagna." Sam walked in and was greeted by the hostess with a smile.

"Hey, Sam! Haven't seen you guys in a while. Table for two, right?"

"Three! My big brother is in town visiting." Sam beamed at her, reaching out to take her hands in greeting. "How are the wedding plans coming? Are you excited yet?"

Bowie chuckled softly and shook his head. "He's still a busybody, huh?"

Tommy snorted. "It's amazing. He makes friends everywhere we go. I'd been coming here for years before I met Sam, but when we walk in, it's always him they say hello to."

The hostess and Sam chatted all the way to their table, and he was handed a menu as soon as he sat down. "Wine list." She gave the board to Sam.

"Thank you, ma'am. My brother isn't a wine guy—do you have something in a blond beer or an amber?"

Bowie lifted an eyebrow. Listen to that. Adorable.

She turned bright blue eyes on him. "Will a Dos Equis work?"

"Absolutely, honey. Thanks." He eased himself around in his chair until he was settled and comfortable.

"Bowie and I were just talking about how you can talk to anyone." Tommy winked at Sam.

"Yeah. Momma always says I can talk to trees, and I like folks."

"And they like you." Bowie grinned as he socked Sam gently on the upper arm. "Weirdo."

"So, Bowie," Tommy handed the server his wineglass to fill. "What's on your agenda while you're here? Anything you really want to do, or were you just escaping your parents? They're lovely people, but I found them to be...a lot of company. And they're not even my parents."

Bowie sat there a second, thinking about how much of

the truth and how much lie to tell. "I just needed out. I haven't lived there as an adult. I'm not going back. I think I'll just wander around for a while until I can't go anymore."

Sam shot him a look, and Tommy must have caught it, because the man's whole demeanor changed. "Well, you stay with us as long as you like. There is certainly plenty to occupy you in the city."

"I know y'all don't need company. I just needed a place to start. I'm thinking about heading for California, maybe."

"I'm sure you feel at loose ends; you take your time. We'll figure it out." Tommy caught his eye and gave him a meaningful look. "We have room for family."

"Thank you, man. I do appreciate it. I need some time to breathe." He looked over at Sam. "You cool, baby boy?"

"Yeah. I'm going to have to start working during the day, but you're welcome with us."

Tommy gave him a nod. "So. Lasagna?"

"Lasagna." *Fuck, yeah.*

5

Gabriel's shower was hot. He'd turned the tap all the way up, high enough that all he could think about was the way it stung his skin as he washed the shampoo out of his hair.

Jesus, that had been a rough fucking shift. Longest twelve hours he'd had in a while. But it was done now, right? Now all he needed to do was let it go. He could do that. Hell, he'd spent the last hour obsessing over the bacon avocado cheeseburger he was going to order at dinner with Tommy and the O'Reillys until it was practically the goddamn holy grail.

He hauled himself out of the shower, trimmed his beard and brushed his teeth, then dressed in his favorite destroyed blue jeans and a threadbare gray hoodie.

He texted Sammy as he left his building. *Shift ran long. Omw*

K. Here. Having a beer and onion rings

Oh, man. Onion rings. He was fucking starved. *Save me one I could eat half the city. Order me a bacon avocado with cheddar and jalapeno, well*

On it. We'll order another round. Oh, Sammy was good to him.

You're a good man c u soon

That was what he needed. Food, friends, maybe a beer. Life was good to him.

The subway ride was quick, something else to be grateful for, and he was greeted by air conditioning as he headed into the restaurant.

Bowie spotted him right away, raising a hand up in the air to get his attention, and he grinned wide and made his way over. "Gentlemen."

"Angel!" Sammy stood, eyes lit up, and hugged him, squeezing him hard. "Good to see you. I ordered you a beer and your burger."

It did feel good, that warm greeting. He gave Sammy a quick squeeze. "Just what the doctor ordered." He let Sammy go, gave a nod to Tommy, and clasped hands with Bowie. "Good to see you, sir. You're against regulation, I see." Bowie's beard was longer than his own.

"Freedom beard. May never shave again." Bowie gave him a grin that Gabe felt down to his balls. "You're looking good, sir. You must be living good."

"Life is good." He took a seat opposite Bowie and picked up his beer. "Welcome home." Something about the beard made Bowie's eyes look completely different than he remembered. Lighter.

"I'm tickled shitless to be out and about, thanks." Bowie's lips quirked, but the expression was more self-deprecating than sarcastic.

"I bet. Pass those onion rings, man. My stomach is rattling my spine."

"You're hungry, Angel? That's unusual." Tommy picked up a glass of wine and sipped it.

He raised an eyebrow. He could volley that right back. "You're the only asshole I know that drinks wine with a fucking cheeseburger."

"I told you, Tommy, man, it's unnatural. This whole wine thing is just wrong..." Bowie raised his glass to Gabe.

"Grape juice is for children." He touched his glass to Bowie's and took a long sip and, oh, that hit the spot.

"When the goal is buzzed, does it really matter how you get there?" Sammy clinked his beer into Bowie's; then Tommy laughed and got his wineglass in there too.

This right here? This was the antidote for the roughest day in the world.

"So what did you guys get up to today? Are you seeing the city some?"

"My baby brother insisted on working all damn day, so I replaced the light fixtures in the guest room and the front room. Made myself useful."

Tommy and Sammy shared a little bit of a long-suffering glance.

"Oh, bullshit, you dick, we watched TV and had ice cream too."

Bowie winked at his brother and laughed.

"Your baby brother is writing a book, man. It's like one of those things you have to keep doing every day. Or so I hear. Though it is Saturday. What were you doing, Tommy?"

"Laundry, groceries, gym, haircut, cleaning up after Bowie's other DIY projects..." Tommy snorted.

"Busy, busy. Well, I'd have put you out of your misery, man, but I was on shift."

"I also took off work a couple three days this week, Bowie, and the new light looks amazing."

So they were still working out the schedule, huh? That was understandable, but he could do the math. It was

Saturday, and Sammy was sitting here at dinner without his stripes. "I get it, you want to keep busy. Even New York can get boring when you don't know people. I'm wide open tomorrow if you're looking for something to do." It might be nice to sleep in some, though.

"Well, I'm still trying to get around, so I haven't explored too far. If you're willing, I can hang out." Bowie looked a little desperate himself.

"I'm in." He could spend a little time with the guy; Bowie was easy company. Easy to look at too. "We'll find something to do." Taking Bowie out on his bike was probably out, though, the two of them together might flatten his tires. He grinned—that was a picture.

"Oh, this looks good." Tommy leaned back in his chair as their burgers arrived.

"Mmm. There's nothing like the smell of a good burger, hmm, Mister?" Sammy was heavy-lidded, leaning toward Tommy, and Gabe didn't see how anyone could miss the need there.

"You look hungry, boy." *Damn.* Tommy said that with a straight face. A deep voice, but a straight face.

"You're coming to Mike's, right, Bowie? I want to buy you a beer."

"Sure. I'm up for that." Bowie glanced at Tommy but then turned his attention to Gabe. "It's been a while since I've been at a bar. My last leave, I guess."

"Sometimes they forget there are other people around." He glanced over at Tommy and Sammy as well before turning to Bowie and shaking his head. "You'll like this place. It's a biker bar, but a friendly one. Gay-friendly, scene-friendly...otherwise about what you'd expect. And on a Saturday night, it's busy. On fight nights? It's packed. Fun."

"Yeah? I'm in. There's nothing like having a bar where you can just sit and drink, meet some folks."

"Damn right. Friendly folks too." His mouth was watering, so he picked up his burger and dug in, the cheese and the jalapeño hitting just the right spot. He nodded to Bowie, mouth full and grinning.

Bowie ate like a soldier—focused and quick, no hesitation. It was impressive, really. It took Bowie a matter of minutes to finish up and settle back in his chair with his beer.

He remembered doing that for a bit when he first got out, until he realized that a cheeseburger sat a lot heavier than rations in his stomach. Especially washed down with a beer. Didn't take him all that long to figure out he should go easy.

He finished second anyway. Tommy and Sammy were chatting about something he knew would be lost on him. He heard something about midcentury cowboy art and picked up his beer. Good they were getting a minute to connect, though. Sammy looked animated and happy, gesturing with one hand and holding a glass of beer with the other.

Bowie's eyes were on him; he could feel them. He looked over and held them, leaned back in his chair, man-spreading some, and took a sip of his beer.

It felt good, that heat and admiration. It felt damn good, to be honest.

"So, do you live close to the boys, man?"

He laughed. "No. Nope. I do not. That's a tax bracket I'm not familiar with. I'm downtown, East Village, Alphabet City. Bit of a different neighborhood." He wouldn't live up near Tommy's place even if he had that kind of cash. He felt more comfortable with ordinary people. Plus he needed to park his bike, and he'd found a shared garage with a couple of other guys a block away.

"Yeah? More my speed then, I'd bet. I'm just an old grunt."

"I gotta believe that's true. Takes one to know one. I'm trying to think if I've worn a suit a single day in my life. People up Tommy's way wear suits. Unless they're brainy cowboys, I guess." He grinned.

He could see Bowie downtown with a bike of his own, maybe working at one of the custom places as a mechanic or something. That would totally suit him. But probably New York wouldn't keep him interested that long.

"Yeah, well, I didn't get the brains of the family, I got the brawn."

Sam snorted and looked over. "And he's a mechanical whiz—cars, boats, bombs, lights, you name it, he can fix it or blow it up."

"Right on, baby boy."

"I don't know, Sammy's got an awful lot of brawn for a little guy."

"Call me a little guy again." Sammy gave him such a look.

He laughed and shook his head. Too bad Bowie wasn't sticking around; he knew every bike shop owner in the city and a few in Brooklyn too.

"Mm. Yes. I recall a fascinating story about blowing up a boat...?" Tommy grinned at Bowie. "I'm sure James would have been proud."

"You know it. The stuffy little fuck would have pretended to be all offended to Momma and Daddy and then come out and helped us."

He nodded. He hadn't known that part of James, but Sammy had told him stories. It was weird trying to make them fit with the schoolteacher Tommy had led around on a chain most weekends, but that was kind of part of the game, he guessed.

Tommy set an empty wineglass on the table as their server brought the check. "I got this one." No one had time to even think about arguing, not that anyone would have won anyway. Tommy liked to treat. At first Gabe had thought it was snobby, or showing off, but really it was just wanting to do something nice for friends.

"Subway or cab?" Tommy asked the table in general.

"Aw, man. I'm too full for the subway, I'm taking a cab. You want to join me, Bowie?" He'd worked his ass off today; he deserved not to have to go down into a stinky summer subway platform. Plus, that was a lot of stairs for Bowie at the end of the day. Win-win.

"Sounds perfect. Thank you for supper, Tommy. I appreciate it. I'll cook y'all steaks tomorrow." Bowie stood up, sliding his hand in the cuff. "You joining us, guys?"

"Yes. We'll ride along if you don't mind. Get us all there faster." Tommy stood as well, offering Sammy an arm. "Come along, sweetheart."

Shit, that was so fucking sweet his teeth hurt.

He got the door, Tommy caught the cab, and he rode up front with the driver all the way downtown. His neck of the woods He felt more at home already.

6

Mike's was busy, of course, but he'd texted Darla on the way to dinner and told her he'd be in with a vet that would appreciate a bar stool, so he already knew someone had been warned they'd have to give up their seat.

"You guys hitting the lounge?" Gabe asked Sammy quickly, as they went inside. Sammy was once a barback and bouncer at Mike's and always got swamped by people that missed him.

"Mister?"

"We are. We need it. You and Bowie okay?"

Gabe thought Tommy would be heading for the lounge even if he said no. They needed some time together; Sammy needed Tommy and versa vicey.

"Looks like you're stuck with me." Gabe gave Bowie a wink. "We just have to...oh. Down this way. Come on." He pushed through the crowd toward Darla, cutting a wide path and making sure Bowie stayed close until they got to two miraculously empty seats at the bar. "Hey, Darla. How's your Saturday?"

"Not too bad." She looked at Bowie and blinked. "Jesus Christ—you're like Little Sammy with good nutrition."

Bowie started laughing, the sound ringing out, just filling the air.

He grinned. That kind of laugh was good for the soul. "Bowie, this is Darla. She is everything you need in this place. Also married to the owner, so watch your Ps and Qs. Darla, this is Bowie, Little Sammy's big-ass big brother, the Army Ranger."

That was an introduction he was happy to make.

"Thank you for your service. First round's on the house." Darla held out one hand, and Bowie took it and shook.

"Thank you, ma'am. I hear y'all were the first ones to give Sammy a job."

Darla shrugged. "Well, then you heard wrong. We didn't give it to him, he fucking earned it. He wasn't taking no for an answer."

"No shit. I remember that night well." He remembered getting Sammy home after the initiation, beat to hell. That was only the second time he'd ever laid eyes on the cowboy.

"Don't look to me. I fight back." Oh, he bet Bowie did.

Darla put a hand on Bowie's, grinning. Flashing her cleavage. "If he'd fought back, he'd have lost his spot. The point was how much he could take, not how much he could dish out. But I saw him fight many times; he's no one to fuck with.' She gave Bowie's hand a pat. "Let me get you that beer.'

"Thank you, ma'am." Bowie met Gabe's eyes, gaze serious. "I would have taken them whaling on my baby brother poorly, I admit."

"Yeah. Tommy took it all very poorly after that night. He was pissed for a while. I had to listen to him complain about this place, but he always insisted that Sammy had to figure it out for himself. And I don't think he understood the level of support Sammy had here. Your brother earned a lot of respect. It's hard to explain to people that aren't...in it."

"I get it. I was in for sixteen years. I done shit most folks don't need to know. Doesn't mean that Sam isn't my baby brother."

He held Bowie's eyes for a second, then gave him a nod. Yeah. That was the truth. Every word of it.

"Don't be shy, Bowie. Give me a wave when you want another." Darla sat two beers on the bar. "You guys good?"

"Thank you." Bowie smiled at Darla and lifted his glass. "To freedom, hmm?"

"To freedom." He lifted his as well. "And beer."

"Hell, yeah." They drank deep, settling on their stools as the bar crowd moved around them like ants.

"It's good to see you again, man." He wasn't sure where he was going with that, but it was true, so he said it.

"It's good to be seen. There were a few minutes there it was up in the air."

He nodded. "Well, you O'Reillys are stubborn. You did a whole year of rehab, huh?" He'd heard a few stories from Sammy, but not many. Just that it had been a long road. Still, it was a road. He didn't like to think about the number of soldiers his team had brought in that never got one. That was a slippery slope.

"It was. Give me another six months, and no one will ever know I was hit." Bowie grinned at him, the look wicked and wonderful. "You know they said I'd never walk on it again?"

"I had heard that, yes." He'd heard it from Sammy, who'd been just as sure it was bullshit as Bowie had been ready to prove it. "Sammy told me you'd prove them wrong.

I fully expect you'll do exactly what you intend to do. Where are you going to do your therapy?"

"Don't know." Bowie leaned in toward him. "I got to tell you, I don't know shit right now. I know I can't stay with the boys, but...I can't bear the thought of going back to my folks."

That was the closest anyone he was at all interested in had gotten to him in...well, since the last time Bowie had done it. He swallowed and focused. "Nobody wants to go home to their parents at thirty...whatever you are. Five? Six? You've been out and on your own too long. I don't know if New York is your thing, but with your skills, I can help you find work here if you want it."

That didn't solve the issue of where Bowie could stay, but with a job the guy could probably put some cash away for first month and security in a couple of months.

"Thirty-four, and you get it, don't you? I've been on my own since I was eighteen. Well, been with Uncle Sam since. I can work. Shit, I've been earning danger pay for years, man. I just need to find my people."

"I get it. I enlisted at eighteen too. That was the summer of 2000." The towers fell a year later. By twenty, he was in Afghanistan. "When I got out after two tours, I didn't even know if I had people. This is as good a place to start as any." He hadn't started here, though. He'd tried to go somewhere quiet, away from noise and people where he could relax. That had been a bad idea. He didn't handle the quiet well at all. Or downtime. He was better off keeping busy.

"I wanted to retire. I had another nine years in me. I did, but...Jesus, these last few months, I've been tempted to do stupid shit. I had to get the hell out of Dodge. So where did the boys end up?"

Yeah, they had a lot in common, which wasn't so

surprising. But he accepted the change of subject, they weren't here for a therapy session. "They're downstairs. Mike has a nice lounge for Doms and their subs to hang out. Darla is Mike's. You'll meet him at some point."

"Good deal." Bowie chuckled softly. "You know, what do you say about your little brother being in the scene? Both little brothers? Shit, both little brothers with the same man?"

"You say it must run in the family." He gave Bowie a meaningful look. "I can't say I'm not enjoying that image."

"I guarantee you, my friend, Tommy is not my type." Those light eyes looked him over, bold as brass.

Jesus Christ, he liked that look. "Good. Because I wasn't referring to Tommy." He didn't even twitch.

"No?" Bowie's lips curled into a smile. "I'm not much into playing games, which I think you remember."

"I remember. Though I might know one you'll like." He tipped his beer glass up and drained it.

Bowie's laugh this time was more husky than booming. "Are you coming on to me, Angel?"

That. That right there—the laugh, that tone? He could handle some more of that right now.

"What? Fuck, no." He grinned, letting everything that husky laugh had done to him show in his eyes. "I came on to you five minutes ago, and you already accepted. I'm walking distance. Even for you."

Oh, that was a good one. That oughtta strike a nerve.

"Don't make me beat you. I'd say your place or mine, but I don't have a mine."

He pulled out his phone and texted Tommy so Sam didn't worry. *We're leaving. Bowie is with me.* He hit send and showed his phone to Bowie.

"Perfect. You ready? I don't need another beer."

"I'm ready."

Was he ready, though? A stupid little voice in the back of his head was saying things like, *That's Sammy's big brother*, and *What if he stays in New York?* It wasn't like last time. Bowie didn't have to be on a plane in the morning.

He decided to go with the voice that said, *He'll probably be leaving in a couple of days.* It wouldn't get prickly. He wasn't messing around with his best friend's family, it was just a one-night thing.

Like the one-night thing they had nearly two years ago.

A one-night thing memorable enough that it had kept him company more than a handful of nights since.

So what? Bowie wasn't looking for a thing—he was looking for a good time. The man needed out of his own fucking head, and Gabe knew how to give Bowie what he wanted.

Bowie pegged him with a sharp, quick knowing look. "Hey, man. I'm not looking for stress. I'm looking for mutual orgasms. I'll grab me a hotel room if you want. Make it easy."

Well, fuck. He grinned. "That obvious, huh? I just have this asshole voice in my head that likes to tell me shit I don't need to listen to. It's not you, it happens with everything. Work, play, even grocery shopping. I'm totally on board. Come on." Fucking voice tried to make him doubt himself constantly.

"Tell it to shut the fuck up, right?" Bowie grabbed his cap from his back pocket. "Lead on, MacDuff."

And damned be him that first cries, hold! Enough!

Ha. Worked for him.

Took him his whole first tour to read through the Complete Works. He memorized soliloquies and passages he liked from the tragedies and history plays on the second. Had to keep his brain busy.

"All right, Shakespeare." He led the way out into the downtown city air. "Oh, it's a gorgeous night. Damn. I love nights like this, warm but not stifling, you know? Feels like summer but you can still breathe." He looked at Bowie and chuckled. "But this is still comparatively cool for you, I bet."

"It feels great. When I first got CONUS, it was the humidity that liked to kill me." Bowie shot him a grin. "I do like being able to grab a beer at will, though."

"I've got lots in my fridge to grab if you want one. The humidity here in the summer is the worst. I have a little AC unit in my bedroom window, and I live in there in July and August."

"I bet y'all work your asses off in the summer, too. Lots of folks keeling over."

He turned off Avenue B and headed east toward the middle of the block. This area had changed so much in the last ten years. It was already changing when he first moved into the neighborhood, from mostly immigrants, drug addicts, and starving actors to this way more gentrified and totally bohemian artsy vibe. Avenue C was still Spanish-speakers, and a lot of folks in the know still referred to it as the Loisaida. "Yeah. Heatstroke, idiots trying to grill shit, stuff like that."

"Mmm...grilling. I do a lot of that. Setting shit on fire is sort of my jam."

"Don't get too excited. Grilling is mostly illegal in the city, Bowie. No propane or anything. You can do the charcoal thing in a few places near the water, ask Sammy. Tommy bought him a tiny Weber last summer. I don't think I've ever seen Sammy look so horrified. I think his exact words were, 'How the fuck do you expect me to grill on that?' He did, though. Decent steaks. One at a time. We all ate eventually." He got out his keys and led Bowie inside, first through the breezeway, then into the building.

"That's unnatural. You know that, right? Burning meat with fire is written in our genetic code."

"The only thing written into a New Yorker's genetic code is a healthy suspicion of everything and a need for coffee." He hauled on the elevator gate. "Gonna be a tight squeeze, you and me. Hope you're feeling friendly."

"I can be friendly." They got into the elevator, and Bowie drew him right in. The man was built like a brick shithouse, just solid and hungry for him. Bowie held his gaze, not a bit shy about what he wanted.

He managed to pull the gate shut behind him and grab the freight handle, but it wasn't easy. The elevator groaned its way up three floors, very slowly, clearly not happy with the payload. He was happy, though. Bowie was just about everything he could see, and that worked for him. He grinned as he backed off the elevator. "We made it."

"Go us." Bowie followed him, and he swore he could feel the weight of Bowie's gaze on his ass.

Yep. He was about to get himself happy. *So fucking there, twelve-hour shift from Hell.* It paid to stay positive. He opened the door and went in, holding it for Bowie. His apartment was spotless, but it wasn't much to look at with white walls and minimal furniture. He was proud of his big-ass TV, though. Great for football and porn alike.

Bowie didn't look like he gave a shit about the interior design. "I seem to remember you kiss, Gabe."

He hadn't forgotten that Bowie did too. Well.

"I do." He stared at Bowie, stepping close. "I also bite, lick, and suck, so watch yourself."

"Perfect." Bowie put the crutch to one side, then slid one

arm over Gabe's shoulder and tugged him in. They stared at each other, waiting each other out.

The last time they were together, they'd had a few shots and a couple of beers and they barely made it into Bowie's hotel room. They never had this moment. This moment was fun. He reached a hand up and tightened it at the base of Bowie's skull and let his grin fade, eyes flicking down to the soldier's lips and up again. "Come on."

Bowie kissed him like he was storming a beach. Hungry and wild, Bowie took his lips, tongue pressing in to taste him and steal his breath. He tangled his tongue with Bowie's and leaned in hard with his chest, pushing Bowie back a step and into the closed front door.

One hand wrapped around his head, holding them tight together. The other slipped around his waist, and Gabe could feel every single fingertip.

Oh, yeah. That felt good, right up to the point where he wasn't just breathless, he actually couldn't breathe. Son of a bitch, that was one of his tricks. He tried to maneuver his head a little this way and that for air but wasn't having a lot of luck. He finally got a knee between them and ground his hip into Bowie's groin.

Jesus Christ. He could sharpen his kitchen knives on that stone.

Bowie groaned, lips popping off his as he sucked in a breath. He breathed deep, too, and let himself grin. *Fuck, yeah.* He got hold of Bowie's shirt and pushed it up and off, then let it go and pulled his hoodie up and over his head.

They crashed together, skin on skin, and damned if it didn't feel right.

"Fuck, man." He leaned into Bowie, their hips rocking. They didn't even have their jeans off, and this was already a four-alarm fire. About three alarms above his usual fuck buddies.

Bowie nipped his bottom lip, one hand supporting him under his ass.

He dragged his hands over Bowie's chest. Everything about Bowie was tight and powerful: shoulders, pecs, hips, thighs....He was made to be touched, made to be explored. Someday maybe he'd have time to do it right, but not right now. Right now they were both too ready to fly.

He groaned and tugged hard on Bowie's belt, getting the buckle open.

"Lucky I didn't get my johnson blown off, huh?" Bowie found his belt too, hand stretching over his crotch.

"Yeah." He nodded and leaned into the touch, his eyes crossing with the heat. "Thank God."

Uh.

Oh. Jeans. Right. He slipped the top button of Bowie's jeans open and lowered the fly, making room for his hands to push past Bowie's waistband and around to the man's ass. He found heavy scars, but Bowie leaned back into his touch, encouraging him.

He didn't worry about the scars—he expected them, and God knew he'd seen plenty.

"God, your ass." Something else to explore more fully. For now, he was loving the feel of it, lean muscle working under his fingers. He dared to wonder if Bowie might let him have at it but dismissed that image quickly and took another kiss.

Bowie grunted and began to fuck his lips while those smart fingers found his cock and measured him, base to tip.

He sparred Bowie's tongue with his own and moaned, the pitch of the sound just right, ringing in between the high ceiling and the hardwood floor. Fuck, he wanted out of his jeans, but he wasn't ready to give up their kiss. Not yet. Bowie tasted like beer and need.

Bowie seemed perfectly happy to stroke Gabe, make him shake and luxuriate in their kiss.

Finally, his jeans feeling like a prison, he dug his fingers into Bowie's ass one last time, took a few steps back, and kicked his bootjack away from the wall. It took him no time to get his boots off; then he got out of the way so Bowie could use it, moving in the direction of his bedroom. With a curse and a groan, he shoved the offending denim to the floor.

Bowie followed him, moving just a little carefully, holding his jeans up with one hand.

He watched Bowie, stopped and waited, and as soon the man got close enough, he smiled. "You can let those go." He made sure he had Bowie's eyes, admired them. "I don't give a shit about your leg, I'm just glad you've got one. I'm interested in this." He slid his fingers under Bowie's briefs and scraped his palm down that hard prick until he found Bowie's balls.

Bowie grabbed hold of Gabe's arm, balanced himself, and stepped out of his jeans. "I was more worried about going ass over teakettle. I earned my scars."

"Good. I agree." He must have been drunker than he thought that first time, because he didn't remember Bowie being this hung. Or smelling so good.

Bowie nodded and encouraged him to move toward the bed. "Come on, stud. I need to sit and explore."

Mmm. That sounded good. He moved quickly to a small lamp on his nightstand and turned it on, the red bandana he'd thrown over it muting the white light. The huge tapestry hanging over the bed made the ceiling feel lower in here, made the room feel smaller than it was, and he liked it that way. "Sit. Sprawl. Whatever you like."

Bowie sat gingerly, then drew Gabe in, hands dragging up along his thighs. He looked down, pushing both hands into a curly mass of dark hair, and combed it back so he could watch Bowie's face, watch those hands move over him. So clever and quick—he'd never been touched quite so curiously, like he was being memorized.

He had his share of scars, though most of them weren't combat related. He had one, though, and he watched Bowie circle a finger around it on his right thigh, where he'd taken a bullet through the open door of the medevac chopper. He snorted. "The big red cross wasn't a deterrent that day."

"Scars are hot." And that didn't sound like bullshit, coming from Bowie.

"If that's your thing, someday I'll tell you about the spectacular wipeout that destroyed my first Harley." He had scars from ankle to shoulder on the left. Fun times. He ran a hand over Bowie's shoulder, letting all that hair fall back in place.

"We'll compare over beers one day." Bowie lifted his chin, dragging his beard over the tip of Gabe's cock.

He raised one foot, braced it on the end of the bed next to Bowie's thigh, and leaned in, his knee bending up by the man's shoulder, leaving no question what he wanted.

"I remember this. Fondly." And with that, Bowie swallowed him down, blazing heat surrounding him in a rush.

He gasped and everything tensed—his ass, his balls, his thighs. For a few horrifying moments he thought maybe he'd been too close, but really, it just felt that fucking good. "Yes. Fuck." He curled his fingers into Bowie's hair and let his head roll on his shoulders.

Bowie cupped his ass, helping him balance, keeping his hips moving, driving into his lips.

Hell, yeah. That was a sweet invitation. Bowie's mouth was the perfect mix of give and resistance and he groaned with it, tightening his grip in those thick curls and tugging, trusting Bowie would let him know when to back off. There was no hesitation, Bowie's rough groan echoed around his shaft. Gabe was going to have bruises on his ass, his hips, and he was ready to feel every single one.

He looked down and watched Bowie take him, the soldier looking hungry as fuck, cheeks going hollow under that beard. "Christ," he swore as his thighs started to tremble and the blood rushed in his ears, everything narrowing to that sight and a burning need at the base of his spine.

Bowie growled, the sound vibrating around his cock, the sensation making it all too much, too good, too big.

"Bowie!" He ground the name out through gritted teeth and from behind the fog he knew his hips were doing crazy shit, bucking and humping. His climax slammed into him, like someone had punched him between the shoulder blades, and he gasped and groaned, spurting hot seed onto Bowie's tongue.

Bowie lapped and licked, slapping his now-sensitive cock, trying to drive him out of his fucking mind. He let himself twitch and shiver until he couldn't take another second before shoving the man off, using his weight to push Bowie's shoulders into the mattress.

"So goddamn good." He lowered himself down and kissed Bowie deeply, pinning the man with one hip and giving Bowie something to work for.

Bowie's cock burned against his skin, long and thick and

diamond-hard. Bowie rocked steadily—keeping himself revved up rather than racing for the end.

Knowing the Ranger wanted to ride that wave for a while, it was good to have the edge off. He'd catch his breath and build up slow while he tried to drive Bowie quietly insane. He grinned and looked into those hazel eyes, lighter than either Sammy's or James's, then winked and went after a nipple with his tongue, flicking and swirling it.

"Oh, damn. That's good." Bowie grinned at him, winked, and stretched tall, pressing into his lips.

"Mmm." He moved to the other, just teasing and tasting, and dragging his fingers heavily along the outline of Bowie's muscles. Thick and strong—these weren't the gym muscles of Little Sammy, this was years of PT, years of hard work, massive strength.

And it was hot as hell. Hotter.

He explored lower, tasting skin, nipping at muscle, mapping out the ridges with his tongue. Jesus, this was such a gift today, this hard body and harder cock. He hadn't wanted anything as much in ages.

He found a ticklish spot, surprising a laugh from Bowie, those muscles jerking and drawing up tight.

"Oh, look at that." He chuckled. "Just when I thought these abs couldn't get any prettier. Damn." He did it again, just to watch.

This time, Bowie rolled up, shoulders leaving the mattress and curling up. "Tickles." The low growl made his eyes cross.

"Y'think?" Big, bad, Army Ranger was ticklish. How wonderful was that? He let it be for now so he didn't pull Bowie out of the moment, but that spot would be remembered. He could search for more.

But first he went after a nipple again, pinching the tight

bud between his teeth. Bowie sucked in a sharp breath, eyes rolling up. *Nice.*

Time for a little of that crazy. He started tasting again, down past Bowie's navel and lower, over one seriously cut hip. He let his hand drag over Bowie's hip and thigh, sliding over the scars as he nibbled and licked. The bumps and ridges fascinated him.

He kept exploring those scars; every bit of rough skin, raised muscle and angular hollow told a story that he wanted to understand. He encouraged Bowie to bend his other leg up, lips tasting the inside of that muscular thigh.

"Sweet fuck, Gabe. That's sweet."

"Yeah? You're a fan, huh?" He scraped his teeth along a meaty section of thigh and followed with a soothing tongue.

He got a grunt, followed by a long, low moan. Oh, that was tasty, so he did it again. With a heavy sigh, Bowie's leg fell open wider and the quiet offering sent electricity straight into his balls. He nibbled farther up that powerful thigh, Bowie's musky scent drawing him in.

Bowie was surprisingly loud for a man who he assumed had to have been incredibly quiet during sex his entire life. He loved it. Raise the goddamn roof.

He palmed that gorgeous cock, lifting it out of the way, and dragged his tongue over Bowie's balls. He went slow and deliberate on the first couple of passes, but soon started to lick and suck, over, under, anywhere his tongue could reach.

"Gabe." Bowie reached out, fingers dancing over his head. "Losing my fucking mind, man."

Oh, wasn't that a lovely idea?

"I'm not sorry." He tightened his fist and pumped Bowie's cock a few times, driving a thumb through the slit, spreading fluid over the head.

Bowie's eyes went so wide they pulled at the corners. "Fuck. Do that again."

He did, scrubbing his tongue along the base for good measure and listening to the deep, musical groans. Gabe teased his way up Bowie's shaft, circled the dark head with his tongue, then drew that heavy cock in, letting it slide right into his throat. Bowie fisted his hands into the sheets, a tremor buzzing through the big body.

It could have been an earthquake. It vibrated through him, setting his skin on fire. *Fuck, yeah.* He closed his eyes and went to work, head bobbing and tongue scrubbing.

"Close." The single word was bitten out, the sound wild.

Bring it.

He slipped his fingers under Bowie's balls and massaged the sensitive skin there, letting them slide farther back and over Bowie's hole. Bowie arched, cried out, and shot, cock throbbing as he came.

Bitter and salt and musk filled Gabe's senses, waking his cock and he swallowed blindly, taking everything Bowie had and asking for more. He moaned around Bowie's prick and pulled up for a deep breath.

Bowie stared down at him, dazed, melted, his expression pure bliss. He admired the look, highlighted by the sweat on Bowie's forehead, and couldn't remember the last time he felt this satisfied.

He stalked up Bowie's body and took a kiss, tangling his fingers in a sea of dark curls. Bowie held him close, one hand heavy on his hip, keeping them so close that air couldn't pass between them.

"Well...damn." He grinned, but he caught himself searching Bowie's eyes, finding them more comforting than he probably should.

"Damn is about right." Bowie patted his ass, the touch hard enough not to tickle.

He snorted and rolled, landing on his back and stretched out. "That was worth the...what, eighteen-month wait?"

"Mmhmm. We got three orgasms out of the last one. So, we each have two left."

"I'm almost ready for number two." He laughed and shifted his hips. "And I'm off tomorrow, so we could even break our record." Maybe. If they laid off the beer. "And order pizza."

"I love pizza." Bowie reached over, cupped one hand over his cock, massaging just enough to make his mouth dry.

"Mmm. That's just perfect." He rested a hand on Bowie's forearm, stroking his fingers from wrist to elbow. "How about a shower?"

"You. Me. Water. Soap. I'm in."

Mmm. The only thing better than all that muscle, was all that muscle wet, slippery, and covered in soap.

7

Eggs. Eggs and bacon and...
Hrm.

Bowie dug through Gabe's fridge, looking for tortillas, jalapeños, tomatoes. The things for breakfast tacos. Or migas. Something.

Gabe didn't hardly have a stick of furniture, but the man had a well-stocked fridge. He found everything he was looking for, plus a big onion and a package of stoplight peppers too. No bacon but there were a handful of breakfast sausages wrapped in butcher paper that would work.

Cheese, tortilla chips, and a jar of salsa. Migas it was.

He called up some old-school rock on his phone, turned it low, and started chopping, letting the rhythm and ease of playing in someone's kitchen work on him. Maybe he could get a place. Have a kitchen of his own. He'd never done that —never filled up his own fridge with steaks and cheese and salsa. Huh.

He figured out Gabe's fancy coffeemaker and was elbow deep in things sizzling on the stove when Gabe shuffled out of the bedroom in a pair of sweats that were so threadbare and rode so low, they were almost pointless. "I just had the best dream. There was this ridiculously hot man in my kitchen, making me breakfast." Gabe flashed him a grin and headed for the coffeemaker.

"Weird, it's almost like it could come true." He handed Gabe his coffee cup. "Fill me up?"

"On it." Gabe brushed a couple of fingers over the back of his hand and took the cup. "Good morning."

"It is. Very." In fact, he was as happy as the proverbial pig in shit.

Gabe didn't smile *at* him exactly, but he caught a glimpse of it anyway, and the lift in the man's shoulders too. "Yep. I even slept some. Black?" Gabe set his coffee down next to the stove.

"Yessir. Please." He stirred the veg and meat, then added salsa.

"That smells fantastic, and I absolutely could eat." Gabe leaned against the counter and he felt the way those eyes were eating him up. "You're a good time, man."

"You aren't three-quarters bad yourself." He shot Gabe a wink. "Thanks for letting me bunk with you last night. How do you take your eggs?"

"Well done, please. Any style is fine, I'm—"

Bowie's phone started ringing. Gabe stopped talking, stretched out, and dragged it over from where he'd left it on the counter. It was Sammy. He swiped and hit Speaker.

"Yo, baby boy."

"Hey. You...you okay?"

"Yep."

"Did you crash with Angel?" Gabe didn't say a word, just grinned, crossed his arms, and sipped his coffee.

Bowie grinned back, waggled his eyebrows. "Yep."

Crashed. Sucked. Stroked. Licked. Orgasmed. All the good things.

"Okay. I was just...what are your plans today? Are you and Angel uh...hanging out then?"

He looked over to Gabe. Were they? "We haven't talked it out. Do you need me?"

"N-no." There was a soft sound, almost a hiccup. Oh, someone was being utterly inappropriate for a phone call to his brother.

Gabe nearly doubled over, trying not to laugh out loud. The man got it together after a second, though, and put a finger up in the air as if to say, "I got this."

"If you two are busy, I can take him off your hands today. I'm sure we can find something to do. What do you think, Bowie? Cribbage? Croquet, maybe?" Gabe was just beaming at him, grin full of teeth.

"Oh, Tiddlywinks. Hours of that and naked mayonnaise Twister," Tommy's voice was dry as dust. "Call before you head back. Please. Bye."

The phone went dead, and they both stared at each other for a second before they cracked up.

"I don't think I've ever played Tiddlywinks, do you...do you know the rules?" For a big guy, Gabe had quite a giggle.

"It's like Quarters, honey. I bet you're damn good at it."

"Oh. Well, in that case, I'm all over that." Gabe took a breath, eyes still twinkling. "I guess you're mine for the day then. Whatever am I going to do with you?"

"First, you're going to let me feed you." He crumbled the tortilla chips into the migas and started scrambling eggs. "Then we each have one orgasm to catch up to the last time. Plates?"

Gabe nodded, reaching into a cabinet and pulling out

dishes. "Works for me. I usually eat at the coffee table. I should really get a table in here I guess, but I never have guests that... uh, that stay long enough to need to sit anywhere."

"Shit, I can sit on the dirt." He couldn't get up off the floor, but he could eat while he was down there.

"Well, you won't find dirt; I'm a little neurotic about that. If my couch eats you though, I promise to think about helping you up." Gabe held the plates out so he could serve.

"Rock on. Migas for two. I shredded cheese if you want some." It looked pretty fucking good, if he said so himself.

"I'd love some." Gabe moved around behind him to get to the cheese, dragging one finger along his waistband.

He hummed and leaned, letting the little zing work for him, make his toes curl. He didn't know if he'd ever get used to that as long as he lived—casual touches. Maybe he didn't want to get used to it. He liked the buzz.

"This looks so good. My stomach is growling." Gabe pulled out forks and handed him one, then headed for the couch. "Remote is on the table there if you feel like surfing."

"You can tell a shit-ton about a man by his remote." He didn't know if he was ready to let Gabe know he was a Jurassic Park addict and completely into the Food Network.

Gabe laughed and winked at him, playing. "Why do you think I asked you to go first?"

"Fair enough. I'll get to see what it opens up to." He let one corner of his lip curl up. "I bet you're totally into the Hallmark Channel."

"Yeah, no." Gabe snorted and took a bite of his breakfast. "Oh. Mmm. Oh, man. So good."

He grinned. The sounds Gabe was making weren't that far off from the ones he'd heard last night. He turned on the TV, noting that those sounds weren't far off either. Gabe grinned at him, not looking embarrassed at all. "Not Hawrmahk," Gabe said with his mouth full.

Bowie chuckled and took a bite himself. Oh. Not bad. He'd do better with jalapeño, but this didn't suck at all.

He looked at the guy on his knees, sucking two dicks like he was fixin' to die if he didn't. "You ever wonder if their calves cramp?"

"Right? I don't think my knees could take that either. But I'm creaky, so what do I know. Wanna see what's on the Food Network?"

"Sure. It's Sunday, so they'll have one of their shows on a marathon."

"So, you're a good cook. I'm impressed. James was a good cook. But Sammy? He lived with your parents too long I think." Gabe took another bite of the migas, clearly enjoying it.

"I think Momma was going to keep him home by making sure he couldn't manage. I like it." One of the secrets to Army life was to have something to offer the married guys so there was a place to couch surf on the weekends when he could.

Gabe shrugged. "I like it too. I work a bunch of long shifts, then have long stretches off. I like to make sure the fridge is stocked, so I have something to keep me busy. Something other than sitting in a bar. I mean, I do my fair share of that too, but at least I've eaten well first. I gotta keep busy."

"I hear you. Idle hands and all." Bowie chuckled at himself. Lord, he sounded like his daddy.

"Yeah. Idle hands, idle mind...not sure which is worse. So tell me about your mechanic work. Was that all in the service? Did you ever do hobby stuff?"

"It's all hobby stuff. I built bombs for work." Bowie

chuckled. *How to Fuck Your World in 30 Seconds or Less: The Handbook.* "I restored a ton of shit with the guys on post—motorcycles, cars, lawn mowers. Hell, we even restored a plane."

"No shit? That's awesome." Gabe smiled at him. "I gotta take you to see some friends of mine. They do bike restoration and custom stuff. You'll love their place. You got any pictures in your phone?" Gabe put an empty plate down on the coffee table and moved closer on the couch.

"Sure." He grabbed his phone and found the images from before the bomb went off, back in Bragg. There had been a little group of guys that had fucked off on the weekends—repairing shit up and donating it to wounded vets.

He showed one picture after another of grunts and vehicles and him, all clean-shaved with his high and tight. Lord. He'd looked young then.

"Good-looking bunch. Look how adorable you are." Gabe laughed and looked at him. "Man, you need to tidy up a little. Look less like a guy that doesn't know what to do with himself." He got a wink and a knowing smile. "I have a great barber."

Gabe's beard was short with white at the chin and kind of deliberately scraggly; you could tell the man had it looked after, but it wasn't obviously shaped.

"Like you got room to talk, stud." He reached out and tugged, just enough to make Gabe feel it.

Gabe swatted at his hand. "Yeah, okay. I'm overdue. That kid is cute, though. Do you remember being that young?"

"Not even a little bit. I mean, I was, I guess, but I sure don't remember." He found a picture of the bunch of them, shirtless and sweating. "I'm on the right."

Gabe took his phone to get a closer look. "Oh, man. I'd've been drooling over you. I could totally tap that."

"That was a few years ago." He was bigger now, especially across the shoulders. All that rehab and getting in and out of the chair.

"Yeah, you're better now. You've lived. I'd still like to tap that." Gabe gave him a grin, then pulled a goofy face. "Maybe I should have kept that last thought to myself."

"Why? Feels good to be wanted. We'll see how it works, if you can take what you want." He chuckled at himself. That was highly unlikely, but the challenge would be fun as fuck.

One of Gabe's eyebrows climbed into that scraggly hairline. "Don't tempt me with a good time."

"What? I'm supposed to tempt you with a shitty time?" That seemed stupid.

Gabe snorted. "It's an expression, dimwit. What I really mean, Bowie, is you're asking for it."

"Dimwit? I will beat you, man." The threat was lazy, but there was a little explosive buzz in the air that promised to be something...interesting.

"You can try." Gabe scooped up their plates and headed for the kitchen. "I realize I'm not quite the lunkhead you are, but I wouldn't get your hopes up too high."

"Well, you manage okay, I'll give you that, but..." He watched Gabe walk, the tight, firm ass like a beacon. "My muscles were made on the sand, not in the gym."

Gabe glanced up at him, then started doing dishes. "It's not all about brawn, Shakespeare. Oh. You blew that quote, by the way. I didn't want to point it out at the time in front of other people and embarrass you, but it's actually 'Lay on, MacDuff,' which is also far more appropriate at the moment."

He snorted and levered himself up to go help. "Like I've ever read a book. I'm not the brainy one."

It wasn't exactly true. He read a lot of novels, especially the serial killer ones, but it was the point of it. He wore big and dumb easily. It served him well and kept people off-balance while he set a bomb in their toilet paper roll.

"You need help getting up?" Gabe glanced at him again, this time with a fucking evil little grin that meant it was a joke, but also meant to get at him.

"Honey, I told you, my cock is whole and hard." He grabbed his crotch, fighting his laughter with all he had.

Gabe's head dropped with a sigh and a chuckle. "Should have known better than to try to get a bomb expert riled up; you're too fucking laid-back."

"Yeah. Your life depends on it. Steady hands, steady eyes, steady heart." If they told themselves that enough, it worked.

He started putting food away, wrapping things up. He liked how Gabe organized his kitchen; he liked it a lot.

Gabe grabbed a dish towel and dried the pan he'd used. "No worries, medics don't give up until we know there's no hope. I think there's still life in this one." The skillet landed on the stove and Gabe stepped closer, crowding him. "Maybe it just needs mouth-to-mouth."

"Nicely done." Point to Gabe. He grabbed Gabe's hip, stepping right in. "Come revive me."

Gabe's eyes narrowed, and both hands quickly reached out and grabbed his head, pulling him into a hard kiss, a hot tongue pushing past his lips. His entire body flared to life, the excitement a jolt of electricity slamming down his spine. Hell, yes.

Their chests bumped together, Gabe moving in on him, leaning in heavily until he had to retreat one step, then another to keep his balance. He had to grab for Gabe to keep upright, and it suited him to the ground, the way Gabe held him, no question.

His hips hit the kitchen island, and while he was still off-balance, Gabe managed to spin him. Heavy hands slid up his spine from hips to shoulders, followed by a hungry mouth.

"Fuck!" He'd never thought of his back as an erogenous zone. Never. He would now.

Gabe's low chuckle was punctuated by a hard prick pressing into one ass cheek. Fingers moved over his skin, working into muscle in some places and lightly gliding in others the attention not letting up for a second.

Come on, Bowie. Focus. The temptation to stand there and feel for a minute was vast. Gabe's fingers were magical, constantly in motion.

Teeth nipped at his shoulder blade. One hand snaked around and ducked under his waistband. He felt those teeth again, only higher this time, up on his shoulder, making their way across until he felt hot breath on his neck and heard a rumble in Gabe's chest.

He curled his fingers around Gabe's, dragging their fingertips over his lower belly, his cock. Gabe didn't hesitate, cradling his cock in a warm palm, thumb swirling over the head. The teeth that had been teasing him started to grip instead, clamping down harder and harder on the thick muscle where his shoulder met his neck.

Bowie's eyes went wide, his whole world that bite, those teeth. He sucked in a deep, deep breath, his chest swelling with his prick. Gabe grunted around the bite and leaned into him, doubling him over the counter, hips rocking.

He tried to straighten up, but he didn't have the leverage, not with his hand caught with Gabe's around his cock.

Neither of them spoke; the kitchen was filled with grunts and moans.

Heat rushed to the spot when Gabe released his shoulder, making it throb, making him take notice of it all over again. Gabe kept their fingers tangled and stroked him with one hand and the other landed on the back of his neck, gently, but firmly holding him down.

"Muscle made on the sand, hm? Sand can so easily give way under your feet." Gabe's voice was rough and dark.

"Fucker." He rolled, testing Gabe's will and his own as their hands worked to make his hips buck.

Gabe put weight behind the hand on his neck and leaned against his ass. "Fuck, that's beautiful. Try again."

Bowie braced himself on his free hand, body working to lift from the island, steady and slow, his muscles fighting hard.

Gabe groaned. "Oh, that is something to see, Bowie. God." He felt the pressure on his neck, the weight pinning his hips ease up slow. "Okay, Bowie. I'm done. Relax." Gabe released him completely and stepped away, giving him room to move.

Bowie stood, schooling his face into something not totally wrecked and goofy, then turned and met Gabe's eyes. He was hard as a rock—nipples, abs, cock—and there was no hiding that, so he showed it off.

Gabe was in a similar state and looked him over, hunger and heat apparent in those dark eyes. They were both moving slowly, closing the gap between them until their lips met again, tongues and teeth clashing. They rubbed together, and when Bowie found the place where their pricks slid, side-by-side, they both moaned, the sound damn near raw.

"Fuck. Want...God." Gabe huffed out a breath and grabbed his hips. "More."

"More." Fuck, yes. He was all about that. He slammed their lips into one another, as he drove them together, humping against Gabe like a naughty puppy.

Gabe groaned into the kiss, rough and open-mouthed, the sound pure need. Fingers dug into his hips as Gabe struggled to meet his thrusts and keep upright at the same time.

"Jesus. Gabe. Horizontal." They could have so much more fun without the imminent crash issue.

"Yeah. Yeah, come on." Gabe steadied him and led the way back to the bed they'd already destroyed last night. Gabe shucked his sweats and climbed up onto the bed, holding a hand out toward him. "Naked first. Come on."

"Fuck, yeah." He stripped in a flash and went to Gabe, crawling up along those heavy muscles. Fuck, miles and miles of playground to explore.

Gabe met his eyes and held them for a long moment, grinning at him. "You set me on fire, Bowie, I swear."

"There's no bad there. You got me riled." He leaned in and captured Gabe's lips. Gabe moaned, pushing a hand between them and running it over his abs before moving lower to grip his shaft and give him a tug. Bowie arched, then curled and got them both in his hand.

"Yeah." Gabe got out of his way, fingers sliding over his hip and digging in. His teeth sank into his own bottom lip and he started stroking, making sure to work the tip with every upstroke, squeeze their bases on the way down.

Gabe pressed their foreheads together. They were so close, he could feel every breath, hear every single sound. Close enough to hear Gabe whisper, "Harder."

He groaned softly, but he tightened his grip, dragging his

thumb along the shaft good and firm. He was rewarded for his effort with a long groan, and Gabe bent a knee up, hooking it over his hip.

"Jesus." Bowie blinked up at him, lips parting. It fascinated him, the way that he was jacking himself and Gabe was touching him and they were buzzing.

"You..." Gabe reached down and wrapped long fingers around his, helping, adding pressure and drag, and took his lips and his breath with a kiss.

Whatever sound he made was trapped between them, stuck in their lips. Fuck him, this was everything.

Gabe kissed him until their hips were rocking together and they both needed air, then broke it off with a gasp. "Fucking close. You? Together, huh? Let's try."

The best he had was a nod and a grunt. Bowie was all over that. Just give the word.

"God, listen to you." Gabe kissed him again. "Now, Bowie. Fuck! Now."

Like it was drawn from him, Bowie let go, emptying his balls in a wild rush. He could feel Gabe shudder, feel the man's harsh breath on his neck as the scent of them washed over him. Gabe's hips bucked and that leg curled around to his ass, pulling them even closer.

He sank down, his eyelids getting heavy—that was some damn fine exercise right there.

Gabe sighed and curled fingers behind his head, pulling him into a slow, lazy kiss, smiling against his lips. "Third time's the charm."

"We got to wait another year and a half to go again?"

"Hell, no." Gabe laughed, eyes lighting up. "Maybe an hour and a half, though. I'm old."

"Oh now, for an old bear, you do just fine." Just fine indeed.

"Be nice or I'll hold you down by the neck again." Gabe's tone was teasing, but his eyes weren't. At all.

His prick jerked weakly, the little jolt of arousal fine as fuck. "You can totally try, Bear. Bring it on."

"Mm. Later. Now? Nap." Gabe kissed him again, eyes closing. "Yeah. Nap."

He was all over that shit. He made sure his leg was in a good spot, and that was all she wrote.

8

Gabe grabbed his sushi off the counter and flopped on the couch with it, turning on the TV. Day two of three twelves and he was feeling it. He'd never complain; it was nothing like the twenty-four seven on a fourteen-day shift in the service. If he could do that, he could do another twelve and shut up about it.

But really, he'd just like to sleep. And he would. Soon.

The twelve hours off were a whole other problem. He knew what was going on—he remembered this feeling from the first time with Bowie. The man was just hard to put away.

He tuned to the history channel, let it drone on at him for a while, then switched over to some cupcake show on Food Network that was more colorful and more entertaining.

His phone buzzed, and he stared at it. Huh. Little Sammy.

Is it tacky to threaten to kill my brother?

Then immediately, a text from Bowie.

Want a beer?

He laughed. Oh, this was good. He put his food down and started texting. Didn't matter which one was first, they each got, *Yes.*

And then, before things could get really out of hand, he texted Tommy.

I'm on it.

Oh, thank God. He's talking about buying lumber for bookshelves in the guest room. You truly are an angel.

Jesus

He needs something to do other than drive my boy insane. It's going to take me hours to get Sam loose enough to even think about breaking him down.

Then from Sam, there came, *He's so bored and I need...*

When? Where? Bowie was way more direct. He dealt with that first.

Mike's. Half an hour So much for sleep. *Eh.* His friends needed him. That was more important.

He'll be leaving in two minutes. I'll get him drunk and send him home tomorrow. Take care of Sammy, tell him I got this.

I owe you

I'll collect

Gabe grinned. He liked the idea of Tommy owing him a favor. Another one.

On my way

He couldn't stop grinning. Stupid, but true. He wanted to play with Bowie again, wanted to push again. Hell, he wanted to sit with the son of a bitch on the sofa and yell at Bobby Flay.

He cleaned up, brushed his teeth, and was out the door in a hurry so he could get to Mike's first. He wanted to be the guy at the bar waiting on someone. It had been a long time since he'd been that guy.

There was a reason for that, he reminded himself as he

walked out into the warm summer night. This was fun for now, but he wasn't in the market anymore.

Mike's was slow, enough people in there to have a low buzz, but quiet enough he could watch the door easily. When Bowie walked in, hair tied back, tight black T-shirt, worn jeans—those pale eyes found him immediately, and Gabe swore they lit up. Bowie crutched over to him like he was the only person in the room. "Hey."

"Hey." *You look fantastic. I think I missed you.* "Have a seat."

"Thanks." Bowie smiled and nodded to him. "Good to see you."

"Good to see you too. Last-minute. What the fuck is going on in that apartment?"

"I've been fixing some of the shit the guys have been too busy to do. You know—lights, put a new shower head in, painted the guest room. They need built-ins in there."

"Yeah?" *Oh, boy.*

Darla appeared and set a beer in front of Bowie. "Nice to see you again. You're on Angel's tab." She smiled at Bowie but winked at him.

"We'll settle up. Thank you, ma'am." Bowie sighed and turned to him. "And no, not really. I'm fucking bored, man. Seriously. I need to get a job, get out of their apartment. Sammy is starting to get all weird."

Okay, well, that saved him having to tell Bowie to back off. He looked at Bowie meaningfully. "If Sammy wasn't your brother, would you say he was 'getting weird'? Or would you maybe say he needed his ass spanked?"

"You and I both know the answer to that. I can be all Zen and shit, but he's my brother. I don't want to see it." Bowie took a deep swig. "More? I don't want to hear it. That's fucked up, you know?"

"Yeah, it's totally fucked up." He took a swig too, then squinted at the row of bottles behind the bar. "Are you thinking about staying in the city, then? Or is the plan still LA or whatever?"

"There's nothing for me on the West Coast. I'm running out of time with Tommy and Sam, though. So I have to figure shit out." Bowie met his eyes, head-on. "I'm not interested in looking in Sam's neighborhood. This here? Way more my speed."

Goddammit. Those fucking green eyes. The simplest answer was really the most complicated one, but fuck him if he wasn't about to offer anyway. "I have that extra room."

"You looking to rent it out?" Bowie never so much as blinked.

"I could, or if you'd rather, you could just crash at my place until you get settled, get a job and...find your own place." *Jesus.* Nothing said "insecure idiot" better than being passive-aggressive. He took a long sip of his beer.

Bowie did look away then, and there was a definite blush. "Sorry, man. I jumped to conclusions. How was work? You save a bunch of folks?"

"I didn't save anyone, but I'm going to see if I can save this." He snorted. "I did warn you about the little voice in my head, right? Move in. We'll...figure it out from there."

"You ought to kill that little voice, Bear. He sounds like a fucker."

He nodded slowly. "Yeah. I should." He sighed and sat back on his stool, crossing his arms over his chest. He knew what it would take. "I'm coming off two twelves; I have to be on duty at eight a.m. for the third. Today was about a seven. No one died on the bus."

"A seven is better than a five, I reckon." Bowie lifted his

glass. "Thank you for coming to have a beer with me, man. You got to be tired. I appreciate it."

"Hey." He put a hand on Bowie's shoulder and caught those eyes when Bowie looked up. "I meant it when I said it was good to see you."

"You know what, I've been itching to see you since I left. You're fine company."

Well, then. That was unexpected. Welcome, but unexpected.

"You've been on my mind a lot too." He grinned and went on after a sip of his beer. "You're gonna learn quick I'm way better at show than tell."

"Works for me. I figure you're tired. You want to go get off before you crash?"

He laughed. "You know, we're never going to be able to stay long enough to have a second beer, are we?" He drained his glass and set it on the bar.

"If we want a second beer, I can drink one, but what I'm offering is better."

God, no shit. Whatever it was Bowie was offering, he'd take it. He climbed off his bar stool. "Way better. Let's go."

"You got it." Bowie put some cash in the tip jar and nodded to Darla. "Have a good night, ma'am. Let's go get you ready for your shift tomorrow huh, Bear?"

He smiled, surprisingly touched by Bowie's tone, the care, the pet name. The whole thing. He wanted to say so, but he waited until they were out of the club, out on the street in the quiet night air. He still wasn't sure he knew how to say what he wanted to, so he just stepped in front of Bowie and gave the man a quick kiss, finding that the connection cleared his mind a little. "Thank you."

Bowie's eyes went wide, the shock only lasting a second before it became pleasure. "You're more than welcome."

He took a step backward and fell in step with Bowie again. "Just so you know, 'on Angel's tab' means the drinks are on the house. Mike calls me a few times a week to come doctor somebody up after a fight—like I did that night with Sam. I haven't paid for a drink there in years."

"Oh. Well, I'll make sure to tip enough to make the difference. Sam sent me some pictures. He took more than I could've. I would have killed someone."

Gabe knew that wasn't blustering or posturing. Just a fact.

"When Sam sinks his teeth into something, he's in a hundred percent. For whatever reason, he decided he needed that job and so he did what it took to get it." A hundred percent and half his soul. He kinda thought the job thing was about more than the bar.

"True that." Bowie grinned. "He lived, so it must've been okay."

"Tommy made it okay." He believed that. Tommy saw Sam. Kind of how he felt like he might be starting to see Bowie. Hard to believe, but he knew what Bowie brought out in him; that couldn't be a random thing he was making up.

He hoped. *Please let me be right. Thank you. Amen.*

He let Bowie into the building, shaking his head about the elevator again. "After you."

Bowie chuckled softly. "Good thing we're not claustrophobic, hmm?"

"I kind of like this." He gave Bowie a wide grin and squeezed himself in closer than he actually needed to. Bowie chuckled and swelled up, pressing them even tighter together.

Jesus, all that muscle and those shoulders...Bowie was

hotter than the sun. "Good God. Knock it off, Sarge, I can't breathe."

Bowie snorted out a laugh but immediately backed off, giving him room. He caught the laughter and the two of them snickered their way off the elevator. "If you're going to make it that hard to breathe anyway, I might as well start taking the stairs."

He let them in and hung his key up on the hooks by the door, literally the only thing he'd ever put up on the walls. "Oh." He pointed to the rack. "You can have that one."

"Thanks, man." Bowie put his cap on the rack. "I keep waiting for my hair to get long enough to braid."

"Is that why you're growing it?" He didn't think it needed to be braided; it was thick and soft and totally touchable. He reached up, pulled out the hair tie, and combed his fingers through it, letting the curls slip and tangle around his knuckles. "I like it like this."

"I'm growing it because...well, because I never got to before." Bowie leaned toward his hand, the act easy and natural.

He grinned and hung the hair tie on the rack with Bowie's key. "I did that for a while. It got to be a pain in the ass. My former sub liked it, though. He was upset when I cut it." He'd had it down past his shoulders for a long while, but all the braiding got to be a nuisance and it was heavy.

"In your line of work, I can see that. You deal with a lot of people in a panic."

"There's that, and I bend over people all day too. It was more work than it was worth." He put his arms around Bowie's waist, pleased by how well they fit together despite their combined bulk. "Yours works for me, though."

He was trying to be chill about going from living alone to a roommate that was really more of a live-in lover in the span of a week, especially since he wasn't confident he was relationship material anymore. But Bowie jumped on that wagon so fast, it was kind of rolling down the road before he knew what was happening.

God. Sammy's fucking brother. He really needed to not fuck this up.

Nope. Not stressing. Tired. Getting off and going to sleep.

He took a kiss and concentrated on the man in his arms.

Bowie hummed softly and slowly muscled him into his bedroom, never once breaking the kiss. Impressive.

He ran his hands over Bowie's chest, smiling against the man's lips. "You know this shirt is awfully tight, right?"

Bowie flexed, the material complaining. "I do. Shows me off."

Shows you off. Damn right, he knew he hadn't been the only one in the bar that noticed. "That wasn't a complaint. You could fill your closet with these, I'd be good with that. I'm taking it off, though." He got his hands under the hem and lifted it, exposing those heavy pecs, the deep ridges of abs.

What was it with the O'Reilly boys?

Oh, ha! He got himself an O'Reilly. That was pretty funny actually. They were highly coveted items in his circles. He pushed the shirt off and grinned, catching Bowie's eyes and holding them as he dropped his fingers to Bowie's belt.

Bowie sucked in, giving him room and letting him watch the muscles ripple. Pretty.

Very, very pretty.

And he should be very interested but really, he was feeling very...tired. "Hey, I don't know how much I have in me, man. I'm feeling pretty beat."

"I hear you. Orgasm and bed. You need to set an alarm?"

Bowie stripped his shirt off, his jeans, baring him like it was nothing. So fast.

"Yeah. Six-thirty. You got me?" He should find his phone, set it himself, but then again, he did have a live-in roommate with benefits. Couldn't that be one of them?

"No worries." One hand wrapped around his cock, easy as pie, the pressure and heat warm and fine. Steady and meant to get him off.

"Mmm." Oh. Okay, that was nice. He moaned and pulled Bowie in for another kiss. Bowie gave it, letting him relax, letting him have that lazy rush that left him boneless, melted.

He tugged on Bowie and they moved up onto the bed, barely breaking contact. "Feels good." Like getting high but better. He didn't think about a damn thing, just lost himself in Bowie's scent and their kisses until he was breathless.

He'd return the favor after a nap.

9

Bowie left Gabe sleeping about one. He took a picture of Gabe's schedule from the counter so that he wouldn't make the same mistake again before he headed out to look for a twenty-four-hour diner.

He wanted a burger and a Dr Pepper. After that he could find an extended-stay hotel for a few days. Gabe had made the offer of a spare room, but Bowie had heard the regret as soon as the offer had been made. That was why that house was empty—buyer's regret. Gabe had it bad.

Bowie would find somewhere to crash for a week, then he'd make some decisions, give Gabe his out, give Sam his space.

He found an open restaurant with a decent-sized crowd and headed in. He ordered his burger and Coke and started searching on his phone.

Sometimes it was easier to have those rules, to know where you were supposed to be, to have a place where you knew you had to be.

Christ, he'd become that grizzly old soldier.

He grinned at himself. One day he'd be in a VA home, one of those old fucks that waited for the weekly visits from the enlisted boys.

He wasn't there yet, though. Not for fifty years or so.

Until then, he'd better find himself a place for a few nights, and a job. He wasn't sure how much call there was for an explosives expert around here. He could do all sorts of things—hell, he was handy. Maybe someone would let him fix up a place like he'd done for his houses in Galveston. He'd been damn lucky; Harvey had done minimal damage, and he had an old Army buddy managing them. It had been damn fun fixing them up over his leave.

Passive income and shit.

Huh. He'd have to ask Gabe how a guy got into construction work here.

He found himself a hotel room close by with decent reviews and booked for a week. That would give everyone the space they needed. He wasn't used to living alone, that was for sure, and he was happy to rent from Gabe, but he wanted the son of a bitch to be sure.

Otherwise they could hang out, no big.

He grabbed a napkin and begged a pen off the waitress.

1. Find hotel. Check
2. Text Sam
3. Get stuff from Sam's
4. Text Gabe
5. Find job
6. Fig out where to live (talk to G when not tired)

ALL RIGHT, THEN. BURGER. CAFFEINE. PLAN.

Hoo-rah.

Hopefully Gabe was sleeping hard. Hell, hopefully Sammy and Tommy were too. He'd eat his burger, and he'd find himself a bed and do the same.

10

Gabe sat up suddenly, swung his feet over the side of the bed, and got to his feet. His eyes weren't even fully open when he reached out to steady himself on the wall in his dark bedroom, but his heart was racing, and the adrenaline rush made the blood pump in his ears.

Bedroom. It's just the bedroom.

He took a deep breath, running his fingers through his hair and sat back down on his bed, glad he hadn't woken Bowie. He was unsure what sound had woken him until he saw his phone on the bedside table. Bowie hadn't turned on the Do Not Disturb function. His sleeping brain sometimes thought the buzz notification, probably from some incoming SPAM email, was the squelch of his radio calling him to the chopper.

He usually took something to help him stay asleep on these nights between shifts, but he'd been plenty tired, and Bowie had been kind enough to provide him a sweet lullaby. He really thought he'd be okay.

He grinned though, knowing just how to deal with the

adrenaline, and reached for Bowie. An armful of Ranger ought to set him right.

Except Bowie wasn't in bed. He listened, but the apartment was quiet, and he discovered after a quick tour that Bowie actually wasn't there at all.

Well, fuck.

He opened a shade to find the sun was starting to come up and his phone read 5:45 a.m. Hardly any point in going back to bed, so he headed for the kitchen to make breakfast.

Bowie hadn't taken the key, hadn't left him a note, or even a text. Guess he wasn't all that interesting if he was too tired to really fuck around, huh? He'd read something all wrong. Well, at least he knew where he stood.

He wondered where the guy had gone, considering Tommy and Sammy weren't expecting him last night, but decided it wasn't any of his business.

He made a hearty breakfast, cleaned up and pulled on his uniform, then headed out for his shift. Keep busy. Today wasn't a problem.

Tomorrow was another story.

11

Bowie texted Gabe at eight a.m. with, *Have a good day. Let me know when I can see you next. Got your sched so I won't interrupt*

Next he texted Sammy with *Coming to get my stuff*

Then he headed to pack his duffel. He really didn't have all that much, and he wanted to get on the whole "get a job" thing. One way or the other, whether Gabe decided to rent a room or not, he needed a job.

"Are you moving in with Angel?" Sam stared at him, eyes bloodshot, wearing a little tiny pair of shorts.

"I've got a place to stay for a few days, don't stress. You okay?"

"Fine. Where are you going?"

"Renting a room."

"Gonna tell me where your room is?" Sammy crossed his arms over his chest.

"Gonna tell me why you look like you've done too much coke?"

"Jesus Christ. The pair of you. If you don't start actually talking to one another, I'll take a paddle to you both."

Tommy took the coffee he'd just poured for himself and headed for the bedroom. "I'm not joking." The voice drifted down the hall as Tommy disappeared.

"Gabe asked me to stay with him, then he changed his mind, then he changed his mind again. I got a hotel room for a couple of days to let him sleep and make up his mind for sure."

"Why not just stay here?"

"Because you and Tommy need your space, and I need some time to figure shit out. We'll have supper in a couple days. Have some fun, y'all." He hoisted his bag on his shoulder. "Love you, Sammy. Holler, huh?"

"Love you. Don't be a stranger." Poor Sam looked confused as all fuck.

"Go to bed, Sammy. You look wrecked. Seriously."

He headed out, texting Gabe on the way. *Gorgeous day. Going to find food.*

Bowie headed out the door and toward the elevator. Time to do this thing.

Miss your face, Bear.

12

G*oddamn protocols.* Today was already a fucking zero out of ten, and it wasn't anywhere near over. There was nothing worse than getting fucking sidelined over nothing. Over a stupid little cut on his arm. If he'd been riding with his usual crew, this wouldn't even be a thing, Skip or Casey would have slapped a couple of butterfly bandages on him, and they'd have gotten on with their day.

But no, Chief had to mix and match today because they were short a lieutenant, so he got bumped to a bus with a newbie. That in itself wasn't a problem. Jake was a team player, a fast learner, and Gabe was happy to share knowledge. He did plan to retire one day, after all. But by the book wasn't always the most efficient way to do things, and Jake called in the injury before he got a chance to explain that.

So now he was in the damn ER, waiting on a nurse to come sew him up and a doc to say he wasn't going to die of infection, or require workers comp, or whatever the latest hang up was in the department.

He could do it himself; he was sorely tempted, but he'd

have to scrounge up the supplies. They'd get to him fast enough and he wasn't doing anyone any good sitting here. Everyone would rather see the team sitting in the waiting area, *not* sitting there.

He pulled out his phone to see if Mike had taken a turn in Words with Friends, but no luck. He should have known it was too early yet. He did find a couple of texts, though.

One from Sammy asking what was going on with him and Bowie—*Dammit*—one from Zeke about his new, custom fenders, and the others were from the big lunkhead himself. He sighed and tapped on Bowie's name.

So...one text looking for a booty call when his schedule allowed, and the other was a weather report.

Wow. He really was in a shitass mood. Six more hours and he could get some rest. He tried to make himself read the texts again without his asshole glasses on.

Okay, so on a second read, maybe one was "Hey, I want to see you again when your schedule's not crazy," and the other was "I'm thinking of you," with a super casual offer to bring him lunch.

He knew what he wanted; he just wasn't sure he should be wanting it. He'd had that kind of relationship once and it had dissolved, slipped right through his fingers. He learned then that it was possible for some people—even long-time submissives—to fall out of love, and that wasn't something he ever wanted to experience again. He'd been avoiding getting close, second-guessing himself ever since.

He hated it, but he hadn't been able to shut that voice down.

He was a Dom, though, right? He was supposed to be the ultimate decision-maker. He just needed to start making a couple, so he looked like one. That was the man he wanted

Bowie to see. Hell, it was the man *he* needed to see. He answered Bowie carefully.

Sidelined with fucking paper cut. Dinner tomorrow?

The answer came with heartening speed. *That papers a stone cold bitch. Yes pls. You want me to cook?*

Okay. A second chance was a good thing, right? He still didn't know why Bowie left in the middle of the night; maybe he'd just figure out how to ask.

Deal. You need me to hit the market?

I got this. Enchiladas or pot roast?

Oh. He could learn something new. S*how me how to make enchiladas - about 6?*

Perfect. Watch out for random paper hmm

That's the plan. He grinned and gave Bowie something to think about as the nurse finally arrived. *Come hungry tomorrow. For everything.*

You got it. 6 tomorrow

Half an hour, eleven stitches, and one police report later, he and his team were back in rotation. Eight o'clock came quick after that; they got one call after another until their relief took over.

He picked up sushi on the way home and finally texted Sammy from the elevator, which he found to be much less fun without Bowie in it.

What do you mean? He needed to know exactly what Sammy was asking. "What's up with you and Bowie?" Could mean almost anything. He didn't know what Bowie had told Sammy.

He says you asked & changed your mind & asked & he wants to give you time to know 4 sure

What? What? Asked and changed his mind? *Jesus.* He was too tired for Sammy's puzzles. He gave up and called instead.

"Hey, bud!" Oh, Sammy sounded positively giddy. "How goes?"

"I'm coming off my third twelve-hour shift, but otherwise I think I'm pretty good. How are you feeling? You sound like you got some stripes."

"I feel amazing. I intend to continue feeling amazing for a few days."

He laughed. "Good for you. So what is this about Bowie?"

"Oh, he moved out. He said you'd offered to rent him a room; then you changed your mind like twice, so he was going to get a hotel or something and let you make up your mind when you weren't tired and shit. He's a turd, but he's sort of thoughtful. Weird, huh?"

Ah. Yeah. He'd been a bit of a turd himself. "That's exactly what he is. A thoughtful turd. I'll offer again." And the rest was Bowie's to tell. "Ask Master Thomas when you can if he wants to have dinner next week, all of us." He grinned. Tommy had to be as smug as the Cheshire Cat right now.

"I will. Get some sleep, Angel. Bye!" *Click.* Oh, yeah. Smug as fuck. Tommy would be unbearable.

He flopped on his couch to eat his dinner. Then he was going to go to bed and make sure he was human by the time his Ranger showed up tomorrow night.

13

Tortillas. Beef. Guajillos. Chicken stock. Cominos. Cheese. Sour cream. Avocados. Ice cream.

Life was good.

The elevator was even better because bags and groceries and crutch and stairs were not a match.

"Hey." Gabe opened the door with a smile and held it for him. "Can I take those?" Gabe reached for his grocery bags without waiting for an answer.

"Thanks. You get some rest?" Rested, Gabe looked about ten years younger, and that suited the motherfucker to the bone.

Gabe nodded and took the groceries to the kitchen. "With a little pharmaceutical assistance, I slept for thirteen hours. I feel like I could fly. What have you been up to?"

"Looking for work. Working out. Watching a lot of Food Network." Bowie chuckled. "About a thousand hours of hot showers."

"I will never take unlimited hot water for granted ever again." Gabe started unpacking bags, setting everything out on the counter. "I don't know what you're looking for, but don't forget I can introduce you around if you're interested in working as a grease monkey."

"I just need something to keep me busy and out of trouble." Bowie popped the ice cream in the freezer and the sour cream in the fridge.

"All right, maybe we'll take a walk tomorrow. Grab a couple of beers while you're in there."

"You think we can get to two in?"

Gabe laughed and leaned closer. "Well, we have dinner involved this time, so it's possible, but I wouldn't call it a goal."

"Hey, there." Bowie stepped right up and kissed the fine son of a bitch. He loved seeing the lines ease around Gabe's eyes, the smile.

Gabe met him halfway, answering his kiss with interest, slipping a tongue past his lips and one hand into his hair. He leaned into the touch a little, opened up, and hummed. Oh, he'd been wanting that.

They let it play out, nice and easy; then Gabe leaned away just enough that they could lock eyes and smiled at him. "You forgot your key."

"I didn't want to take advantage of your tired." He wasn't a bad guy. He didn't take advantage of people.

"Why leave in the middle of the night?" Gabe didn't seem upset, but there was something else in the man's eyes. Something more personal than just curiosity.

"I waited until I knew you were out, but I was restless and starving, and I knew you were wiped the hell out."

"I was pretty done, that's true. But I was a little freaked to find you gone when I woke up. Sammy told me why, and I get that, but I didn't know where we stood, and I couldn't get back to sleep, and..." Gabe shrugged. "Maybe a text might be good next time, hm?"

"I texted as soon as I knew you'd be at work, but sure." That was easy enough, made sense. "You want that beer?"

Gabe held his eyes for a second and gave him a light kiss. "Yeah. I do."

"Rock on." He grabbed two bottles and opened them. "You want to start cooking or sit a minute?"

"Let's cook. We may never get around to dinner otherwise." Gabe grabbed his ass and picked up a beer.

"You want to chop an onion for me, then? You got a blender?" Bowie grabbed the broth and the chiles and started the process of rehydrating in a pan.

"I do. And there's a food processor on the counter over there. Choose your poison." Gabe grabbed the onion and started peeling it.

"The blender will work just fine."

They worked together well—cooking meat and onions, drinking beer, telling the periodic "no shit, there I was" story. He was tickled as a pig in shit.

Gabe was so casually physical too, a hand on his back on the way to the refrigerator, a kiss on his shoulder with a compliment, a naughty hand on his ass now and then. And smiles, lots of smiles.

"Did your mom teach you to cook? Or did you just pick it up?"

"Mom taught me some. I got a good buddy that went from army cook to chef." Cooking was a lot like building a bomb—follow your instincts and your recipe, in equal amounts.

"Nice. It's a great hobby. Keeps me busy and feeds me well. I guess we need a table, huh?" Gabe was cleaning up, wiping down counters.

Huh. Okay. Looked like someone had made his mind up

for sure. "If we're going to cook together, makes sense we have somewhere to eat together."

"I'm off for two days, I'll hunt one up."

"You want help?" He could help with the cash part and the finding part. Hell, he could build a table, although that would be messy.

Gabe smiled at him. "Yeah, if you're up for shopping together, I'm in. What's your...whatever. Your style?"

"I have no idea." He tasted the enchilada sauce. Nice. He spooned up some for Gabe to try. "Sturdy. We're big men."

Gabe took the taste he offered. "Oh. Hell, yeah. That's great." He got a pat on the back and another on the ass. "Big men. Is that a style? Hi, we'd like the big man furniture department, please." Gabe snickered.

"It ought to be. That would make life pretty easy. Bed for five hundred pounds of fucking, please."

Gabe laughed loud, the sound free and relaxed. "I'd like a table big enough for us to eat at and strong enough for me to bend him over, please."

"See?" He chuckled and started rolling enchiladas. "We need a sofa that will take a nice hard pounding but is still soft enough for long blowjob sessions."

They were cracking his shit up.

"Maybe a breakaway coffee table in case it gets... contentious." Gabe turned the beer bottle up, finishing it off.

"Oh. Oh, man..." That tickled him, and he began to howl with laughter. "That would be dangerous. Funny, but dangerous."

Gabe's grin was wicked. "There's a reason I don't have much furniture."

"Are you having wrestling matches in the front room?" He covered the enchiladas with the red sauce and cheese.

Gabe snorted. "I haven't in a long while, no."

"I'm pretty sure it requires mats and shit."

"Not necessarily, the kitchen counter worked just fine for us the other day." Gabe grabbed two more beers and opened them.

His cheeks heated, because he still had a mark and it was still hot as fuck, so he just ignored the comment. "Look at us! Beer two."

"It's a record!" Gabe took the bottles out to the coffee table and set them down, then came back for plates. "This looks so good. Silverware is in the drawer by the fridge."

"It should be. It's Momma's recipe. You want to dish up here or bring the casserole there?" He grabbed the sour cream to dollop on.

"Probably better here." Gabe set the plates on the counter for him. "Tommy said he liked your parents. He said they're good people."

"They are. Solid as rocks. A rancher and a schoolteacher." And they hadn't made a single son that wanted to take over the ranch.

"And you left home and never went back, hm? When did you get involved in the scene?"

"It was less a scene than something that happened. We had to be careful. There are a couple places in Germany that taught us things, and there's always the Internet. You'd be surprised how much typing went on."

"Wild." Gabe led the way out to the coffee table. "Did you ever have anyone serious?"

"Nope." He didn't think it was safe—you had the guys in your unit and you couldn't be stupid with them; you had the young guys, and he didn't want to be accused of pulling rank, and pretending to fuck online? Weird.

"Well, you've got a whole life to live, then. Here's to a new beginning." Gabe raised his beer.

"I do." He clinked their bottles together. A new beginning. That worked for him, down to the bone. "Cheers."

Gabe dug in like he hadn't eaten in two days, which was more or less the way he always saw Gabe eat. Focused. "Mmm. So good."

Bowie started eating, humming deep in his chest. *Oh. Oh, hell yes.* They'd done good, the two of them. They sat, thigh to thigh, pressed together.

"You like Italian? We could make stuffed peppers tomorrow."

"I love food. All of it. That sounds great." He could enjoy damn near everything—from falafel to shakshuka to burgers to lasagna.

"Awesome. Sammy and Tommy can burn water, you know. They're no fun to cook with. In fact, I've never known anyone I could cook with. We're going to eat well, my friend." Gabe took another bite and hummed happily.

"There's nothing wrong with that. I work out." And thank God for it. He didn't need to compete with his baby brother, but he didn't need to go to pot, either.

"I think food is the only reason I still do." Gabe laughed and sank back into the couch with a sigh. "That's not really true; it helps to be in good shape for work too. So I can wrestle nutjobs with knives." Gabe pressed a hand over the bandage that just barely peeked out under the sleeve of a dark-blue T-shirt.

"That the paper cut?" He knew about those, but he still had to wince. "Does it itch like fire?"

"Fuck, yes." Gabe laughed. "It's fine for a while, and then it just drives me apeshit."

"I'll be gentle with you, I promise."

Gabe raised an eyebrow. "Yeah? I'm not making the same promise."

"Well, I ain't broke." And he was hungry. He spread a little wider, giving himself room.

"It takes more than a cat scratch to break me, Sarge." Gabe reached over and rested a hand on his nape, massaging.

"Mmhmm." He liked that touch, so he dropped his head forward for a second.

"Feels good?" Gabe put his plate down, shifted on the couch, and added the other hand, moving to his shoulders and digging strong fingers into the muscle.

"*Uhn.*" That was an answer, right? That counted?

"Clint, at the club? He has a fantastic masseuse. I'll introduce you sometime. He kind of looks like a wishbone, but he's surprisingly strong. He did this thing where he walked on my spine. Oh, my God." Gabe's fingers kept moving, finding hot spots and working them out.

"The little guy from Sammy's party." He remembered.

"That's right, I forgot you met him. I don't know if I'd call him little, but he's littler than we are, anyway." Gabe laughed and took his hands away. "I'll tell you what. Let's get the kitchen cleaned up, and I'll let you stretch out for some real attention."

"Mmm." He nodded and stood, humming in the back of his mind as they worked to clean up. He'd been cleaning up as he cooked, so it didn't take much—the pan and the casserole dish, the two plates.

They didn't have enough to save for a meal, but he was always up for a snack.

"I think this will pass muster." Gabe stepped close, stroked his beard. "Got a little trim, hm?"

"I just cleaned it up some." Okay, that was the wildest

sensation, someone touching his beard. He reached up, mimicking the touch on Gabe's much shorter chin hairs.

"It looks good." Gabe's eyes narrowed, and he got a quick smile before Gabe kissed him. He wandered a half step closer and brought their bodies together. They fit, shoulder to shoulder, hip to hip. That was just about perfect and unusual enough to send a buzz through him.

They moved together toward the bedroom, slowly making their way without really breaking their kiss, their hands roaming and tugging on one another. They didn't waste time undressing each other once they got there, just slipped out of everything and climbed into bed.

If Gabe's arm was bothersome at all the man didn't let on, but the white bandage over the stitches was evident in the half-light. "Stomach? I'll pick up where I left off."

He wasn't going to insult Gabe by asking if the son of a bitch was sure or if he was okay or any shit like that. "Sounds like one hell of an idea."

Gabe seemed to like it too and helped him roll and get settled, chuckling. "I don't have Bryan's fancy oils, so don't expect too much." Gabe straddled his hips, placed hands on his back, and leaned into his shoulders.

"Like I'm fan—oh, fuck." Everything in his shoulders popped, the sound and the pressure release making him dizzy.

"Whoa. Damn." Gabe's fingers dug deep into muscle. "Bet that felt good."

He grunted in total agreement. That felt like a fucking orgasm. A bone orgasm. A joint orgasm. Something.

Gabe worked his shoulders for a bit and moved lower, getting a pop here and there out of his rib cage as well. As Gabe's fingers reached his hips, the touch grew lighter, more sensual. He turned his head, trying to figure out that sensation. Part of him wanted to stretch up tall, part of him wanted to spread his legs. It wasn't a tickle, but it was waking him up, almost like wearing his TENS unit.

"Good?" Gabe's voice was low and husky. "I've rarely had a better view." Hands started working his glutes, rolling the heavy muscle under flat, warm palms instead of fingers.

"Damn, Bear. That's...new." He'd never had someone rub his butt, much less massage it.

Gabe laughed softly. "New, like, 'What the hell you perv?' Or new, like, 'It's weird but I kind of like it'?"

"New like new. I like how you touch the scars." He wasn't ashamed of them; why should Gabe be?

"They're interesting." Gabe traced a pretty gnarly divot with one finger. "They're just another part of you I want to get to know. Someday I'll ask about their story, but for now, they're heroes. They deserve equal time."

"Just another part of me." He did stretch then, rubbing against Gabe—all of him, hands and body both.

"Mmm. Look at that. You feel great." Gabe moved over him, covering him shoulders to knees, and dropped a kiss between his shoulder blades.

A long, low groan left him, like the pressure just pushed it out of him. Gabe swept his hair aside and picked up there, kissing and tasting his skin, finding sensitive spots. When Gabe found that spot where he'd bitten before, Bowie grabbed for Gabe's hands, twined their fingers together.

"It looks amazing." Gabe gently wedged a knee between his and coaxed his legs farther apart, that heavy cock rubbing against him.

"Feels fucking hot. Can't believe you did that." Couldn't believe it, but it had burned, and the dark bruise looked just fine.

"No? Sounds like you like it. What's not to believe?" Gabe licked it but let it be, hips starting to rock gently.

"It's good to be wanted, Bear." He rocked, his eyes falling closed.

Gabe groaned, and the bear's forehead dropped to his shoulder like a stone. "You're wanted. Fuck, I want you."

They had a good rhythm, a solid rocking together, Gabe's strength and heat matching his.

Gabe put a hand on his hip and sat back, straddling just one thigh, and reached under him to stroke his balls. That was distracting, but what got his attention was the pressure of Gabe's thumb as it stroked over the skin behind them and up over his hole. "Your ass is perfect, Bowie."

That was new and unexpected—both the touch and the praise—and he wasn't sure what to do with either. Gabe wasn't tense, though, so he let himself breathe too.

Gabe kept it up, switching up that new sensation, stroking his cock, rolling his balls, then back to that pressure again, not giving him a lot of time to focus on any part of it for long. He brought his focus to Gabe, clamping down on the man himself and letting that guide him.

Gabe pushed his knee up, his strong leg, baring him more, making him feel exposed, and moved again. A heavy hand settled on his neck with all the intention it had in the kitchen, just less weight. Gabe's voice was rough, his tone even. "I want you, Bowie. I want inside you. I need to know what you want."

He'd never been fucked, but he'd done it to other men enough that he knew it could be good. He made sure he made it good. If Gabe didn't, Bowie would know he wasn't who he said he was.

"Make it good, Bear." That was a challenge, a directive, an order—all at once.

"I promise." Gabe moved off the bed and opened a drawer in the nightstand. "Roll over."

Bowie missed the heat and the pressure on his back, but he did as he was asked, settling deep into the sheets.

"It's better. You can see me this way, you know?" Gabe climbed back into bed, making it shift under that bulky frame, and moved over him. "And, I get to kiss you." Their lips met, and Gabe was suddenly all heat and teeth and tongue and need. Now that was something he could get behind. In front of. With. Whatever. He pushed right back, meeting Gabe with all his answering need.

He was dimly aware of Gabe futzing with the lube and maneuvering between his legs as they kissed, but the desire in it was everything. It stayed that way until a slippery finger gently tried to breach him and Gabe whispered, "Trust me, and I can make you fly."

He wouldn't be here if he didn't. He nodded once before he took another kiss. He needed somewhere to unpack all the desire twisting up inside him. Gabe moaned for him, right through the kiss, and that finger eased inside.

It was different, having someone else touch him, enter him, and he shifted, tensed, and relaxed, letting himself feel it.

Gabe gave him time to adjust, time to feel and react, moving that finger inside him slowly. After a bit, his bear kissed his chin, his neck, and south to one nipple, which he teased with a determined tongue and added a second finger. Bowie grunted and rocked, his eyes burning down at Gabe. His arms were tense beside him, so he forced himself to roll his shoulders, reach up and touch Gabe's hair, his temple.

"Breathe, babe." Gabe leaned into his fingers, though, obviously appreciating the touch. "I've got you."

"You do." He knew that tensing up wouldn't help either one of them. Not now.

If Gabe was concerned or nervous, it didn't show. Bear was breathing evenly; those big hands were steady and sure. The relaxation suited him to the bone, and he stroked skin, petted Gabe's arm, feeling how Gabe was fingering him from those muscles too.

Gabe sat back, knelt between his legs, and looked him over hungrily down his abs, across his chest, then firmly gripped his cock with the other hand and started stroking.

His eyes went wide, and his belly tightened. *Oh, fuck me.* That was good, and when Gabe started working the tip, it was fucking perfect.

"Yeah." Gabe's eyes were on him, heated and focused, and those hands were busy making him hot, making his heart race, making him feel. Trying to drive him mad waiting. He rode it, panting and rocking, every ounce of his focus on letting the sensations flood him.

Gabe lined up and pushed into him before he even realized it was happening, going so slow, watching his face, still working his cock.

"Damn, Bear." He groaned, his body making room for Gabe. The stretch burned, and he rolled up, trying to get more. Gabe eased him back, that hand inexorable.

"No rush, babe." Gabe chastised, jaw set and brow damp. "But, fuck, that was hot anyway." He watched Gabe switch to an overhand grip, still stroking, rolling a palm over the head and down the other side. Up and over, up and over again as his bear filled him.

Bowie forgot how to breathe. Simple as that. He was nothing but heat and need and Gabe. He reached up, cupped Gabe's face, and brushed his thumb across Gabe's lips.

Gabe opened up and caught his thumb between white teeth, then took it right in and sucked on it, humming as his eyes slid closed.

"Fuck..." His body clenched on Gabe's cock, and suddenly it felt so big, so thick inside him, taking him.

Those eyes flew open, and Gabe let his finger go with a pop, gasping. "Jesus!" Gabe let go of his cock as well and fell forward, bracing a hand on either side of him as they started to move together, thrusts still careful, but definitely in earnest.

He found the rhythm, bracing one foot against the mattress to meet Gabe's thrusts now, one after the other.

"That's it. It's good now, right? Fuck." Gabe bent and kissed him. That worked for him, because he wasn't all that coherent. In fact, he was working on pure sensation and need.

Gabe curled fingers around his cock again as those thrusts grew heavier, stroking in double rhythm, quick and purposeful. He gulped in air, his balls drawing up so tight that they ached. He grunted a warning, but he couldn't manage words.

Gabe stroked him through his climax, and he could feel his bear starting to tremble. "Beautiful...oh. Fuck." Those hips picked up speed, thrusts growing shallower, and he was treated to a raw, uncensored Gabe, taking...or maybe claiming, what the man wanted. The sight satisfied him, just as much as the orgasm had. Maybe even more. This was truth and proved his gut was right.

Gabe's climax hit hard, an intense and drawn-out moment that made them both shudder. "Bowie," Gabe growled, his name equal parts gratitude and possession.

"Bear." He blinked up, trying to be focused, but damn, he was...not.

He got a quick kiss as Gabe hung over him, and a surprisingly gentle smile, before Gabe slipped free of him and rolled to stretch out long beside him, one arm over his chest.

Bowie took a deep, slow breath, then let it out with a long exhale.

Apparently tonight, he should stay.

14

He'd startled awake again.

But this time, the heavy arm Bowie had around him had stopped him, kept him from flying out of bed, and prevented the worst of the adrenaline rush. He tangled their fingers together and wondered if the way Bowie had pulled him in closer was instinct, or if his lover was awake enough to know what he was doing.

Bowie could've known. He and Bowie understood each other on a level most people couldn't, not because people didn't try, because they did all the time, but they just hadn't been there. Bowie could easily understand his neurotic responses to shit, just like he totally got a statement like, "It's good to be wanted."

That was anything but simple, right? And he'd heard Bowie loud and clear. It was good to really be wanted. It was good to know someone wasn't just another willing hand in the dark or a meaningless lover of convenience, but a man who genuinely and specifically wanted *you*.

That he got. The need he definitely got. That weird thing people do when two words really mean twenty? That he also got. But there was something about Bowie he didn't have a handle on yet, something interesting. Something he thought was probably important.

That was okay; it took time to know people, and it wasn't any kind of deal breaker. He trusted Bowie, and it was pretty damn clear that feeling was mutual. And, by the way, he was a fucking stud, and Bowie appreciated that. What more did he want?

Bowie's hand settled on the center of his chest, heavy and warm, a solid weight that drew his attention. No ink. No jewelry. No decoration barring the scars and calluses—this was just a huge, square, solid hand.

He hummed low, the sound vibrating through Bowie's fingers into his own, and his eyes slid closed again.

It was light—like, bright morning light—when they opened again. He was drawn out of bed by the smell of bacon, so he pulled on sweats and followed his nose. He could get spoiled by a man cooking him breakfast, that was for sure. And look at that fine specimen right there. *Damn.* He could get used to *that* man cooking him breakfast, as a matter of fact.

"Good morning." He kissed Bowie's shoulder as he walked past, headed for the coffeemaker. "Smells so good."

"Bacon and pancakes," Bowie grunted and nodded at him, then smiled. "Morning."

He reached for the coffeepot and winced, glancing at the streak of blood that had soaked through the bandage on his arm, then shook his head and poured himself some coffee.

"You're hired." He took a sip, set his mug down, and pulled a couple of plates out of the cabinet. "Sleep okay?"

"Like a rock. How's the arm?" Bowie started making plates—three big pancakes, three pieces of bacon each. It looked pretty damn good. "You want milk with?"

"Sore. I'm good. You want butter?" He dug in the fridge and found the syrup.

"Please." The touch to the small of his back sent tingles up along his spine.

He grinned and grabbed the butter too and set them both on the counter. This was fantastic—*fan-fucking-tastic*—having someone to putter in the kitchen with. Someone hot and half-dressed to putter with was even better. "Man, I'm hungry. You rock."

"I figure everyone likes bacon, and you had it in the fridge." Bowie was relaxed and easy, loose-limbed, even. Gabe had wondered about day-after regrets, but it didn't seem like Bowie was into that.

"What's not to like?" He poured a lot of syrup on his pancakes, too much, but he liked it that way, and dug in right there at the counter. "How are you feeling this morning?"

"Sore in new spots. Nothing bad, just noticeable." Bowie grinned at him, the look pure evil. "I'm an overachiever. I didn't start small."

He blinked. *What the fuck?* Was he blushing? Must be all the syrup, he didn't blush. *Jesus.*

"Go big or go home?" He grinned, teeth showing. "I did try to follow orders, Sarge. How'd I do?"

"You passed with flying colors. Congrats."

Silly or not, that felt good. He leaned over and kissed Bowie, playing. "You were spot-on yourself."

"Hell, I spotted all over myself."

God save him, Bowie had no shame. Zero. Worked for him. Lovers with no shame promised fun. "Regular Jackson Pollack." He snorted. "You're a nut."

Bowie leaned against the counter and ate—pancakes first, then the bacon. "I did good. Excellent."

"You did. Bacon's perfect. So...showers and table shopping? And I want to take you over to see my buddy Zeke about work. My new fenders are in anyway." He couldn't wait to see them, get them on his bike.

"Works for me. I got no plans except for maybe checking out of the hotel, since it seems we got our minds made up."

"Sorry. It's been a while since I needed to think along those lines. I wasn't sure what I was offering. I am now." Minds made up, huh? He really didn't know what they'd made their minds up about exactly, but he knew he wanted Bowie, and he wanted Bowie here. That was about where he stood. There were other things simmering, but they needed more time for him to figure out.

"Fair enough. If things change, you'll let me know."

He squinted at Bowie. Okay. So...what, then? Should they shake on it? "I don't think it works like that."

"No?" The question wasn't the slightest bit sarcastic or bitchy, simply curious.

"Well..." He didn't want it to feel like he was starting something, Bowie was obviously touchy about that kind of thing, so he started washing dishes and trying to sound casual. "If things change, it's because we are changing them, not because I am, you know? This is kind of a two-way thing, don't you think?"

"Ah. Yes." Bowie nodded and began to put things away. "I meant your offer. If you change your mind, you'll tell me."

"Oh, I see. Won't happen. Not that way. If something isn't working, we'll talk about it." The last time he met anyone this literal, they were five.

"Works for me." He waited for Bowie to put the next plate away; then he took a kiss—firm and sure, all-encompassing and somehow joyful.

"Good. Me too. Go get your shower, babe. I'll take mine,

and we'll go enjoy the day." Bowie had all that hair to deal with, he was more wash and wear. He winced as he moved his arm just wrong, it was possible it got too much of a workout last night. He just hoped all the stitches were still in place or that Bowie knew his way around a needle.

"I'm on it. Holler if you need me to check your arm." Bowie never missed anything.

Not surprising when your job was to make sure people didn't get blown up. Details were pretty much his bailiwick. "After my shower. Thanks."

He'd get in with his lover, but they'd never leave the apartment. Naked equaled orgasms. It was like a base imperative for Bowie. Fun, but today they needed to go places.

His phone chimed and he picked it up to find a text from work, saying they needed a swing for the night shift. He started to say he'd go in when he heard the shower turn on, and he looked up. He always said yes, right? They were texting him because they knew he'd say yes. But he only had tomorrow; then he had another two days on, and he had plans. He didn't have tickets or anything on the calendar, but he still had plans. They were in the shower.

He looked at his phone and texted that he was unavailable.

15

Bowie put his duffel in Gabe's extra room with the motorcycle parts and books. He had a job starting tomorrow working on engines. He liked Zeke well enough —straightforward guy, relatively honest, liked being the boss. Assuming he could learn to leave Bowie alone, they'd get on like a house afire.

Speaking of learning to leave him alone—Bowie grabbed his phone. *Got job. Staying with Gabe.* That should be enough for Sammy.

He got back, *Good deal*, and a text popped up from Gabe. *Day was an 8. Eaten yet?*

Nope. What you want? His leg was reminding him he wasn't sixteen anymore, but he could go get food or cook or whathaveyou.

Something I can sleep on. Sushi? Greek?

Works for me

How did this work? He wasn't sure exactly. *You want me to go pick something up? I am here at the house*

He got a text with a Google Maps link to a Greek

restaurant a couple of blocks north of the apartment. *Give me 15*

k

He made sure his hair was tied back and his shirt was still clean, then went out and down. He had his crutch with him, but he'd done without it all day, so he was pleased. Soon he would put it away and tell the doctors who said he'd lose the leg to fuck off.

That was a nice little fantasy, wasn't it?

Gabe was waiting for him outside the restaurant, still in uniform and playing on his phone. Bear's happy smile lit up those deep blue eyes as he got closer. "Hey. How was your day?" Gabe moved in for a kiss.

Bowie would never be used to the casual public touches. Never. He gave a soft, awkward buss and grinned at his own nerves. "I have a job. I start tomorrow."

His first nonmilitary job. Interesting.

"Yeah? Did Zeke call you? Or something else?" Gabe held the door for him.

"I went to see Zeke again. We talked." He had a knack for putting things together, and motorcycles were straightforward.

They went inside, the smells of garlic and onion and parsley magic. "You had an eight, huh? That's impressive."

They were seated at a table in a corner. "I did. I left that place whistling, it was such an easy day. The guys said I was too nice today, and they think I got laid. Go figure." Gabe winked at him.

"They owe me a beer." Maybe two. He was worth it. "Glad to hear it."

Gabe laughed. "Did Zeke have my fenders on yet when you got there? I dropped my bike off this morning."

"They're on. Look great." He'd put them on himself as

part of his "put your money where your mouth is" test. "You picked a good set."

Gabe leaned forward, excited. "Does the Alien Queen look even cooler on the bike than it did in my hand? He does amazing work."

"They look sexy as hell. It's a great visual, and it works on the bike like it was meant to be there." He was happy to enthuse about the bike. Obviously it was well-loved and taken care of.

They ordered a couple of beers and got menus. "Did you text Sammy? Did you remember to call your mom?"

"I texted Sammy. He'll call Momma." Sammy was good like that. He was all obedient and shit. "I brought my bag and backpack over."

"Oh, great. There's some room in the closet, but we should get another dresser. Did you find the laundry thing? It's in the closet by the bathroom." Gabe sipped his beer.

"I did." It wasn't like there was a lot. He had four sets of BDUs, two pairs of jeans, four T-shirts, six briefs, six pairs of socks, and his coat. Just exactly what he needed. "I can live out of the duffel until we find something."

"Saturday. The table is coming in the morning. Oh. What are you eating?" Gabe ordered the chicken souvlaki and looked at him expectantly.

"I want the combo plate, please ma'am." Whatever that was, he was interested in trying it. "I need to clean out the area, huh?"

"Shouldn't be too bad. So hey, what's your work schedule?" Gabe was full of questions tonight. Must be wound up from work. "Is it full-time?"

"Zeke says he'll pay me by the project. Works me. Gives me something to do, you know?" But he had time off when he wanted it.

"Oh, that's cool. Because my five of nine doesn't really match any other schedule in the whole world." Gabe laughed. "How's the leg feel today?"

"I spent most of the day without the crutch." That was a non-whiny answer that was still the truth.

"Nice. Way to go." Gabe smiled at him and reached for his hand. "I thought about you a lot today."

Bowie took Gabe's hand, squeezed it, thumb rubbing the palm. He'd never met anyone so tactile. "Did you? I worked on your bike, got it cleaned up for you." So he got it.

"You did?" Gabe grinned, and those eyes lit up again. "Wait, you put my fenders on yourself?"

"I did." He had to grin, had to.

"Well, how about that? That's incredibly cool. Thank you. I can't wait to pick it up in the morning."

He grabbed his phone and showed Gabe the picture he'd snapped of the bike. "*Ta-da.*"

"Oh, look at her. You polished her up and everything. She looks great! Wait until the guys see." Gabe was smiling wide as anything. "Thank you, babe."

"It was my pleasure. Thanks for introducing me to Zeke. He'll be decent to work for."

"He will. He's a straight-up guy. I've known him a long while now. Honest and fair. Probably a better artist than a mechanic." Gabe winked at him.

"Well, I'm not a bit of an artist, but I can build shit."

"Perfect."

Their food arrived, and Gabe dug right in, talking between enormous bites. "What are you planning for tomorrow?"

"Getting the table in, stopping by the garage for work, possibly making fried chicken. You off at eight?"

"Yep. Eight. And then I have two more days off. Fried

chicken sounds great. I can make some potatoes when I get home if you want. Or just bring a six-pack and dessert home with me." Gabe snorted. "I'll probably be pretty beat, but I'll perk up after a nap."

Food. Orgasm. Sleep. That would be Gabe's tomorrow. He wanted to organize the spare room. Make it somewhere to work on things, maybe.

"This is so good. How's your sampler thing?"

"I like the hummus and the falafel, and this gray goo is delicious. I don't care for the chunky stuff as much."

"What even is it?" Gabe reached over and forked a bite.

"Tomatoes and garlic and lots of parsley and something...lumpy."

Gabe made a face and put the fork down. "Yeah. That's a no on the lumpy. Water." Bear picked up a glass and drank deep, then set it on the table, grinning. "I'm stuffed anyway."

"Yeah, the rest of it was worth it, though. Falafel is like crazy breakfast sausage. I love it."

Gabe nodded and stuck a hand up, waving for the server, asking for the check. "I'll remember that. Falafel soothes the savage beast."

Bowie hooted. "Ice cream."

"What?"

"Ice cream is my weakness. Falafel is great, but it's ice cream that I asked for in the hospital."

Gabe started laughing. "Ice cream. That's even easier. What flavor?"

"Anything with fruit—strawberry, blackberry, peach, cherry—but I can do any flavor."

"Yeah, I like strawberry too. And coffee. You all done? You want a cone on the way home? It was hot today. Getting sticky."

"I do." He loved an ice cream cone, and the thought of

watching Gabe lick an ice cream intrigued the hell out of him, if for no other reason than he could just watch, straight up.

"Come on, then." Gabe unfolded from the chair with a groan that turned into a laugh. "God. I'm not old enough to groan when I get out of a chair."

"Come on. We can walk a ways and work out the kinks." He grabbed his crutch with one hand and Gabe's arm with the other, to make it around the table.

Gabe was a strong support, and his bear smiled at him and tucked his hand in against a solid torso too. "All good?"

All good? Was it? Well, if Gabe wasn't worried, he wasn't. "You know it."

"Ice cream is only a block out of the way." Gabe got them through the door and out onto the sidewalk, where the night air was muggy but not horrible, and claimed his hand again, hooking it around a thick forearm. "Tell me honestly. Does this make you uncomfortable?"

"I never thought I'd walk through the street holding on to my lover. I never thought that could be a thing. So, it's not comfortable, but that doesn't make it bad." And it helped. He was hurting.

"That sounds fair. It can be a thing. It should be a thing. And I have ice cream in the freezer if you'd like to get a cab home." Gabe chuckled and looked at him. "Huh. Home is a big word."

"Yeah. Is it too weird?" His home was in Texas, he guessed. That was his home of record.

"No, no. It's not weird. It just hasn't meant what that word oughtta mean in a long while." Gabe tugged his hand in tight again.

"I understand that. This is my first place. Funny, huh? I own five houses, and I've never lived in one as an adult."

"Whoa. Whoa, hold up. You do not own five houses." Gabe stared at him like he had five heads to go with them.

"I do. On the beach. I bought them for next to nothing after a bad hurricane, fixed them up, and I rent them out." He needed to do something with his savings.

"Beach houses. You're a landlord. Huh. Sammy never said." Gabe stuck a hand out, and a cab pulled right over.

"Don't know that Sammy knows. We've never talked about it. I've had them forever. They're super simple. Places for folks to come see the water." He grunted as he sat, his leg trying to cramp up.

Gabe moved around and got in the other side, so he didn't have to slide across, and gave the driver the address. "I'll rub that for you when we get home."

"I'd like that. It's tender. Thank you for supper. I'll cook for us tomorrow."

"Looking forward to it. And to my next beach vacation." Gabe grinned at him.

"Just say the word. We'll go. I love it out there. I'd love to show you about."

"I'll see when I can get some time." The cab pulled up, and Gabe let him cover it and headed around to give him a hand out of the car. "Jesus, I had to pick a gigantic lover, huh?"

"Well, Sammy was already taken." He hauled his ass out of the cab. "You could've just thrown him over your shoulder."

"I was tempted. Tommy got to him first." Gabe grinned. "And actually, even though he's probably a little spitfire in bed, he's not what I need."

"Probably. I wouldn't know. I know he's happy with Tommy. Really." And he had to smile, because Gabe seemed willing to need him, here and now.

"They're just right." Gabe supported him inside without a word about it, got them into the elevator. "When you find it, you hang on to it."

"Amen." And there wasn't a whole lot more to say about that. Not at all.

16

The only air conditioner Gabe had was in the bedroom. It was warm out here in the living room, and he wondered if they ought to get another one for the window in here. He'd never bothered. Living alone, he'd honestly tried not to be home much. He needed people and interaction. He'd go to Mike's or the club, see people. Have a beer.

He'd only gotten up to pee, so he went back to the bedroom, stopping to watch Bowie sleep for a minute instead of climbing right into bed.

Bowie was in his bed.

That was a concept, wasn't it? And really, it was their bed now. And their new dining table and their apartment. It should probably freak him out more than it did.

He'd say it happened really fast, but it didn't for him. It started eighteen months ago, one crazy night in a hotel room. He'd had a long time to think about it.

But he was sure Bowie hadn't thought about it. Not like he had. He was starting to wonder if Bowie thought about anything, really. At least anything beyond dinner.

He pumped the AC up a little and climbed in beside his lover. One thing he did know? Only people who didn't have a care in the world slept like that, and the only way someone like his lover wouldn't have a care in the world was if Bowie had decided not to.

So that was it. Bowie had unplugged.

The only thing Bowie offered as a memory of their one night together was he remembered Gabe was a kisser. Not how Gabe had felt in his arms. Not how much fun they'd had in the shower, doing their best to make the hotel run out of hot water. Not breakfast in bed. Just that kisses were allowed.

And there was the thing about letting Bowie know if he changed his mind about the living arrangements. And Bowie's noncommittal job with Zeke. Or the fact that Bowie hadn't asked to talk about anything. Like, anything at all unless he brought it up first.

Okay. He got it. He didn't know what to do about it yet, if anything, but he got it.

Bowie reached for him, drew him in, and held him, never waking up. "I got you, Bear."

He hadn't been gone for more than a few minutes, but he'd take it. It wasn't the first time Bowie'd caught him bouncing around in his own head, but it was crazy how Bowie could do it half-asleep too. He'd never had a lover big enough to really hold him. It was kind of nice. Odd, but nice.

Not comfortable, but that doesn't make it bad.

He'd liked how Bowie was thinking. He liked the small ways he was taking Bowie out of his comfort zone. Not that it was hard to do; his lover's "zone" was pretty narrow.

Huh. Maybe he had some marching orders.

God. He'd have to be careful, though. It hadn't taken

much for Bowie to take off for a hotel—just a moment of indecision on his part. He'd fixed it though; right or wrong, he was going to be damn decisive from now on. Think like a Dom, act like a Dom. Even if Bowie wasn't quite what he'd call a sub, his lover hadn't put up an argument with anything yet.

He guessed Bowie was used to giving orders and taking orders both without question.

Bowie's leg drew up, a frown crossing his face, and he reached out to grab it. Hard to tell if he was dreaming or if it just hurt all of a sudden, or both.

Gabe reached as well, covering Bowie's hand with his own. "Hurts, babe?"

Oh, that was a cramp, the quad hard as stone. *Jesus.* He bore down, working the heavy muscle until it let loose. Bowie was staring at him, sweat beading his forehead.

"Thanks."

He gave his lover a nod, still massaging, helping the circulation along. He was totally calm and made sure Bowie saw that. Injuries were right in his wheelhouse. "You're welcome. You want me to get your meds?"

"Let me see if I can stand on it." Bowie sat up, face set in stern, determined lines. "Morning, Bear."

Bowie forced himself to stand, the muscle fluttering visibly as he asked more of it than it had to give. Stubborn man.

"Morning, babe." He wasn't going to baby anybody, but he did hop up and snag Bowie's crutch from where it leaned against the new dresser and handed it to his lover. "You're an idiot, but I'm here if you need me."

"I am." Bowie took the crutch. "I'm going to get rid of the crutch. One day. I will." Then Bowie grinned at him. "Won't be today, though."

"No, seems unlikely to be today." He grinned back. "But you will. I have no doubt." He didn't. Doubt would have had Bowie in a wheelchair. At this point, he might not doubt if Bowie said he would fly too. "Let's make breakfast. You can sit at the table if you want, I'll bring you veggies to chop." He wanted egg wraps. With peppers and mushrooms, all that good stuff. Cheddar. Sausage. His stomach growled loudly.

"Works for me. I mean, we have a table, we might as well use it." Bowie's smile was warm as hell. "What are we making?"

"Egg wraps. With all the good stuff." Gabe followed Bowie into the living room and kept one eye on him until he was seated, then went after veggies to keep Bowie occupied. "Coffee?"

Like he needed to ask.

"Yes, sir. I appreciate it. You mind if I put on some music? Do you like music?"

"I love music. As long as it's not a half-naked twentysomething chick in a bodysuit and wearing too much eyeliner, I'm in." He laughed at himself. There were probably even a couple of those he'd like.

"I'm an old-school rock type of guy, mostly. I like a bunch of the 90s alternative stuff too. Industrial." Bowie chuckled softly. "I got to admit, I had a violent crush on Trent Reznor."

Violent was the perfect word. "Well. Is there anything hotter than NIN?" He set a cutting board and a knife down on the table. It was a nice solid piece. Not solid enough for a throwdown, but solid.

"I sure didn't think so at thirteen. You want to talk about confused."

"Oh. I hear that. How did you cope? Asks the guy that

didn't cope so well." He laughed. He'd been such a disaster. *God.*

"I jacked off a thousand times a day. I swear to you, my dick was going to fall off before I was eighteen."

He brought Bowie peppers and mushrooms to start with. "Please, that was every kid I knew." He grinned. "I got a job so I didn't have to go watch the football games. They were embarrassing."

"I was on the team. James didn't go out for it, and Sammy was too tiny, but I did fine." Bowie started chopping, the cuts incredibly delicate for those huge hands.

"I wasn't going anywhere near a boy's locker room. I had issues." He laughed. Big-ass issues. "Kicked out of school kind of issues. So, I wasn't really a joiner."

"Well, I wasn't a student, so I did shop, metalwork, football. Then I went to Basic the day after graduation."

"I waited about six months but yeah, I knew that was where I was headed. I was a decent student, just had the self-esteem of a drowned cat." Ah, teenagers. "Close on the veggies?"

"All done." Bowie handed them off. "I don't think I had to worry about self-esteem and all. I worried about blowing Jack in the barn, then I worried about getting blown up."

"Lucky Jack." He threw all the veggies in a skillet and took the opening. "Now what do you worry about?"

"Figuring out what to do now that no one needs me, I guess."

He rolled his eyes and sat a box grater and a block of cheddar in front of Bowie. "You're needed." He turned Bowie's head by the chin and kissed his lover like a man with needs ought to, only pulling away when he was very sure Bowie wasn't missing his point. "Now grate cheese." He winked and headed back to the skillet. Time to get the eggs in.

It took a few seconds for Bowie to move, and when he did, there was a slightly dazed expression on his face.

He chuckled and cracked a bunch of eggs into the skillet, scrambling them up with the veggies. He wanted to tell Bowie that digging a little deeper than that wasn't going to make anything explode, but he was starting to wonder. There had to be something under the surface, but it must have a very, very long fuse.

He warmed up tortillas, split the scramble up between four of them, and carried their plates to the table. "Cheese me. I'll get us more coffee."

"I'm on it." Bowie added cheese and folded the wraps up like a pro. "They look good. Thanks."

He brought two mugs of hot coffee and set them down, then grabbed a seat. "Table's great, huh? I really like it." Today's goal: find a button. Something that gets a real reaction. Anything. Find it, push it, deal with the fallout. But first, food.

"It's solid, not fake, put together like someone cared—I approve." Bowie stroked the wood like it was a lover.

Well, that was interesting. "If you're seriously looking for something to fill your time, we could use an entertainment center over there. Against the wall, right? You could build it. Something that fits the TV and the speakers, the cable box, all that crap."

"No problem. I can do that. Do you rent a truck to pick lumber and shit up, or do folks deliver?" Bowie sized up the wall like he was planning on storming a beach.

"Ask Zeke. His buddies have trucks, tools, everything." Okay, good. The beast had a project to focus on. Keeping busy he understood well. He inhaled one of his wraps and swallowed it down with coffee. "Hot in here, right? I think we should pick up an AC unit for the front window. Cooking won't be any fun in July otherwise."

"Have you seen the units that don't have to go in the window? They're expensive up front, but they work like a charm, especially in rooms like this."

"I have not. I'm just trying not to deal with the landlord. He's a pain in the ass. Maybe we should paint." He knew what he was doing. A layer of paint and some furniture didn't make up for what he wanted and wasn't getting yet from Bowie. But he would. He had plenty of patience and even more time.

"I'll show you. These units are small and don't need so much infrastructure. I put them in my rental units." Bowie chatted with him over breakfast, showing him pictures of his little houses. They had been shells, and Bowie had apparently spent his free time fixing them and turning them into something decent.

It was pretty amazing, actually. He'd spent a lot of time on them, knew what he was doing. He was obviously very capable. Bowie was more chatty and animated than Gabe had seen him in...well, ever. He was proud of those houses.

"You fixed them up great. I'm impressed."

"Thanks. I couldn't leave all that money in savings, so the JAG helped me figure it out."

"That's cool. Good for you." All that money. Gabe guessed Bowie must be pretty loaded, considering his time in and pension and disability and all. Good for him. He deserved it after putting his life on the line for years on end. "You all done?" Gabe picked up their empty plates and took them to the kitchen.

Bowie got up and followed, helping out, even if he was moving slow.

He handed Bowie a dishrag to dry and turned on the water. "Tell me what you miss the most about...hm. About the desert."

Bowie snorted softly. "The guys. I had some great soldiers in my unit. Steady as fuck. The desert itself? We weren't having a vacation, so we were all just trying to survive. You were deployed, you said. You have to get it."

He shrugged. "I do and I don't. I saw a lot of soldiers trying to survive, believe me. Trying hard. Everyone's experience is a little different. I miss the sky at night. I'd never seen so many stars."

"Fair enough." Bowie grabbed the plate Gabe washed.

He glanced at Bowie. "But then, I wasn't worried about getting blown up every day. Those are steep terms."

"That was the job. Build 'em up. Tear 'em down." Bowie shrugged one shoulder. "Good reason to excel at your job."

"Yeah, right?" He pulled the pan off the stove and scrubbed it. "Are you in touch with anyone?"

"Not from my unit. The guy that manages my properties were in with me. Got a couple godbabies from a friend in Basic."

"Yeah? That's cool." He handed Bowie the pot he was washing and shut the water off.

Bowie nodded and put the pan away. "Were you a medic while you were in?"

"Yep. That's what I did. Flew in under the red cross, grabbed whoever we were there for, and flew out." He grinned. It sounded very tame put that way.

"Good deal. That's good work."

"It was. Nerve-wracking, but good work. I'm sure you can relate. Every time my radio went off, someone's life was in my hands." Gabe leaned on the counter. "So, shower? Get dressed? Back to bed?" He hooked an arm around Bowie's waist and let his lover lean.

"So many choices." Bowie did lean against him, trusting him to hold on. "I vote for shower and sit around in our skivvies, making out, and watching movies."

"Oh. Perfect. I'm so in." And that would also give him time to see what it would take to rattle Bowie a little. "You want to sit for a bit first or head on in?"

"I'm easy as pie." Bowie chuckled. "And that is where James would say, 'Mmm pie.'"

Gabe grinned, leading Bowie toward the bathroom, steadying him. "Were you two close?"

"I think so. Closer than me and Sammy were, growing up, for sure."

"James never talked about either of you, you know. I didn't even know he had brothers."

"That doesn't surprise me. I didn't know he had a lover."

He shrugged. He wasn't going to pretend to get it. He ducked into the bathroom and started the shower. "You miss him?"

"Well, sure. I talked to him once a month, no matter what. Talked to him the night before he died, in fact. He seemed happy."

"Tommy says he was. But he and Sammy are special. Everyone sees it." He helped Bowie undress and get into the shower. "Sammy says James used to run interference between you. Did you two not get along?"

"We're a lot alike." That was a non-answer answer.

He followed Bowie in and grabbed the shampoo to wash his lover's hair. "What does that mean?"

"You know how it's hard to get along with people that are just like you? Like Momma and James fought hard. Me and Sammy can butt heads sometimes."

"What about?" He massaged the lather into all that thick, long hair. He never saw himself with a guy with hair like...well with anyone like Bowie at all. The hair, Bowie's size, his lover's past...none of it was what he expected.

"Now? Not a whole lot. When we were younger, I didn't do right by him. That feels good, Bear."

He had no idea how you didn't do right by your brother, especially when you were overseas all the time. "What could you be expected to do? You weren't home. He had James. Rinse."

Bowie leaned back into the water, rinsing his hair. "It was bullshit brother stuff. You got siblings?"

"My little sister, Gilli, is in Denver." They talked about once a month, they got along okay, but they were...different. They didn't have a lot to say.

"Well, we used to tease Sam, tell him he couldn't possibly be gay, that he was just copying us. How could three brothers be gay?" Bowie shrugged. "I'd say that I wouldn't do it again, but that's silly. You do what you do and you learn."

"Well, in your defense, how could they? It seems impossible." It was remarkable. "But I see what you mean." He ducked under the spray. "I couldn't make fun of Gilli, she did everything right. Still does. And I couldn't even make fun of her for that."

"That was James. He was the good one. Me and Sammy? We're scrappers." Bowie reached for him, washing him, hands exploring his skin.

"James was a good boy for sure." He grinned a little; he'd always admired the way James served. Like Tommy was the only one in the room and the planets revolved around Master. It was flawless. "Mmm. If we're staying in, you should take something to help those muscles relax."

"Yeah. I try to not, because they make me...off, but I can't afford for them to tear either."

"We're watching movies. Off is okay." He rinsed, then crowded Bowie into the shower wall. "Guess we should get out."

"Mmm. Or we could just stay until the hot water runs out." Bowie winked at him.

"We tried that once. I was exhausted." But duly noted that it was memorable after all. He winked back. "Wouldn't want to make you stand too long."

"Exhausting, but I remembered that over a lot of months in the hospital."

He'd never been so happy to be all wrong. He smiled and hooked some of Bowie's wet hair behind an ear. "I'm glad. You were on my mind...often."

"Yeah? Thank you." That was sincere and warm, Bowie obviously pleased.

He reached over and shut the water off, deciding they had all day to get off, this was too good a moment to overshadow. "Do Sammy or Tommy know? Do you want them to?"

He climbed out of the shower and grabbed towels, handing one to Bowie.

"Know that I'm interested in you? That we're lovers?"

He smiled wider because Bowie just said they were lovers, out loud. "Just that much, yeah. Is that okay? Or would you rather we keep it to ourselves?"

Bowie stopped him and stared at him, face so serious. "I would not be with a man that I had to hide. I did my service. I am not ashamed of you, most especially not with Sammy and his man."

"Oh. Wow. That deserves a kiss." He rested a hand on

Bowie's jaw and pulled them together, giving his lover a kiss the man could hold on to.

Bowie's hands rested on his hips, solid, sure, trusting him to balance that big body. "This whole kissing at will thing does not suck, Bear."

"No, it's pretty good, right?" He took another quick one. "I thought I was a fool to be thinking about you all that time." After all, what were the chances of him seeing Bowie again more than a handful of times? He would never have wished an injury on the man, not ever. But Bowie was home now, and in his bed, and he had to believe that was a good thing.

"I always asked after you, even when you and Sam were growling."

He scratched at his scalp, embarrassed. That hadn't been one of his better moments. He'd let emotion blur the line between right and wrong. "He told you all of that, huh?"

"He called for advice. I told him that he chose to be a sub; this was part of it. He needed to figure out what was bothering him and be clear."

"He was very clear. There was a lot of gray area for me, but Sammy, like any good sub, doesn't live in the gray. I needed to get clear too. Anyway, no one told me you were asking. But I guess they couldn't have known it would be meaningful to me. It is, though. Did Sammy send my hellos?"

"He told me about you, but really, his phone calls were for advice, support about James and the fallout from before the arrest. Big brother stuff."

"Sure. That's what he needed. Big brother stuff." He smiled and gave Bowie an arm to lean on so they could go get not-dressed. "I don't really know what to say, you know?

I'm sorry you got hurt, man. I'm sorry you got sent home. But I'm happy you're here. It's weird."

"Regret is a waste of time. None of my people died, and neither did I, and now I'm here." Simple, straightforward, sure—Gabe wasn't clear whether the words were meant to soothe, but he thought maybe they were.

"Got it, Sarge. I'm happy you're here." He smiled at Bowie and pulled on a pair of briefs.

Bowie pulled on the tiniest, most-worn pair of PT shorts known to man, took a pill from the bottle near the bed, and they sat together.

He turned on the TV and threaded his fingers with Bowie's, hoping maybe his lover would bust right out of those shorts. That would be okay. Easy access for their mutual hand jobs.

17

"Good job, O'Reilly. You're quick." Zeke looked pleased as he checked over the bike, the motor purring like a kitten. "You want another project today or..."

"I have air conditioners to install at the apartment." He'd built and stained the entertainment center, painted the front room, and organized the spare room into somewhere he could putter when Gabe was sleeping. Now he had two air conditioners to put in, one in the front room and one in the spare room.

Sammy was meeting him to help because he and ladders weren't friends right now.

"Fair enough. Text me when you're available again." Zeke pulled some cash out of his pocket, counted out twenties, and handed him a stack. Then Zeke lit a cigarette, taking a huge first drag. "You're working out good. Any time you want to make this a real job, you let me know, okay?"

"Thanks, man. I like to keep a little flexibility."

Gabe was off for the next three days after today, and he figured he ought to be about.

Bringing burgers. Fries? shake? He looked at Sammy's text. Food. *Score.*

Yes. Yes. Strawberry. Heading to the apt

Sammy was a good egg. It was something vaguely wonderful, having his baby brother close by and be not home, all at the same time. Lord, it was strange, learning how to be a civilian and a local brother.

On it

He buzzed Sammy in about half an hour later. His brother came through the door with a giant takeout bag and handed him a flat with two strawberry shakes. "Those might be a little melty, it's sticky hot out."

"Yeah. At least we're better equipped back home, huh? I bought these little units to cool it off in here." They tore open the food and dug in. "Thanks for the grub."

"No big. I was hungry too. You been busy?"

"Working on motorcycles and this place, you?"

"Yeah. Writing." Sammy grinned at him. "I'm taking Thomas to Rome."

Bowie blinked. "No shit?"

"No shit." His baby brother looked stupidly tickled, and he had to chuckle.

"Go you, man. That rocks."

"Mhm." Sammy chewed, grinning. "He bought one of those 'learn a language in five minutes' things. His accent sucks, but it's kind of cute. How's Angel? Is he a decent roomie?"

Roomie? Gabe? That seemed like a flip term, but whatever. "He's good. We fit together. We cook a lot, which is cool. I'll like it when our bedroom isn't the only room with AC."

Sammy looked at him, raised an eyebrow, and instead of

saying anything, picked up a strawberry shake and sucked on the straw.

He didn't have to explain, did he? If Sammy wanted to know specifics, Sammy could ask.

"Do they actually make a bed big enough?" Sammy grinned around the straw.

"Do you end up disappearing under Tommy in the middle of the night?" he countered.

Sammy snorted. "I'd hate to be your downstairs neighbors. Jesus Christ."

"Like your next-door neighbors don't dread beating day." Oh, that was pretty good.

"So, when y'all whale on each other, no one cares?"

He arched an eyebrow. "Seriously? We don't whale."

"Oh, so you two dress up in lace and ribbons and make sweet, sweet love?"

Oh, he was going to beat Sammy to death. "We prefer chain mail. It makes a great noise."

Damn. So close to shake-out-the-nose. Next time.

"Seriously, I'm not sure I approve. I think there's a conflict of interest. I don't know who to use my 'If you break his heart, I'll break your neck' speech on."

"Oh, you know me. They didn't issue me a heart in the Army."

Sammy laughed. "True. You better find one, though. Angel's is made of chocolate and roses."

"I'm totally capable of providing chocolate and beer." Bowie stood up and grabbed the detritus of their lunch.

Sammy picked up what he'd left behind and followed him. "Well, I'm happy for you guys. I feel bad for the landlord, but I'm happy for you. Hopefully the guy has good insurance."

"Hey! I'm fixing the place up, right?" He popped Sammy on the hip.

Sammy cut eyes at him but didn't move. "I thought so! I've only been here once but I remember it being way more...empty. That's cute. You're playing house! Who's the...*whoa*. No. Never mind. Don't want to know."

"Play nice now." *Shithead.*

"Sorry." Pretty fucking funny how Sammy blushed, though. He didn't know people could turn that color. "Uh. Air conditioners, right?"

"Right." They started unpacking the machines, both of them steadfastly avoiding the question that Sammy had almost asked. Bowie had no intention of explaining anything, especially something he and Gabe hadn't even touched on.

It was easiest just to not.

"So, how's the job going? Angel said your boss is one of his biking buddies?" Sammy went up the ladder like a monkey. There was something to be said for a low center of gravity.

"Great. I go in when there's a project and I want to." He had guilt about that, but part of him said that he'd worked for sixteen years, whenever and however the Army wanted. He'd given a whole chunk of his leg.

"That's cool. Good to have the same guy on a project till it's done, I guess. Probably lets him take on stuff he wouldn't otherwise, right?" Sammy found the center of the wall and marked it. "Here?"

"Yeah. Perfect." He handed up the drill. "Zeke seems happy enough."

"Good. He should be, you know your shit." Sammy started drilling holes, and it got too loud to talk for a bit.

That gave him a second to notice how good his brother was looking. Fit. Not having to make weight looked good on Sammy.

Hell, having the trial over and that murdering asshole in jail looked good on Sammy.

"Okay." Sammy handed him back the drill. Climbed down two steps and jumped the last few. "I need that... mounting thing. The long thing."

"Got it." He handed it over. This was going to work well. "You like the entertainment center?"

"Looks like Momma and Daddy's. You made that in woodshop, didn't you?"

"Yessir. You made...a tiny little birdhouse?"

"Shut up. Mine's better." Sammy gave him a toothy grin.

Bowie flipped Sammy off, but they both cracked up, just hooting with laughter.

By the time Gabe walked through the door, with Tommy in tow, they had gotten the two new units up and working, without murdering each other.

"Well, well, look who the cats dragged in."

Gabe snorted. "Oh, no. You don't get dragged around by cats when Tommy's around. You get picked up right after your shift in an Uber and handed a bottle of water and a roll of Wild Cherry Lifesavers. Hey! It's cool in here!"

Tommy stepped around Gabe and shook his hand. "Bowie."

"Tommy. How goes?" He was pretty damn proud of them.

He caught Gabe giving Sammy a hug, his brother disappearing in his lover's arms.

"Well. Everything is going very well. You look good. Rested. Gabe says you're working?"

"I am. I'm doing piecemeal mechanic work. It's decent money and flexible. I hear you're going to Italy?"

"I am! Your brother surprised me with tickets for my birthday. I'm really looking forward to it, I've never been. Sam hasn't either, so we'll be exploring together, which will be wonderful."

"That fucking rocks, man. Congrats." He loved that the kids could go.

"I haven't been here before; this is a great place." Tommy started wandering, checking things out.

"Hey, Sarge." Gabe stepped over and pulled him in. "You guys did a fantastic job, they look great. They work great too."

"It's going to be more comfortable for us." He smiled and took a quick kiss. "Good day?"

"Eh. About a six. But Tommy brought me Lifesavers." Gabe winked at him. A six was better than a four. Still, Bear looked tired. Three days on was a lot. "Are we cooking or going out, did you and Sammy decide?"

"We hadn't talked about it. You want to order in?"

Gabe smiled at him, eyes knowing. "I'd appreciate that." He got a kiss too. "I'll get everyone a beer. You guys want... beers...what?"

Tommy and Sammy were staring.

"You want Thai? Pizza? Bacon fried rice?" Bowie refused to let the buttheads get to them.

Gabe seemed oblivious and just looked at him. "Pizza. Definitely pizza. I'm getting these two beers, they need one. Sorry, Tommy. No wine."

"Oh. Uh, not a problem. Beer is fine." Tommy followed Gabe into the kitchen, giving his shoulder a slap on the way by. "Good catch."

"Thanks, buddy." Tommy's words made his eyes roll.

"I appreciate your help, Sammy. It would have killed my leg."

"No big. How is it?"

He shrugged. He wasn't sure. Mostly okay. Sore.

Gabe came back out and handed him a menu and a pencil. "Have a seat, babe. Take orders."

"Yes, sir." He knew what Sammy and Gabe liked— sausage and mushrooms—and Tommy wanted pepperoni, just like him. Perfect. Three of each.

He ordered and paid on his phone before moving toward the guys.

"I like this table." Tommy pulled out a chair for him and sat in another one.

It wasn't all that long before their food was delivered. He put on some tunes, they all got seats, and refreshed their beers.

"Sammy, how did you decide on Italy?" Gabe picked up his slice, folded it in half, and took a bite.

"We both have talked about it a few times, and there's the art and the food and the wine..." Sammy had a blissful look on his face.

"It's right up our alley." Tommy smiled at Sammy and sipped his beer.

"I'm going to try to get some time off this summer so Bowie can show me his beach houses."

"Beach houses?" Sammy asked. "Where?"

"Galveston. I got five."

"No shit? When? You closemouthed old fuck. I could've bought one off you and just lived down there."

"They're a project."

"I'm glad you didn't know, Sam. You needed to come to New York." Tommy's voice dropped deep and a little possessive.

Sammy looked at Tommy, and lord if his little brother didn't go all doe-eyed. *Christ.*

"Well, I'm hearing waves calling me." Gabe took another huge bite of his pizza.

"Are you two working together at the club, then? I bet Clint loves that, all three O'Reillys, he's probably ready to write a white paper on the biology of BSDM or something." Tommy laughed.

Bowie chose another piece of his own. "No. We've gone to the bar, but we've been busy working on the house a lot."

"Bowie's got skills, Tommy. He built that entertainment center in two days." Gabe totally backed him up.

Tommy looked over at it. "That is nice work. Perhaps I ought to have let you put those built-ins in the guest room after all."

Sam laughed out loud, and Tommy joined in. "All right, perhaps not."

"I'm telling you, man. I am not appreciated." Bowie winked at his bear and ate his pizza. Of course, they had three days off together with a fresh air conditioner. They could appreciate the fuck out of each other.

Gabe picked up his beer and leaned back in his chair. "So, Tommy. How's work?"

Tommy talked for a while about donors and money, and something he wished he'd paid more attention to about Civil War era weaponry. He was pretty sure the man said some things that made sense to Sammy, but Gabe looked as glassy-eyed as he felt by the time Tommy was done.

"That's great, man. Good for you." Gabe sipped his beer.

"Fucking A." Lord, that man had a lot of words in his mouth.

"One as bad as the other." Sam snorted, but he got a wink.

"Angel, I'm sure you're exhausted. Did you say this was your third shift in a row?"

Gabe nodded. "Yeah, pretty standard stuff, but it'd be a lie to say it doesn't take it out of me."

"Well..." Tommy stood; then Sammy stood with him. "We'll get out of your hair and let you get some sleep."

Bowie stood, hugged Sammy with one arm. "Thanks for your help, man. I appreciate it."

"We had fun. I was glad to take the afternoon off."

"Yeah. Thanks, Sammy, for making sure your brother didn't drop something on his head." Gabe headed for the door and opened it for them.

Tommy took Sammy by the hand. "Thank you for the pizza. Next time we'll invite you to our neck of the woods."

"Sounds great, man. See you soon."

"At the club. We might go this weekend." Tommy raised an eyebrow at Gabe.

"Maybe. We'll see."

"All right. Goodnight, you two."

Gabe waited for them to get in the elevator and closed the apartment door.

"Hey, you." He went to Gabe and rubbed his shoulders. "Happy your Friday, huh?"

"TGIF." Gabe groaned for him. "Oh, fuck. That feels good. Did you and Sam have a good day?"

"Just fine. He was a huge help." He hadn't been looking forward to climbing the ladder.

"They work great—it's really comfortable in here now." Gabe turned to face him and combed fingers through his beard. "We have three whole days."

"We do." And he was looking forward to them with an almost goofy anticipation. God, it fascinated him, how Gabe touched him. It was so easy.

"We should probably start them off with a nap." Gabe slid warm hands under his T-shirt, finding his nipples and rolling them gently.

"I know how to nap." Lord, it didn't take much for his voice to go all gravelly, did it? Just that little, sweet buzz.

Gabe liked it. Didn't matter that his lover was tired. Bowie saw the way Gabe's broad chest puffed up, the little flash of heat in those eyes. "Bedroom, then."

They made it to the bedroom, the AC unit in there doing a good job now that it wasn't having to struggle. He helped Gabe out of his boots, his uniform.

"It's good, you know. Coming home to you." His bear was watching, not really helping, eyes all over him.

He nodded and let himself touch, stroke here and pet there. "Zeke can't understand why I don't come on full-time, but I do. I get it."

"I love my job. Even the hard days. But the schedule makes things complicated. I know what you're doing, and I get it too." Gabe reached out and gripped his nape, holding his eyes. "I get it. And I appreciate it."

"Good deal." That made things work. Mutual respect. He leaned into Gabe's hand. It was a weird, wonderful sensation and Bowie intended to feel it.

He got a nod, then a kiss heavy enough to knock him a little off-balance. On purpose. Gabe was right there, the other arm wrapping around him pulling him in.

Bowie grabbed for Gabe's shoulder, but it was more instinct than worry. Gabe had him. The son of a bitch was strong.

Gabe grinned, a low hum vibrating between them, and stepped him toward the bed. "You trust me. That's good."

Bowie slept with Gabe, dreamed next to him. He nodded and sat, drawing Gabe down with him. They moved up into the pillows and into each other's arms, and he lay his head on Gabe's shoulder as his bear tangled fingers into his hair. It didn't take any time for Gabe to fall asleep.

He rested there, planning a shelving unit for the spare room, and before he had it half-designed, he was asleep too.

18

G abe had been pleased to discover Bowie liked a clean ship too. They'd spent part of the morning cleaning, part of it food shopping and running errands. It sounded like Bowie wanted to turn the spare room into a sort of workshop and office thing, and they'd looked at paint colors online for that.

He'd made chicken salad sandwiches for lunch, and now he felt justified sitting his ass on the couch with Bowie and watching TV.

"Hey. You think we need a new couch? Do you think this thing is looking ratty with all the new stuff?"

"Who cares what it looks like? This couch is comfortable as fuck and fits us both. I love this sofa."

"Cool." That was the right answer; he loved it too. "Me too." He leaned right into Bowie, flipping channels, knowing eventually he'd end up with the Food Network, but surfing anyway. He heard Bowie sigh and grinned, flipping a few more channels, watching a minute, and flipping again.

Bowie chuckled. "You're doing that on purpose, turkey."

"Doing what?" He snorted. He was bad at this game and

he knew it, but he flipped again, to some talking head neither of them wanted to listen to.

"Don't make me take it away from you, now." Bowie leaned in close, heavy against him.

He liked that weight if he was honest, and Bowie's teasing tone. He shook his head and flipped the channels again leaning back hard. "Fat chance."

"Uh-huh." Bowie dug into his ribs, enough to tickle, not enough to hurt.

"I'm not ticklish, lunkhead." He was a big fat liar, but he tried not to tense up and show it.

"No? Then this won't bother you." Bowie danced those fingers up along his ribs, teasing and trying to bring the remote into reach.

He tried. His toes curled, he bit his tongue, he squeezed the remote hard enough to change the channel again accidentally, but it was hopeless. He flinched and shoved at Bowie's hand, laughing and holding the remote as far away as possible. "That doesn't bother me, it pisses me off!"

"Pisses you off? That seems extreme." Bowie threw himself across Gabe in a sudden move and got the remote.

"Asshole." All the air left him in a rush, so he could barely croak the word. He reached out with one hand and slapped his lover in the ass, hard enough to make his hand sting.

Bowie turned, rolling them both off the sofa with a thud. He landed on top and thought for a second about Bowie's leg, but his lover was already trying to get out from under him and wasn't complaining. He made a grab for the remote, getting his hand on it but not quite managing to get it out of Bowie's grip. He pinned that wrist to the floor instead. "Let it go, babe."

"Not a chance, Bear." Bowie's riposte was to grab the remote with his other hand.

He chuckled. That was a big brother move if he ever saw one. He shifted, wedging his knee between Bowie's thighs. "I'm going to get it one way or another."

"Are you now?" Bowie arched, rubbing on his thigh, managing to almost hide the motion.

"I don't give up easy." He stretched long, reaching for the remote, his thigh pressing hard into his lover's groin.

"I count on it. This is way more fun." Bowie used his whole leg, wrapped it around Gabe and tugged.

"Damn." He wasn't used to playing this game with someone his size. That leg was heavy and strong. Fortunately for him, there weren't any rules. He ducked his head and nuzzled Bowie's chest, found a nipple, and pinched it between his teeth.

"Fuck! Cheating!" Bowie twisted, even as he swallowed a moan, and Gabe found himself under Bowie's rock-hard body.

"Not." He grunted and blinked the stars out of his eyes, biting back a moan as his cock stretched. "Fucking Rangers, so by the book." He needed to stay away from that book; Bowie had the upper hand. "Kiss me."

"My pleasure." Bowie slid one hand under his head, cradling him as Bowie brought their mouths together.

Oh, that was nice. He opened up and tried to swallow Bowie's tongue, making his lover moan, then slid a hand along the Ranger's free arm and plucked the remote from Bowie's fingers.

"Oh, you are a cheater!" Bowie was all smiles and pushed into their kiss, even as he tried to get the remote back.

He laughed against Bowie's lips and tossed the remote

aside, sending it skittering across the floor, well out of reach. "So there." He arched up, pressing their hips together, making sure Bowie felt him.

Bowie settled on him, slowly lowering his weight down.

"Mmm. That's it, babe. I'm not gonna break." He had to admit, the weight was nice, Bowie felt solid and real. He rocked a little, encouraging Bowie to move with him, letting his lover think he was pinned, enjoying the friction as he waited for the man to get himself off-balance. It didn't take long—Bowie had to trust more on that right leg, so he was already at a disadvantage.

Gabe gripped Bowie's shoulder and grunted with the effort of shoving him to the floor on his good side, frankly taking advantage of Bowie's weaker side and pushed him facedown, pinning him with a knee in the center of his back.

Bowie was stiff for about a second; then Gabe felt him try to relax. "You do know that you only get a point if you pin the shoulders, right?"

He rolled his eyes. "You would be keeping score." He leaned forward and added his weight to a hand braced on Bowie's neck. "How many points now?"

"Far as I know, we haven't decided, Bear." Bowie's voice was low, husky. "I never played just like this."

He nodded. "Do the math. This one is a winner every time." He moved his knee so he could straddle Bowie's waist. "How do you feel about that?"

"I trust you, Bear."

"I know, babe. But do you want this?" Because just handing it over wasn't what it should be about.

"Yeah. Yeah, I want this, from you. You've proven you know how to take it."

He leaned lower, bracing the rest of his weight on one

hand flat on the floor by Bowie's ear, and lowered his voice. "Do you need this?"

"You tell me." Bowie rippled underneath him, pushing back, testing him.

He held steady but that was damn distracting, all that beautiful muscle working as Bowie tried his resolve. "You do. You know it too, Bowie, you've been looking for a new point of reference."

He dragged one hand down along Bowie's spine, loving the low groan, the way Bowie bucked underneath him, damn near unseating him.

He made sure he had his balance and let that hand travel farther, fingers finding scars. "Because if I asked you right now who you are, would you have an answer? Do you?"

"Bowie O'Reilly, all the way."

He let his voice drop, eyes trained on that hand on Bowie's neck. "I didn't ask your name, *boy*. I asked who you are."

He knew that Bowie was trying to find a new space, a new identity now that he was a civilian. He also knew Bowie didn't have an answer.

"That is who I am."

He bent forward and kissed Bowie's shoulder. "Okay, I understand. What does it feel like to be...Bowie O'Reilly right now?"

"Right now? Fucking amazing."

He had to smile. He felt pretty fucking great himself. "Good. Well, I know who you are, boy. Other than Bowie O'Reilly, that is. You're mine."

He could feel the heat climbing up along Bowie's body, feel the way Bowie shifted to make room for his trapped erection.

There. That's a hitching post for you, cowboy.

He eased up on Bowie's neck, just as ready to find some room for his need as *his* boy was. He could say that in this context, he was pretty sure. Maybe even very sure. He shifted and sat on the floor, reaching to lift Bowie's hair out of those pale eyes.

Bowie didn't shy away from Gabe, but he did turn so he was resting on the good side, the scarred leg propped on top.

Gabe stretched out with Bowie, gave the boy a smile, and took a kiss. Just a slow one, letting them simmer a little, enjoying it. Bowie hummed, tangled their fingers together, and held on.

"Need a hand up?" He offered softly. "Or do you want to crawl like a good boy?" He let himself grin, just a little, just enough that Bowie would know he was joking. Mostly.

"I will beat you, Bear." Bowie rolled up onto his elbow. "I haven't ever been a good boy. It's a genetic impossibility."

Right. Because neither Sammy nor James was a good sub. This had to be genetic too.

He got to his feet and waited for Bowie to sit up, then hauled his lover up off the floor and onto the couch with him. Bowie made it easy, probably having done it a hundred times since that bomb went off.

Which he was thinking he might ask about tomorrow.

Right now, he pulled Bowie in and kissed him again, intending to make this a very long night. Bowie crawled right up into his lap, settling them close together with a moan.

"Nothing like having an Army Ranger in your lap. Jesus." He pressed a hand against the long ridge in Bowie's sweats. "Mmm. That feels very nice."

Bowie arched into his hand, the move slow and sinuous. "Hell, yeah."

He loved the way Bowie wanted this, wanted him, when his lover let that guard down enough to just do what felt good. Bowie could burn hot, and it didn't take much of that to set him on fire.

He pushed the sweats over Bowie's hips, baring that gorgeous cock. "So pretty." He curled his fingers around it lightly. The elastic on the waistband pushed up under Bowie's balls, presenting his lover like a package.

He hooked a hand behind Bowie's back and leaned up to lick and nibble at his boy's chest and nipples. He'd be happy to get his mouth on every inch of Bowie's skin, feel all that muscle under his teeth. He loved how Bowie shivered, responded to him like a dream. Those nipples drew up, went hard and tight. Bowie's abs rippled and pulled, drawing his gaze.

He stroked his fist up Bowie's length and rolled his thumb over the head, making sure to pay special attention to the damp slit, one of Bowie's favorite hot spots.

Bowie bared his teeth, breath coming hard and quick for a few intense seconds. "Damn. Damn, Bear. So fucking hot."

That sound, the look on Bowie's face, made his balls ache. Later he'd see if he could get Bowie off just by doing that. "Fuck, yeah. You're burning up. I want your mouth, babe. So bad."

"I'll sit, you can fuck my lips. That work for you?"

"Goddamn it, I love that you just say that kind of shit. Hell yeah, that works for me." Even better than saying it, he knew Bowie could take it. And he was more than ready to return the favor after.

Bowie pushed himself up and over, then held his arms open. 'Come here, Bear."

He shoved out of his sweats and climbed into Bowie's

arms. "Just know I'm going to make you lose your mind after this."

"Fair enough. I look forward to it. I want you." Bowie hauled him up, hands hard on his ass, and slid down a bit, taking the tip in and lapping at it, teasing him.

"Mhm." He chuckled darkly. "You're gonna get me." He reached over Bowie and braced a hand on the back of the couch. Bowie was right, this couch was perfect. For everything.

Bowie opened up, eyes focused on him, and deliberately pulled him in with one slow drag.

"Shit." Jesus, Bowie threw himself into this. He wasn't just good at it; he gave head like he loved it. Like it mattered.

Gabe sank in as far as Bowie would allow, cradling Bowie's head in the other hand. Bowie's tongue worked him, slapping his shaft, dragging over his skin. Then the suction kicked in, his boy focused on his pleasure.

He kept his eyes on those lips, watched as Bowie's cheeks hollowed, but couldn't ignore the way the boy's fingers dug in where they gripped his ass. It was just distracting enough that he knew focus wasn't going to be a thing for long. When his boy did something evil with that tongue, it made him grunt and sent electricity right to his balls. He tried to keep his eyes from crossing and managed a raspy, "Good boy."

So Bowie did it again.

And again.

And again.

"Fuck!" That last one pushed a little too hard, and somewhere in the back of his mind, he knew that was no accident. At the end of his patience, he felt more than heard himself growl, got a fistful of his boy's hair, and took what Bowie had offered him.

He slammed in, trusting in the hands on his ass, the way Bowie's eyes fell closed as he fucked those hungry lips.

He should be careful—make sure he wasn't choking the fuck out of Bowie. There were a bunch of things he probably should have been doing, but he didn't have one fucking ounce of patience for it. Bowie was a big boy. If it wasn't working out, he'd know. His ass would be on the floor.

All he was getting from his boy was that he should take exactly what he wanted. He dove in, again and again, lost in a haze with that heat and Bowie's hands on his ass.

A deep hum built inside his boy, the sound vibrating around his cock, buzzing all the way up his spine. He pulled hard, burying himself in Bowie's throat, the sensation of Bowie swallowing around him nearly unbearable.

Then he froze, totally shorting out, curled over Bowie and let his boy drag him off the cliff. Like he had a choice. He swore, the word coming from somewhere deep and animal and it felt fucking amazing. "Fuck!"

Bowie held him, suction easing, the pressure becoming soft, almost gentle as Bowie eased him down.

The couple of aftershocks were nearly as intense as the real thing, and he panted through them, trying not to look as stunned as he felt. Probably a losing battle. He relaxed back, sitting on his boy's knees. "Fuck, man. That...stars. Like, bottle rockets and...so good." Nope. Words were bad. He leaned in and kissed his boy instead. Hard.

Bowie groaned, the sound raw and rough as it pushed into their kiss. Bowie held him, keeping him close so that the kiss went on and on.

Yeah...that was, yeah. He slid a hand slowly from Bowie's shoulder, down his boy's side, and across that hard belly. He let Bowie anticipate and kept his hand where it was, abs twitching and vibrating under his fingers. He knew Bowie was aching for him, but the big man didn't demand. Not yet, anyway.

Gabe knew though, he knew how to draw the boy out, he'd seen it earlier. He held off a little longer, keeping Bowie breathless in that kiss, teasing with his fingers, until he felt it coiling on its own. Then he broke the kiss off abruptly and leaned close to his boy's ear, nuzzling that thick hair. "Mine."

Bowie grunted, hands on his hips tightening and trying to encourage him closer. "Need you."

Gabe nodded and let Bowie have what he wanted, moving in close, fingers wrapping tight around the base of Bowie's cock. "What do you want, babe? Ask me."

"Touch me, please. Work the tip. Won't take much. I'm revved."

"Mmm. You sound it." Please. From a six-foot-something tank of a man. Damn, he was a lucky bastard. He did exactly as Bowie asked, releasing the base and sliding his hand up to the head, adding a little of that sweet pressure to the tip and pushing his thumb deep into that sensitive slit. "Got you."

"Bear!" Oh, hell yes. That was a beautiful noise—honest and gruff and wild and his.

He drew his fist down and back, a quick stroke, and tunneled his thumb in again, watching his boy's face, feeling Bowie rise under him.

Bowie's chin lifted, lips open in a silent scream as he shot, his entire body convulsing beneath him.

"Yeah." His own voice was barely above a whisper, feeling oddly respectful of his boy's powerful, silent release. He couldn't be any more smug, honestly. He stroked Bowie slow and gentle, his other hand fussing with Bowie's hair, stroking that beard, touching.

Bowie relaxed, easing beneath him, breath slowing. He caught Gabe's fingers with his lips, teasing them gently.

"You." He grinned and leaned in for a kiss, this one just gentle, just a connection. "Fuckin' A."

"Uh-huh. All the way."

He climbed off Bowie, groaning like he was seventy, and fell back onto the couch, beside his lover with a sigh. "Yeah. This is a kickass couch."

"I'm telling you. Don't matter what it looks like. This is our sofa."

He rested a hand on Bowie's knee. No question, this was their sofa. Their apartment. The beginning of their relationship, as strange as it was perfect. And totally their own.

19

There was something on the air. A whisper. The dust devils too close to the tents. An itch behind his ear.

Bowie shook his head, frowned deep.

"This is a bad idea."

He wasn't sure who said it, which one of them had said it, but it was true.

This was a bad idea. It was going to be a bad fucking day. All the signs were there.

Neill and Moore stood out in the center of the circle of tents, looking down at a box. Everyone had been evacuated; all the babies had to do was disarm.

They'd practiced this every fucking day.

Every...

He heard the ticking, knew they were wrong about the how and more wrong about the when. He ran for his men, throwing Neill and shoving Moore hard, covering her body with his own as the world turned to fire.

"Run!" he bellered. "Goddamn it! Run!"

He felt a weight cover him, and somehow the flames

didn't burn like they should. It was hot, and he still couldn't breathe, but something was different.

Bowie grunted, confused, things going squirrely and off.

"Hey, I got you." That wasn't right either, that voice, but Moore was still good.

"I don't..." He didn't understand, but he would, dammit. "Come on, soldier. Focus."

"Bowie. You hear me, babe? You're good." There were hands on him. "Look at me. Open your eyes."

He blinked awake in a wild rush, his heart trip-hammering. "Fuck. Fuck, sorry. Dreaming."

He was up and moving, stumbling toward the bathroom, toward a cold shower.

Gabe didn't stop him, but he followed close behind, speaking slowly, calmly, one hand on his back. "I'm right here. Breathe. Tell me what you need."

He didn't know. He never dreamed. Never. He knew better. "I'm sweaty. My fingers will be slick."

"You want a shower, huh?" Gabe ducked around him and started the water, kept a hand under the spray, and held the other out to him. "Come on, I'll get in with you."

"Yeah." He reached out, shocked to see his fingers trembling.

Strong hands gripped his and led him into the shower, and Gabe kept him steady as he stood under the spray. "Were you dreaming about the accident?"

"I was dreaming about the bomb." Was it an accident? Had it been Neill? Was it just time for one to blow on them?

Gabe encouraged him to get his head under the spray and started working fingers through his hair. "The bomb wasn't an accident?"

"It was an outside drop. Meant to take the unit. Not a pro job. Not one of mine."

Gabe's hands hesitated for a second; then his lover exhaled and reached for the shampoo. "Back up. Tell me what happened. Why were you there that day?"

"I was working. Running training drills." He had been about to take Paul and go into the town to cause a little shock and awe, but that was over most of the guys' pay grade.

"So was it a training exercise gone wrong, or a real-life job with newbies?" Gabe's fingers massaged his neck as they worked shampoo into his hair.

"Real bomb. Decent soldiers, but they hadn't learned how to know." That was the secret. You had to anticipate. You had to be a hair before the moment.

"So tell me what happened." Gabe turned him under the spray, so they were eye to eye. "Tell me everything. Your guys were trying to disarm it?"

"They were. I was NCOIC. It should have been up and down. It wasn't." It had just been a bad day, a bad bomb. "It was just a bad day." And he didn't want to talk about it anymore, he didn't think.

"Well, it was more than a bad day, don't you think?" Gabe's tone was casual, but a hand slipped into his and held tight. "That bomb tried to take your leg. And your people."

It took his career. It gave him pain and shaking hands and...he shook himself. Regret was a waste of time.

"Hey, say it out loud. Whatever is it, babe, say it out loud. It doesn't go any further than me, I swear. That bomb fucked with you. It fucked you up."

"I knew. I knew it was going to be a bad day." He didn't know what else to say. He'd known. "I never dream."

"It wants out. That's why you dream." Gabe leaned in and gave him a kiss. "Your instinct told you something was off?"

"Yeah. It was everywhere. On the wind."

"So you were on your guard. That's good. Imagine if you hadn't been."

"Yeah. They lived." Moore took a psych out and Neill lost an arm, but they lived.

"Bowie." There was that hand again, heavy on the back of his neck, Gabe's dark eyes holding his. "*You* lived."

"I did. Lots of guys didn't." Paul hadn't, not even three weeks after he'd been taken to Landstuhl. "But I did."

And he wasn't going to waste it. Not a second.

"Tell me who didn't. Tell me their names." Gabe just wasn't letting it go.

He shook his head. That was a ghost story. Another life. Not a lover, not at all, but a partner. Someone that knew his secrets. Someone that had died with his secrets. "Some things just need to die, don't they?"

Gabe searched his eyes. "No. You know you're not okay, right?"

"I got scars, but I'm not letting it stop me." He had a bad dream. It happened. He wasn't broken, though, dammit. He was still whole. Useful. Functional.

"Your leg healed, sure. Up here?" Gabe tapped his temple, then leaned in and kissed the same spot. "The wounds are still open. You're not letting it stop you, but it can. At some point it probably will." The water rained down on his shoulders and Gabe slipped arms around his waist. "What happened when the bomb went off?"

"What do you mean? What did I do?"

"Yes and no. You, them, how it felt. What happened? Do you remember?"

"I heard the sound, and I knew it was too late. I ran in and threw Neill and it was too late for Moore, so I tackled her. Then the impact hit. The bomb was shit—took Neill's arm, a bank of computers, a few burns here and there."

"Did you feel it? Were you scared? Did you black out? Do you remember where you woke up first? I'm asking about you, babe. Not a bank of computers."

"I remember that it was so hot that it hurt to breathe. I remember that it was quiet. Everything was very slow and silent." He had wanted to stay right there more than anything, knowing what was waiting for him. He'd never been so scared when the world snapped to real time with its agony and screaming and fire. He'd been safe and whole, in those quiet seconds.

Gabe reached past him and shut the water off. "Can I take you back to bed?"

"Sounds good." He reached out and grabbed them each a towel. "I didn't mean to wake you."

"I jumped into this with both feet." Gabe gave him a half smile. "I'm guessing you didn't mean to have a nightmare either."

"Nope. Wasn't on the schedule. I got to watch that."

"Hey. Dream your dreams. I'll be here for all of them." Gabe grabbed his comb and started working it through his wet hair.

"I like that. I vote for good dreams, though." Him and Gabe at the beach. In the mountains. Having Christmas and Thanksgiving. Lord, he was going to be able to have a Thanksgiving where he could cook with Gabe. All this good shit. Who needed nightmares?

"Yeah, me too. Not to worry, you'll get a chance to throw me in the shower too at some point." He heard Gabe laugh behind him, the comb gliding easily through his hair now. "Nightmares happen—the important thing is to understand where they're coming from."

"I don't tend to have them, I don't think. Guess that means I was sleeping hard."

Gabe set the comb down and wrapped thick arms around his chest, hugging him close. "Mmm. And I guess that means this feels like home."

"I guess it does, Bear." He leaned hard, nodded. "Come on, back to bed with us. When we wake up, we'll do something fun for breakfast."

"You know I love breakfast." Gabe hustled him out of the bathroom.

"Yes, sir." He did know that. He loved that. "Anything with syrup and bacon."

"Anything." Gabe made a goofy show of fluffing up the pillows and climbing into bed, arms open for him. "Come on, lover. I'm going to dream about waffles."

"Works for me." Bowie pushed in close, finding the places where they fit together, where he was comfortable.

Gabe hummed, kissed him, tangled fingers in his hair. "You feel good. Sweet dreams."

He took a deep breath and closed his eyes. He was beginning to need that touch a little to help him find his rest.

20

Gabe paced outside the squad house, waiting on the Chief. He told himself to breathe, told himself to cool off. He'd been telling himself useless shit for ten minutes, and it wasn't doing him a damn bit of good.

When Derringer finally came around the corner, heading for him, he took a deep breath and told himself to bite his tongue. For all the good it was going to do him.

"Rogers."

"What?" Gabe rolled his eyes.

"We're giving you a week off."

The fuck? "You put an asshole on my bus, and I end up on the sidelines?"

"Nelson didn't throw a punch."

"Oh, please. That wasn't a punch. Bring him over, I'll show him a punch."

"Rules are rules, Gabe. And this isn't the first time. You're out. See you Monday." Derringer turned around and headed back inside.

"Are there rules about touching my bike?" Gabe shouted after the Chief. He could handle a bigot, he could handle a fuckup. But that fuckup shouldn't have touched his bike. "I'm sending the city the bill!"

But first he was going to Mike's. Maybe throw a real punch or two.

He was on his second beer—and Mike was letting him rant—when his phone buzzed. Bowie.

The text simply said, *Sandwiches? Too hot to cook*

He shook his head and texted back. *Im good drinking my dinner Mikes got AC*

good deal

Darla grinned at him. "Little Sammy coming down?"

He looked up at Darla. "Texans have a hundred ways to say 'fuck you.' You think 'good deal' is one of them?"

"Never heard that one. Maybe it's like o-o-okay?"

He looked at his phone. "Yeah. Maybe. Can I get another?" He slid his glass over. *Day was a o bring bail money*

Np. I got you. You want me to kill someone?

wait til you see my bike you'll want to also

?????

Then his phone rang. He sighed and answered it.

"I'm in a bar, lunkhead, hang on. I can't hear you." He gave Darla a wave and pointed toward the stock room and she waved him on. "Okay. Better."

"What the fuck happened? You can't drop a turd in the punchbowl and not expect a call, Bear."

"Short version? Fuckup on my bus, I hit him, he whined and took off in his jeep, but not before backing into my baby."

"I'll get Zeke to pick it up. I'll fix it. I hope you hurt him." Bowie's voice was a low growl.

He took a deep breath. Bowie could fix her. Yeah. That was good. "Not enough. And it figures they'd suspend me, huh?"

"What? Why? How long?"

"A week. I'm thinking if I drink for three days and sleep off the hangover for three more, I might manage not to kill him." This week. All bets were off next week.

"A week, huh?" Bowie paused, confusing the hell out of him, then he heard, "Well, I guess that works. I mean, we could head to the beach instead. I could get us flights to Houston."

Houston? The beach? That'd be a fine fuck-you, right? Go back to work with a goddamn tan? "I'm so in, man." If it was a bad idea, he could blame it on the beer.

"Good deal. I'll get the bike picked up and the flights arranged. You be home in time to get to the airport. I'll text you times. Take care of yourself, Bear." Just like that. Huh. *Wow.* Not even judging.

"One more beer and a turn in the ring out back, and I'll be home."

"Good deal. See you in a bit. Bye, you." And *click.* That was it. No, "I'll come out," or "Just come home," or "Fuck off." Just "See you in a bit."

Bowie got him. Right on. How fucking cool was that?

He headed into the bar, handed Darla his keys and his phone for safe-keeping, and pounded his last beer. That should do him. He made his way toward the ring, looking forward to showing off his bruises on the beach.

21

Bowie got a one a.m. flight, texted Gabe the times, then called Zeke to come pick him up. He texted to make sure one of the houses was open, packed his bag, and got himself downstairs.

They got the bike loaded up and to the shop, assessing the damage—which wasn't too bad, mostly cosmetic—and they shared a beer while they made a plan to have things fixed.

"So you're going to Texas?"

"Yeah, I got a beach house. He's always going on about time off. Why not take it?"

Zeke nodded. "Hell, I'd get out of the city in the summer if I had somewhere to go too. So are you boys a thing now? Together?"

He couldn't believe how many people asked that. "We are."

"Nice. Angel's a friend, and he's been alone a long time. I'm glad for you both." Zeke sipped his beer and didn't ask any more questions.

"He's a good man." An angel? Hardly. Maybe a fallen one with teeth and a temper.

"He is when he's not pissing someone off. I can touch up the custom paint job, but damn. Why are you dealing with his bike? Is he in jail?" Zeke grinned wide, tobacco-stained teeth giving him a sinister look.

"Not so far as I know. I'm just making sure it's safe and not sitting out there waiting for another shot." If Gabe ended up in jail, Bowie would go to Texas alone, as much as he paid for the tickets.

"It's drivable, he could have brought it here himself. If I know him, he's drinking."

He felt his phone vibrate and pulled it out of his pocket.

Home. Packing clean undies, rubbers, and sunglasses. That'll work right?

He could hear the grin. Someone was in a better mood.

Yep. We'll get trunks and flip flops there

"I guess I'd better get moving. I have a flight in a couple three hours. Thanks for your help, man."

"Not a problem. I'll keep her safe until you get back. Parts should be in by then too. Get a sunburn for me." Zeke shook his hand.

"I'm not sunburnable, but I'll tell Gabe." He winked at Zeke, then headed home, wishing by about halfway that he'd brought his crutch.

He got home to find Gabe on the sofa with the TV on and a bag of frozen peas on his hand. "Hey." Gabe smiled at him, got up with that familiar old-man groan and headed over.

"Hey, you. Got your bike to Zeke's." He took an easy kiss. "Ready to go?"

Gabe was freshly showered, tasted like toothpaste, and didn't have so much as a scratch on his face, just a big grin.

"I am. I decided I should pack pants too. Thanks for dealing with my bike. It's probably fine to ride, I just wasn't going to be sober enough to ride it."

"You're welcome. It'll be all fixed by the time we get home." He was ready to get to the ocean, sink his toes in the sand. "I'm going to grab a sandwich before we head to the airport. You want one?"

"I made you one." Gabe's grin softened into a smile. "It's on the counter. Sorry I ate without you, I was hungry."

"You rock. Thanks, man." He bumped shoulders with Gabe and headed to grab his snack. "You looking forward to getting out of town?"

"I am. You've totally turned this week around for me, that's for sure. I haven't been anywhere in years. Unless you count rallies in Jersey."

"It's about time, then." Why not take advantage of the good, right? "I told my guy to save us the house with the red porch."

"Is that the one with the hot tub?" Gabe leaned in, kissed the side of his neck.

"How did you know?" He leaned right back, pleased as fuck that Gabe remembered to put the pickled peppers on his sandwich. "We'll rent a car in Houston and head to Galveston. You got a preference to type?"

"I liked that house, I remembered from the pictures. The only thing with four wheels that I've driven in years is the ambo, so you pick. Something with leg room. This is so weird and impulsive. I never thought of myself as impulsive."

"Leg room. We'll get an SUV, then." He hadn't known whether Gabe was the convertible type or the Escalade type. "I don't mind taking advantage of an opportunity. Not at all."

"You are the quick thinker." Gabe tossed the bag of peas

back into the freezer and stretched out thick fingers, the first couple of knuckles looking purple.

"Advil?" He tossed Gabe the bottle. Someone had been taking out his frustrations on a face.

Gabe caught the bottle easily in his other hand. "Thanks. Fingers are warm. I'm good. Looks uglier than it feels." He wasn't convinced that was true, but it didn't look much worth complaining about either. Gabe was an EMT; he'd know if he was hurt.

"Good deal. I know flying with the pressure can be a bitch, so bring the bottle for me."

"Got it. Speaking of which, you wanna sit down?" Gabe must have noticed how hard he was leaning. "Did you schedule a car for the airport? We could take the train, but it's a haul. You could probably walk it all, but I'm a lazy asshole." Gabe winked at him and stepped up on his weaker side, looping an arm around his waist.

"I didn't. I wasn't sure what to do. I can. And please. I'm wore."

Gabe got him seated at the table and brought him the rest of his sandwich.

"Thanks. So, I can just do an Uber?" Do you do an Uber? Get an Uber? Ube an Uber?

"Yep. You have the app? I've got it if not." Gabe sat with him, watching him with a goofy look on his face.

"I don't. I'll let you handle it." He grinned over at his bear. "In a few hours we'll be at the beach, napping in the sun."

"I can't wait. I really am excited about it, like I'm five and going to Disney or something. No shit. I tan well too. I get dark pretty fast."

"Mmm...I can tan, that's for sure."

"We're gonna be a couple of brown bears." Gabe

grinned, pulling out his phone. "Newark airport...right? That's where Tommy and Sammy—" Gabe looked at him sharply. "This isn't a 'meet the parents' thing, is it?"

"We're heading to Galveston. My folks live north of Dallas." And no. No, it wasn't. It was going to the beach.

"I'm going to assume these places are nowhere near each other because this Yankee doesn't know where anything is in Texas." Gabe laughed. "Okay, we have a car."

Gabe leaned back in the chair. "Man, babe. I was mad today. I don't get that mad much. I'm not sure I even should have been that pissed." His lover's forehead scrunched up. "And I didn't want to come home like that. Bring that here."

"Sounded like it sucked hairy donkey balls. You gotta do what you gotta do, huh?" Whatever got you through the night, so far as he reckoned it. It took a hell of a lot to piss him off, and when he went, it was brutal.

Gabe stood up and took his plate to the kitchen. "It got me a week at the beach, so I guess I can't be too upset about it."

"You can be pissed, but there's no reason not to have some fun and aggravate the fuck out of everyone when you get back to work, right?"

Gabe's grin grew slowly. "Exactly what I was thinking. Show up tan and smelling like coconut rum."

"There you go. Flip-flops and salt water. All the Gulf shrimp we can eat and hours of sun."

"Jet Skis. Fishing. And fucking. Don't forget that. Not in the sand, though."

"No, that would rasp. The house has an outside shower." He grinned at Gabe. "We can rinse off first."

"Oh, I'm all over that." Gabe grabbed for the phone on the table. "Uber will be here in five. I'll get your crutch. Where's your bag?"

"Sitting on the end of the bed."

Gabe disappeared for a minute and came back with his bag, his crutch, and a backpack, with a pair of sunglasses perched in that short-cropped hair. "Come on, beach bunny."

"I'm with you." He took his crutch and bag. "Let's go play, Bear."

It was about time.

22

Gabe smelled bacon. It woke him and got him moving like a siren's call. He rolled over in bed and got up, making a quick pit stop to get rid of his morning breath, tugged on his bathing trunks, and headed downstairs.

When was the last time he stayed in a house? A house with stairs? So weird.

"I smell bacon!" he called from the stairwell and trotted through the living room to the kitchen.

"You do! Bacon and eggs and toast." Bowie looked like a million bucks, hair down, shirtless, looking comfortable as hell.

"You rock." He moved in behind his lover and tugged them together, running his hands over that broad, beautiful chest.

"Mmm...hey, Bear." Bowie rubbed his ass back against him, teasing, playing with him.

He chuckled at Bowie, fingers tangling in thick locks of hair. The sun was well up and the tide was in, and he could hardly believe he was standing here. "Look at that day."

"Isn't it beautiful? I love this view." Of course, Bowie was looking at him.

He blinked at Bowie, surprised as hell at the sentiment, smiling as that look warmed his cheeks right up. That was hot, but also kind of...romantic. He had a sweet reply, a snarky one, but he chucked both and kissed Bowie instead. That said more than he had words for.

Bowie hummed and kissed him back for a long minute before going to rescue the bacon. "You want to sit on the deck? I sprayed it all off last night."

"Yeah, sounds great. You want a refill on your coffee? Where are the mugs?" He started opening and closing every cabinet in the kitchen, looking.

The house was well-equipped with mismatched dishes and goofy mugs, plastic cups and crazy silverware.

"I do, please. Right above the coffeemaker."

Right, because that was logical. He pulled down a mug for himself and got them both coffee. He also grabbed silverware and took everything out to the table on the deck. He put up the umbrella for shade and was about to go back in to see what else he could help with when the view got the better of him.

Bowie's house. At the beach. So weird. He was going to be doing this all day, wasn't he?

"It's gorgeous, isn't it?" Bowie brought out the plates. "The one on the left and the three to the right are mine, but this one's my favorite. I worked on it for an entire month."

"It is. It's incredible. Sorry, I meant to come help, but it's been so long since I've seen anything but the city, I got... stuck." He laughed at himself.

"That's why we're here, right?" Bowie settled in a chair.

He took a seat, not across from Bowie but much closer, where they could enjoy each other, their food, and the view all at once. "Thank you for breakfast." He picked up his fork and dug in, suddenly really hungry, the salty bacon making his mouth water. "Oh. Mmm."

Bowie grinned at him. "Tastes better out here somehow, doesn't it?"

His mouth was full, so he glanced at Bowie and nodded. Damn, his lover really did look good. They'd been here one whole day, but it seemed like Bowie was right at home and relaxed; the damp salt air even seemed to agree with the Ranger's hair. He swallowed and poked Bowie with his elbow as he forked up another bite. "You're better out here too."

"I love it out here. It's simple, rednecky, easy."

It showed. And it was nice. By the end of the week, Bowie might look like a different guy. "So you worked on this one a lot, huh? This deck is fantastic."

"Yeah, man. They were trashed from a hurricane. So I started with the easy one, used the rent to fix the second, and so on. This one is...well, this one feels a little more like mine."

"You should just make it yours, then. Don't rent it. You can come and go when you want to now, you know? We could come back." He had so much vacation time banked, it was scary.

"Anytime you want to." Bowie beamed at him—literally just beamed. "You want to go for a walk this morning?"

"I'll go anywhere with that smile." He leaned over and kissed the corner of that amazing and dangerous grin. If his lover kept smiling like that, he might not have the heart to ask Bowie to come back to New York.

Except...he needed Bowie to come home with him. He totally blew it. He crossed a line he thought he'd never let himself cross again, and now things were getting complicated in his head.

Fuck it, this was the beach, right? Bowie looked gorgeous, and the weather was fantastic. He was gonna eat his damn bacon and watch the waves, and he was gonna enjoy the shit out of it. He didn't need to think very hard about that at all.

Bowie's hand touched his knee—a careful caress, almost ticklish, but not quite.

He took a quick breath and glanced down, tangling his fingers with Bowie's and giving them a squeeze. It was so strange how nothing got past his lover. Bowie was sensitive to everything and just knew. He took the reassurance and gave back a smile and a wink. "Mmm. Bacon." He picked up a piece and took a huge bite.

"Bacon is proof there's a God." Bowie ate, eyes moving constantly over the house, checking everything from the roof to the windows to the paint.

"Damn right." He stuffed the rest of that piece into his mouth and chewed, then glanced at Bowie again. "Hey. You have a project in mind? We could bang something out while we're down here."

"I'm thinking, if I'm taking this one off the market, so to speak, I'll put in a better security system and a speaker system for the whole house. Maybe pull the tub out of the master and put in a nice, big shower for the two of us. I might see if there's another property to fix up, depending on the price." Bowie leaned back in the chair. "It's a crazy hobby, but I've done okay."

"It's more than a hobby at this point, babe. It's a moneymaker." He was all about the nice big shower; he loved showering with Bowie, whether they were fooling around or not. It was just a thing. Water was hot and healing and fun all at the same time.

"Yeah, it was a tax thing at first. Now it's a few thousand

dollars a month income." Bowie wrapped the last of his bacon in his bread and munched. "I'm glad you said yes."

"To coming here? Me too." He sucked down the last of his coffee. "Where are we walking?"

"We can wander the seawall, just go where we want. The park's right here, the pier."

"Do you have to wear a shirt?" He grinned. "I mean, do I?"

"I'd take one in a bag if you want to go inside somewhere."

He laughed. Bowie could pay him a hundred subtle compliments and still not catch the ones he handed out. "I'll just tuck it in my shorts." He stood up. "I'll do the dishes."

"Can I lube you up before we go?"

"Tease." That sounded so wonderfully dirty, it made him grin. "You have something that's not SPF one million? I want to tan."

"I have something so you won't be miserable in the morning, yeah. I just want to rub the lotion on you." Wicked man.

He chuckled and started the dishes. "You can rub me all you like."

Bowie stepped up and kissed his nape, fingertips massaging his hips, thumbs digging into the small of his back.

Oh, that felt... "Mmm. Nice." He put the dishes in the little drainer next to the sink as he worked and thoroughly enjoyed his lover's hands.

This was kind of new for Bowie, just reaching out and touching. It was like he needed permission at first or something, and now he knew it was okay. So Gabe made sure to be clear about appreciating the attention.

He thought he felt Bowie smile against him, and the

massage just kept on and on.

He finished with the dishes, let his head roll forward, and leaned into Bowie's hands. "You're good at that. You got knowing fingers."

"I like it. Touching. You got a bunch of knots."

"Yeah." He knew. They'd been there forever. Years of having to jump at the squawk of a radio at all hours made them pretty much permanent. "At first I tried massages, therapists. I decided I didn't need agony in my life. What you're doing feels good, though. Your touch feels...better. Right."

"Well, I care." So simple. So straightforward.

He smiled, turned in Bowie's hands. "It makes a difference, doesn't it? That someone cares. This way. Our way."

"I think so, yes." Bowie stepped right in, leaned into him, and hummed.

"Hey." He put his arms around Bowie, just to hold him for a minute. Just because it felt good. He took a kiss because that felt good too. No means to an end, not foreplay, just because it made him happy. "Sunscreen?"

"On it." Bowie pulled away, grabbed a rubber band, and tied his hair back. Then he disappeared up the stairs.

It surprised him, how silent Bowie's footsteps were.

"Bring me a T-shirt, babe!" He shouted up the stairs. Then he found the flip-flops they'd bought the day before along with the trunks he was wearing and slipped them on his feet. He pulled out his phone and sent a quick text to Sammy.

Did your brother tell you we're at the beach?

Yep. He sounded bouncy. CREEPY

He laughed. *He's happy down here*

He's a beach baby. Have fun. Eat EVERYTHING

working on it! Be good

Bouncy. Bowie. That was pretty damn funny.

Bowie had a loose white button-down over his shoulders, a goofy straw cowboy hat on, and a T-shirt and a bottle of sunscreen when he came out.

He shook his head. It just kept getting better. "You look way too comfy. Love the hat."

"Thanks." Bowie doffed it, bowed carefully. "Here's your T-shirt. I'm fixin' to grab a couple towels and waters, if you want me to keep it with me."

"If you're bringing a bag, sure." He took the sunscreen and put some on his nose and the tops of his ears. He'd grab his cap on the way out; it was on the table by the door.

"Turn around. I'm not having you being lobster boy."

He sighed and turned around. "Yeah, okay. Lobster would be bad. I don't want to be out of commission." He grinned and flexed his shoulders for Bowie.

"No, you don't. I hope to share a couple orgasms this week." Bowie started "lubing" him up.

"That is setting the bar way too low. I'm kind of in the couple a day camp. I mean, we just had breakfast."

"Oh. I'm in. Vacation sex can be wild."

"I'll remember that and see if I can't get creative." He turned his head and grinned at Bowie, lowering his tone. "Boy."

Bowie flushed a sweet, bright red but didn't say a word. He just leaned forward and did the backs of Gabe's thighs.

So honest. He let it go at that, smug as fuck. "Ready?"

"I am. Let's go wander. I'll show you Galveston." Bowie grinned at him, eyes lit up with happiness.

"These flip-flops were made for walking!" He grabbed his ball cap and tucked it onto his head, ready for whatever adventure came their way.

23

"Bring the salads, Bear." Steaks were done, potatoes were done. Bowie was into his second beer, the Eagles were on the radio, and the breeze made everything feel so good.

He was having the best motherfucking day. Walking. Shrimp. Ice cream. Swimming. Bear.

"On it." Gabe came out of the house with a bowl in each hand and set them on the table. "I'm hungry like you have no idea. Those steaks look so good. You know what Sammy said to me? Eat everything."

"Good advice." He served up the potatoes on each plate and turned off the grill. "Soup's on."

Gabe took the plates from him, set them down, and pulled out his chair. "Sit, grill master."

Oh, well, wasn't that something. "Thank you, sir."

"You're welcome." Gabe took a seat too. "How's the leg holding up? You did great in the sand, I thought."

"I'm doing okay. We'll see how it goes tomorrow, right? I feel...I'm feeling fucking amazing."

"You're looking it too." Gabe winked at him and cut into the steak. "Amazing."

They ate like they were starving, and he had to admit, he had done good. The best food, the best beer, the best music, and the best company. He was buzzed—not from the booze, from the whole day.

"Oh, man. That was so good, babe." Gabe leaned back with a satisfied sigh, looking about as far away from a stressful day at work as a person could get, and glowing slightly where the sun had touched his cheekbones. "Man, if vacation is this good on day two, by day five we're going to be high as kites."

"Works for me, man. Let's shoot for high." He could manage that.

"I can do that." Gabe put a hand on his thigh, palm searing into his skin, and his legs parted like he had a button. Gabe growled low. "Mine."

That gave him the best types of shivers, but he let himself play, just because he could. His bear stood up and straddled his legs but didn't sit, just bent over and kissed him, bracing hands on the back of his chair. The kiss was intense and low gear, like Gabe was ready to make it last until day five. He reached up, hands finding Gabe's hips and holding on.

"Jet Skis tomorrow?" Gabe asked lips smiling against his.

"I'm on it." Lord have mercy. He'd have to take muscle relaxants starting first thing in the morning.

"Assuming we don't stay in bed all day." Bear's hand fell to his belly and rubbed in circles.

"Mmm...we could. We are a day behind on orgasms."

Gabe laughed. "You're keeping track. I love it." He got another kiss and that hand slipped under the waistband of his swim trunks and palmed the head of his cock.

Bowie's eyes went wide. They were outside. Outside and Gabe was touching him and he was getting hard.

The touches kept coming, long strokes and gentle tugs, fingers playing with his sac, and Gabe kept kissing. A thick tongue pushed past his lips, forcing his mouth open and gliding along his own. Jesus, he'd never felt so...wanted, and he wasn't a virgin. Bowie was caught, right there.

Gabe kept him pinned with that kiss a bit longer, hot but in no hurry. Eventually his bear lazily moved to tasting his jaw and lower, along the side of his neck and over his shoulder until Gabe was kneeling between his thighs and biting at his nipple.

"Bear...you got the best teeth..." The sting was crazy-making and wonderful, all at once.

"Mmm. You taste like the ocean. And fresh air. Wild." Bear tugged on his trunks. "Off."

He pushed his trunks down, shocked at himself. It was a private deck, on this lower section especially, but he couldn't believe he was doing this.

"Yeah." Gabe licked across his abs with a flat tongue and right into his groin, inhaling deep. "Fuck, babe. You smell so good."

"Thank you." His toes curled and he spread wide, willing to give everything up.

"You're welcome." Gabe laughed darkly and licked across the tip of his erection.

His belly went tight as bowstrings, and his fingers went white-knuckled on the arms of the chair. Jesus, that was magic.

Bear grabbed his ass and dragged him to the edge of his chair, spreading his legs wider. The evening sea breeze blew across his sensitive damp skin, making him shiver as Bear licked and tasted him from tip to root to the inside of his thighs, savoring him.

Bowie stared, the care and time Gabe took loving on him stunning him into silence.

Gabe looked up at him and grinned. "Mmm. The look on your face, babe. You ready for this?" Gabe's thumb swiped over the tip of his cock and burrowed into the slit.

"Bear!" He curled around that touch, his nerves lighting up. It was dangerous, delicious, a promise of fire.

"Fuck, yeah." Gabe did it again, then bent and took him in, cheeks going hollow, fingers digging into his ass. *Oh, Jesus.* He was going to fucking lose his mind. He didn't know how to fucking feel that.

Gabe was unrelenting, scraping that tongue over his shaft, sucking and swallowing him down.

Bowie's head fell back, eyes wide open as he stared up at the stars. "Oh, God." *So fucking good*. He began to move, to rock up into the suction.

Gabe grunted, and the hands on his ass shifted to his hips and pinned him to the seat, fingers gripping tight, forcing him to hold still. Bear went after the tip of his cock again, tongue sweeping over it and diving into the slit, sweeping and plunging in again.

Bowie stiffened, and for a second he forgot how to breathe, caught as he was between hands and mouth. "Please. Oh, goddamn."

Bear nodded and hummed for him, and he knew his lover got it, heard what he needed. Gabe's tongue dipped deeper the next time, adding more pressure, spending more time between each sweep and probing his opening with intention.

Bowie gritted his teeth against the cries that needed out, against the way his ass clenched in the chair. Gabe groaned but stayed focused on his slit and started stroking him off, pumping his cock in a solid fist. He bit out a warning, but it was too late, he was shooting like a fucking geyser. His balls hurt with the rush of pure pleasure.

Bear swallowed every drop down hungrily, moaning around him, then pulled off him finally, sounding a little breathless.

"Fuck, babe." Gabe was pressing the heel of one hand hard into his groin. "Jesus."

"Yours. How do you want me? Anything."

Bear's eyes searched his. "Can you kneel without hurting yourself? Won't take much, I swear, I'm so fucking ready. But be honest." Gabe unfolded, shucking his trunks and standing up tall, that long cock stiff and needy looking.

He groaned and hit his knees, focused on that fine fucking prick, knowing that he needed to suck as bad as Gabe needed his mouth. He didn't tease; he didn't play. He took Gabe to the root and pulled.

Gabe shuddered and restrained a cry, letting the sound out in short low grunts instead. "Fuck, Bowie." The words were delivered on a long breath, and Bear rocked against him, catching the back of his head with one hand and pushing deep. His lover wasn't kidding—he could feel the tension coiling in Bear's abs and thighs. It made him soar, the power of knowing that he made Gabe need, desperate. He cupped Gabe's ass and encouraged his bear to fuck his lips.

Gabe swallowed a groan and plunged into him, thrusts erratic, some shallow and some deep, and finally arched over him, groping at his shoulder for balance and coming with a strangled sob. *Fuck, yeah.* Bowie took every fucking drop, cleaning the now-sensitive shaft with a soft touch.

Bear huffed out a heavy breath and dropped to his knees, pulling him in with one hand and kissing the ever-loving fuck out of him. He held on, opened up, and let Gabe have him. Every bit.

Gabe let him go, sucked in a deep breath and blew it out, and stared at him, dark-blue eyes looking black in the starlight.

He nodded. He got it. He heard. He loved Gabe too.

Gabe swallowed and stood finally, getting a hand under his arm to help him up off the ground. "You're stunning, Bowie. Just...stunning."

Bowie let Gabe stabilize him, and they rocked together, just for another second.

"Oughtta clean up, huh?" Gabe squeezed his shoulders and let him go. "You want me to do the grill or the dishes?"

"I'm easy. You scrape the grill; I'll toss the dishes in the dishwasher. You want me to get the hot tub bubbling?"

"Yeah, that sounds perfect. Maybe a nightcap?"

"You want another beer or a whiskey?"

Gabe winked at him with the hint of a grin. "Whiskey."

"I'm on it." He gathered plates, feeling loose in his skin, and turned the hot tub on. Whiskey and towels, after dishes.

Orgasm number one, down. Excellent.

24

D ead serious, Gabe had no idea what day it was.

He woke up in a bed that had been a playground day and night to a room that was dim but not dark, and he wasn't sure if it was dawn or dusk, if today was still today, or tomorrow already.

Jesus, he needed a shower. And coffee. But not yet, because Bowie was stretched out next to him and really looked like someone that needed a snuggle. Or maybe that was him. Either way, he rolled closer and slid an arm over Bowie's chest.

He wasn't hungover, not from booze anyway. Could you have a sex hangover? He traced the hours back in his mind, remembering the hot tub, a nap, queso, half of *Gone With the Wind*, a shower, another nap, lots of music, and everything in between was...well, fucking.

God, he loved the beach. He loved vacation. He was going to have to take more of them. With Bowie.

"Mmm. Bear." Look at that smile, like Bowie was dreaming the best possible dream.

He figured he was allowed to feel pretty smug about

that. Not everyone who had done and seen and been through what Bowie had could smile like that. But that was the real deal.

He kissed a warm, bare shoulder and rested his head there, listening to Bowie's heart. Sure and steady, stable and strong as a drum—God, that was a comforting sound.

He concentrated on the constant lub-dub, not thinking about his own. His was off on some boondoggle, and he wasn't gonna dig too deep into that right now. Maybe ever. He wasn't dishonest, he wasn't lying, Bowie got him. It was just...a place he'd never been when he thought he had, and that was more confusing than anything else.

Bowie definitely got him. His lover got a lot of things he didn't say; all those years of fine-tuned senses were a matter of life or death, and they'd become instinct for Bowie now. It was fascinating.

He grinned. Good thing he was at least a well-intentioned fuckup.

Bowie stretched, long and slow, bones popping and snapping. "Want to go to the Mosquito Cafe today, Bear? Have a lazy breakfast?"

Breakfast. So it was morning. Got it. But which morning? This was great, he was totally high like they'd planned. "That sounds great. Lazy about fits the bill." Food sounded good too. Seriously, all he could remember was queso.

"Mmhmm. I'm all about the lazy mornings with you." Bowie cracked an eye. "Supposed to storm this afternoon. I love to watch the storms come in over the water."

"Oh, yeah? That'll be cool. I'm not sure I've seen that before. We could sit up in that big window off the deck and watch Maybe cook?"

"Perfect. Shrimp? We can stop at the wharf on the way home from breakfast."

He nodded. "Big salad. Pasta?"

"Sounds perfect, Bear." Bowie kissed his temple, tickling him with his beard. "We have our plan. I like it. Now I just have to convince my lazy ass to get out of bed."

"Shower." He stuck his nose into that beard and growled playfully.

"Are you suggesting I smell like sex?" Bowie's laughter filled the air, and he blinked. God, that was a great sound. Wild. Bright.

He laughed along. "No. Sex smells good. You stink."

"Butthead!" Bowie pounced on him, rubbing on him and pressing him into the mattress.

He grabbed Bowie by the hips, encouraging him, and kept playing. "Ugh! It's like being attacked by Pig-Pen! I can even see the cloud." He made a show of coughing like he was choking, but he couldn't stop grinning.

"I am going to beat your butt. Pig-Pen, my ass." Bowie pinched his nipple hard enough to sting.

"Ow! Motherfucker." He tried to do the same, but Bowie batted his hand away, so he pressed up on one shoulder and tried to roll them.

"Ow, like that hurt." Bowie scrambled to keep on top, surprisingly good at dealing with that leg.

"It...stung. A little." He pouted. "Boohoo. Whoa!" He turned his head suddenly to one side, eyes wide like he saw something big and scary.

"Lizard?" Bowie lifted his head and looked.

"Yep!" He took advantage, throwing Bowie off-balance and rolling them both, landing full-weight on Bowie's chest. "Big lizard."

"Can you do that tongue thing?" Bowie flicked his tongue madly.

Oh, such a beautiful setup. He stared Bowie down and

dropped his voice. "You know damn well what my tongue can do."

Bowie's hand brushed over his ass, and he felt the full-body shiver. "I am a lucky motherfucker."

He nodded. "I am too." He grinned again. "I fucking love the beach. Real life is going to be hard."

"We can come back at will. You say the word."

"I will. You can too. As long as you smell better."

"Come get in the shower, turdbucket, and I might take you to breakfast..."

He chuckled and rolled off Bowie, getting a really good look at the man, head to toe, before getting out of bed. *Damn.* Someday he'd wake up from this dream. He offered Bowie a hand up. "I'll take you if you don't take me."

"Fair enough." Bowie dragged him into the bathroom with its little tub. "We need to choose a shower, something with a sturdy teak chair."

"Oh, I like that. Glass walls? Couple of shower heads. Big enough for both of us. Not that I don't love squeezing into this tub together." He laughed.

"Right, but I like the idea of being able to fuck in the shower or sucking you off in here." Listen to that. Bowie just said what he wanted.

"I...totally want the same thing. We'll design something." For them. Specifically. Bowie just wrote their future with a shower. "I've never done a bathroom, but I learn fast."

"We'll have a ball." Bowie turned the water on and grabbed the towels. "We work just fine together."

It was pretty damn funny, the two of them in this little shower. Every time they shifted under the water they were one step away from disaster, moving around each other like they were dancing on a window ledge.

Of course it never occurred to either one of them *not* to try to squeeze in there together.

They managed to get clean with a huge amount of laughing and more than one kiss, and soon they were dressed and clean and ready to go.

"So, coffee, food, shrimp, greens, and we'll be home by the storm."

He grinned. "I'm following you." He held the door for Bowie. "I'm trimming that thing on your chin tonight."

"You aren't." Was that a challenge?

He glanced over at Bowie, trying a different tack as they headed down the sidewalk. "It just needs a little taming, babe."

"Yeah? Am I getting shaggy?" Bowie smoothed the scraggly mass.

Okay, that was a better reaction. So, Bowie wasn't giving him authority over everything. Noted. "Vacation shaggy. You're too handsome for shaggy."

"I keep waiting to get tired of it, you know? To just cut it all off. Hasn't happened yet."

"I've never wanted to cut mine off, it just kept getting shorter until it was...right. You want it to be comfortable, and you want to make a statement."

"Yeah, I hear you. I shaved for years, and that's the first thing I stopped in the hospital, even before I was out. They didn't make me shave over the scabs."

"That would have been a mistake, yes." He liked his beard. It was still a little hint of defiance, and it distanced him from the city-dwelling corporate drones. "I have an oil you should try too."

"An oil?" They climbed into the SUV. "That might feel nice. It does get tangled. Sammy says I look old with the gray, but I sort of like it—the sparkle."

"Oh, I like the gray." He smiled, pulling on his seat belt. He gave Bowie's knee a pat. "I own my own, after all. And the oil is great—I use it a couple times a week after I shower, so it stays healthy looking and soft." He kicked back in his seat, letting Bowie drive.

"You'll have to show me. I don't want to be nasty." No. No, his lover was strangely and wonderfully fastidious. "I may fly into Dallas and drive my truck down, keep it here. Although, I have to say, for toodling around, this Acadia is great.'

"I'm comfy. And hungry. We know how to work up an appetite. Huh? Do you remember the last time we ate something other than queso? You won't believe this, but I'm kind of fuzzy on time." Today was Wednesday. Or Thursday. But he was pretty sure it was Wednesday.

"I made steaks and we had tacos on the beach." Bowie pursed his lips. "We've had doughnuts."

"The steaks I remember clearly. And blowing you after the steaks. My God. And then things get fuzzy." It was really kind of wonderful. It didn't actually matter, did it?

"That blowjob damn near killed me. Also, riding your cock in the hot tub was incredibly not bad."

Oh, yeah! He certainly remembered that. Bowie had him just...gone. "It didn't suck. And the shower-proof lube was a good call. I like a man that can plan ahead."

"It's a thing. I've never had a vacation with a lover before. I like it."

"Did you have a lot of lovers you didn't vacation with?" That sounded snarky because it was nosy and maybe none of his business, but how many lovers could a Ranger on active duty have?

"No. Fuck buddies, a couple, but...well, I got to admit, if I had leave time, I wanted to be with my friends and have fun, you know?"

He knew. But he'd always found someone to be with when he was stateside. He'd needed that outlet, to take some control back. He had to wonder whether Bowie had been needing someone to let him let go, but he hadn't known how to get it. "Did you tend to hook up with twinks? Subs?"

"Yeah, for the most part. There's a reputation you can't fuck with. No one can doubt you, you know?"

"Yeah, I get it. You had to be an authority. I didn't but I was a big guy. Kind of the same deal. There were expectations."

"Yeah. I mean, I—" Bowie shook his head, lips twisting. "I had a good friend that I spent my time with. We weren't lovers. That was enough."

"That's good. You gotta find what you need somewhere. Is he still over there?"

"No."

Oh. There was no questioning that tone. "I'm sorry."

"Thank you. He was a good man. We were a great team."

"You were lucky to have each other." Of course he wanted details, but he knew better than to ask. At least not now, not with the way Bowie was answering the few he'd already asked, not volunteering anything. He rubbed Bowie's thigh, just to say it was okay.

"We had a mission planned for after...when I was in Germany. Blew himself sky high along with an enemy cell. He's been wiped off the earth."

Wait. Wait, had Bowie been planning a suicide mission? Is that what Bowie was saying?

"Hey. Pull over. Park somewhere." Better to get off the road for this conversation.

"What?" Bowie pulled into an empty parking lot. "What's wrong?"

"What was his name?"

"Cardiff. Paul Cardiff."

"Paul." He took Bowie's hand. "You were supposed to be on this...mission? When Paul died?"

"Yes, sir. We were a team." Bowie held on to his hand but didn't quite meet his eyes.

"Babe, are we talking a calculated risk or a planned operation of no return here?" He was fairly sure he knew the answer, but he needed to know for sure. He needed to hear Bowie say it.

"He had no chance on his own." That was a non-answer answer, but about the time Gabe started to push, Bowie growled. "We had our orders. That's how it works. We had our orders."

Bowie looked over at him, just once, just quickly, and there was a look in his lover's eyes he wasn't sure how to interpret. "I didn't get hurt on purpose."

"Fuck, of course not. You're not a fucking coward. If you could have been there, you would have been." That didn't give him any clarity, but he hoped it would give Bowie some. "You saved someone's life, man. If that's getting hurt on purpose, then more guys oughtta do it."

"This isn't for anyone to know. You and me. This is ours, Bear." It wasn't even a question. Bowie believed in him.

"Yes. I know, I understand. I promise." He squeezed Bowie's hand and leaned a little closer. "You know I still have a question."

"Okay. Ask." Bowie held on to him like he was a lifeline.

"I know you had orders, I know how that goes. I won't dig any deeper, I promise, but I need to understand....Would

Paul...would you have had a chance even if you had been there?"

"I think so. I hope so. Shit, I don't know, but together we were more than the sum of our parts. Sort of like you and me, but different."

He ducked a little, catching Bowie's eyes as they lowered. "Thank you. For sharing that, for the trust. For being...what I need." Thanks didn't seem entirely right, but what was bigger than a thank-you? He didn't know. Trust, he supposed. Being worthy of the gift. But there weren't words for that.

"I love you, Bear. You get all of me, good and bad. Let's go eat." Bowie put the SUV in drive and headed out.

Right. Those were the words. Of course Bowie would know that. But saying "I love you too," making three words into four, sounded so canned. He'd wait until he could say them first. On his own.

"Mmm. Bacon." He was hungry. For all of it.

25

The storm was coming.

Bowie could feel it everywhere, and he was buzzed, hyperaware, his skin too tight, his nipples hard. He wanted to growl, to run out into the ocean and let it take him, to stand outside and dare the lightning to find him.

He stood in the open door of the deck, goose bumps covering his skin. The wind had just begun to blow after an hour of humid, sticky stillness.

"A breeze! Thank God. The humidity was starting to get to me.' Bear stepped up behind him, resting a hand on his hip. His lover wasn't unaffected by the energy of the storm either, Bowie could feel it—a little tension, anticipation, the hand hot where it touched him. "Feel that. Wow."

He grunted his agreement. Yeah. He'd been in a shit-ton of storms—natural and manmade—and he got it, the buildup, the way the world tightened for a long minute, gathering itself for the blow.

"I've never experienced a coastal storm. Mountains, yes. Drowning on street corners in New York? Sure. But this is different. The wind off the water and the salt in the air."

"Wait for the lightning. It's something." Bowie let himself lean back, breathe, and soak up Gabe's heat.

"You're...vibrating." Gabe sounded a little awed. "You get off on a good storm, babe?"

"I...yeah. They do it for me." All the way. Down to the bone.

"Nice. That does it for me, you know. You getting ramped up." Gabe kissed his neck lightly. "Makes my fingers itch wanting to touch you. Like you're begging to be touched."

That little kiss made him shiver, and he caught himself licking his lips, a low moan filling the air. He didn't bother hiding this. If he couldn't share it with Gabe, then who?

"What gets you about it?" Gabe spoke softly, close to his ear. "The power of it? The waiting? The electricity?"

"Yes." He fucking loved things that were bigger than he was, that he couldn't control. It didn't happen often.

The sky grew dark, and big droplets of rain started splattering the deck as the leading edge of the storm drew closer, assaulting and staining the wood, some of them hitting hard enough to be heard. "Here it comes." Gabe pulled him in tighter, hands maddeningly chaste.

His heart slammed against his rib cage, his eyelids going heavy, and his cock filling steadily. He wanted to rub and push, to hump Gabe like a slut, but he made himself wait, anticipate.

Behind him, Gabe stood still and patient despite the long, firm ridge he felt beginning to press against his ass. Gabe pulled his hair aside and kissed him behind the ear as a gentle rumble of thunder rolled over the house.

"You have everything I am. You can have whatever you want, anything you need. I would...I will let you have this."

"Gabe." He didn't know what to say, how to do anything,

so he took one of his bear's hands and brought it to his mouth, kissing Gabe's knuckle.

"Mmm." Gabe traced the tendon in his neck with a wet tongue, following it until it ended at his shoulder, and kissed the thicker muscle there. Lightning tore across the sky, and a hint of ozone blew in through the open door, followed immediately by a deafening crack of thunder that shook them both.

"Fuck." Bowie let the sound have him, let Gabe hear his need, and when the next jolt of lightning hit, his bear bit, testing his skin.

The warning only lasted a second. Answering the second clap of thunder, those teeth clamped down hard, and Gabe held him there, sucking up a bruise sure to turn darker than the sky. Bowie's toes curled, a spot of wet need growing on his shorts. He wrapped his lips around Gabe's finger, sucking hard as his hips began to rock.

Gabe released him slowly, the spot heating up quick, and gripped his jaw with the remaining fingers, twisting the one in his mouth. Gabe turned him suddenly and kissed him, herding him backward, out the door and into the heavy rain.

He grabbed Gabe's head, and for a second they fought for dominance, clashing together under the pouring rain. The drops slapped against him, stinging his skin.

Gabe reached out with both hands and shoved at his chest to break them apart. When that didn't work, his bear went after his fingers, trying to pry them off, but couldn't manage that either. He only felt stronger as Bear tried tugging on his arms, leaning in with all that weight. Gabe finally had to concede, the kiss changing character, his lover's mouth opening for him.

Love.

He groaned and explored, kissing Gabe until there was nothing else but them and the rain and the wind. He poured himself out until his soul was empty, and it was good, because Gabe was right there, holding on.

Gabe wasn't holding back either, returning every sound he made, hands running over his soaking skin, hips rocking into his. Lightning struck not far away, close enough to startle them both, and Gabe pressed a hand along his cock, dark eyes shining in the light coming through the kitchen window.

"The lightning is something, you're right." Gabe had to shout to be heard over the hum of the wind and the water driving against the deck, but Bowie didn't seem to notice the rain at all.

"It's...huge." He was dizzy with energy, with need.

"Want you." Gabe's voice was loud and gruff. "Want inside you."

"Need you." And that was clear. He needed Gabe.

"Inside. Too cold out here." Gabe pulled him into the kitchen, where they stood dripping on the kitchen floor as he closed the sliding glass door. "We'll make our own thunder. Put this storm to shame."

"God, yes." He felt like he was jangling, like he was fixin' to come undone on some base level.

"Upstairs, boy." Gabe nudged him with a shoulder and led the way. Everything about Gabe was steady and deliberate. It seemed like the more he started to fall apart, the more in control Gabe was. "Come on."

"With you." *Come on, O'Reilly. Focus.*

Gabe led him into the bedroom, stopping at the foot of the bed and taking his face in warm hands. "Breathe, boy. Just breathe, and belong."

He nodded because that was what he did. He breathed. He just was. He didn't think.

Gabe pulled back the curtains, so they got the view of the ocean and its rolling whitecaps. "There's your storm, boy. Shorts off." Gabe stepped out of his own and handed them over.

Bowie folded them, set them on the chair, and took his off, his prick still mostly hard, wet at the tip.

His bear stepped right in, so close, but didn't touch him at all, anywhere. He felt the heat start to build between them, and still Gabe didn't reach for him. The room was quiet except for the sound of the driving rain on the roof, his breath and Gabe's, and they stood there, chests rising and falling.

Gabe held his gaze as they breathed, and he found himself, right there again as he waited for Gabe to move.

He got a slow nod. "There you are." Gabe reached out at last, a hand going to the nape of his neck and pulling him into a hungry kiss that held none of the restraint Gabe had shown him just a moment ago. He opened, accepting that hunger, encouraging it. He leaned into Gabe's grip as the lightning flashed again, like the touch lit the sky.

Gabe groaned and grabbed his ass with both hands, pulling their hips flush and grinding into him, their cocks rubbing together.

He spread, balancing himself, bracing himself for Gabe's need. Bowie held on, trusting in his lover, in his bear.

The quiet was gone, replaced with Gabe's grunts and his moans, the wet and breathless sounds of their kisses. When Gabe started moving them toward the bed, he was ready. "Want...fuck."

Gabe turned him, letting Bowie see the storm as he was bent over the bed. "This okay, boy?"

He bent his knee, bracing himself on the bed and exposing himself all at once. "Better?"

Gabe moaned in answer, and the shock of Gabe's thumbs stretching him open even more, tongue attacking sensitive skin made him growl back.

"Bear!" His belly drew up as he shivered, that touch totally unexpected and wildly erotic.

"Boy." Gabe's tongue was busy, everywhere, teasing him and making his tight muscles tremble. Gabe left him, but only for a second before that same skin was met with cool lube. Gabe gripped his hips and pulled him back onto that cock to the sound of a rolling rumble of thunder. The stretch burned so good, and the way the pressure filled him was like the storm, raging away.

"Christ. Tight. So good." Once his ass met Gabe's hips, Gabe tugged on him hard, forcing him to take even more, and then went still, hissing through gritted teeth behind him.

Bowie panted, his head down as his body worked Gabe's cock, trying to force him to move.

Gabe rocked forward, making them both moan, and he could feel his lover fighting a little, making them wait until neither of them could stand it another second.

He nodded. Yes. Gabe understood. It was all about timing. All about the right second.

How that second happened, he couldn't have said. Gabe groaned, he clenched and arched, making Gabe shout; then they were just moving together. He rocked back and Gabe thrust forward, hard, nearly brutal, and perfectly in tune.

He might have screamed; he wasn't sure. It didn't matter. They had it—both of them rutting as the wind blew, his body taking every inch, the hands on his hips leaving bruises.

It was sensation and sound, waves and lightning, and after a while Gabe's fingers were slipping on sweaty skin and they fell out of rhythm, thrusts growing shallow and erratic. "Fuck. Fuck, Bow...Bowie!"

He nodded, his hips curling, the pressure of that heavy cock sliding past his gland. He needed more of that, and he got it, his teeth clicking together. "So close."

"I got you." Gabe was working now, holding that angle, keeping steady, driving him higher. "Yeah, I got you, huh?"

"Oh." Everything shorted out, that pleasure damn near unbearable, and he was caught. "Bear. Bear, please. Fuck, I need."

Gabe grunted and slid a hand around to his cock, not teasing for a second, going right for a sweep of the head, thumb diving hard into his slit. "Show me."

Lightning hit his brain, cracking him in half as he shot so hard his bones rattled.

"Shit!" He wasn't sure what exactly he'd done, but it set Gabe off too, his bear damn near exploding, hips stuttering reflexively. He nodded and groaned as Gabe covered him, heavy and still.

"Fuck, babe." Gabe kissed between his shoulder blades. "Damn." His lover muttered some combination of those three words several more times before finally moving again, breaking their connection and climbing up on the bed, beside him.

He let himself lean, take comfort now and ease himself down. "Thank you."

Gabe drew him right in close. "The pleasure was mine, trust me on that. I think I could learn to love a thunderstorm." Bear kissed his forehead, nuzzled his hair. "Not as much as I love you, though."

"Good." He nodded, settled on that front. "Very good."

Bear didn't have to say it for it to be true, but it was good to hear. Good to know.

Gabe stretched and he could tell the bear was headed off to dreamland. The storm wasn't done with them; it was supposed to come and go half the night. They sure as hell didn't need to keep up, though.

26

H e'd never wanted to do anything less than get on that plane back to New York yesterday, although having to get out of bed this morning was running a close second. Gabe lay there and ran through what was usually a no-brainer morning routine in his mind just so he'd have an excuse to hold Bowie for another five minutes.

Damn. Re-entry was going to suck.

He wasn't looking forward to running into Nelson, but then again, he had much more "I Don't Give a Shit" today than he did a week ago. Bowie and the beach had refilled his tank for a long while. He was looking forward to the locker room, though. He did have a rockin' tan after all, and he planned to show it off.

Okay, lazy-ass, get out of bed.

He carefully slid his arm out from under his lover—the tan, stacked, fucking gorgeous lover that Bowie was—and sighed as he headed for the bathroom, where he took the first solo shower he'd had in over a week and resented every second of it.

When he came out, there was a cup of coffee waiting for

him on the bathroom sink, and hell if that didn't make him smile. So simple, and so Bowie. Okay, then. Didn't take much to turn his day around did it?

"Good morning!" He called, not caring that they had neighbors. He picked up his coffee and took a sip, discovering something else. He was glad to be home to his fancy-assed coffeemaker.

Okay, so. Fancy-assed coffeemaker for the beach house. He needed a list.

"Morning. Why did we come back to work again, man?" Bowie was laughing, the sound ringing out.

"Fuck if I know. Rent?" He laughed. He didn't have Bowie's stash; he needed a job. "I should bounce at one of the beach nightclubs instead." Imagine that? He'd probably kill somebody by mistake.

"Shit, Bear. We ought to just flip a couple houses. It's fun work. There are two that I'm looking at that are cheap as hell."

"Yeah?" He toweled off and hung it back up, taking his coffee to the bedroom to get dressed. "Right now it's really fucking tempting, I'll tell you." He and Bowie, the beach, keeping their hands busy day and night? Hell, yeah. Wouldn't take much more to convince him.

Honestly, what would it take? What did he need? What was keeping him here?

Nope. No thinking before work.

"Yeah. I'll show you tonight when we get home. It's a good investment. You want to come pick your bike up after work, or you want me to bring it home?"

"Do you have time to bring it home? I don't get off until eight. Then we'd have time to have dinner."

"No problem. I'm thinking I'll order something, huh? Burgers or some shit. Something easy."

He dressed without thinking about it—uniforms were like that. "Easy is good. I'm on a three-day run."

"I hear you. I'll put a few shifts in with Zeke while you're saving lives." Bowie wandered through, tying his hair back. He looked amazing in his tighty-whities and nothing else.

"If I strangle Nelson today, will you bail me out?" He laughed and went to the kitchen to fill up a travel mug.

"Totally. Just holler."

"God. The idea of three twelves after a week of grilling and swimming and fucking does not sound like fun. I need to find my mojo, or this is gonna suck." He filled up his mug and grabbed a banana.

"I'd suck your mojo, but you're running late."

Oh, that was a sweet little ache in his balls. "That works. Now I have something to look forward to. Boy."

"I know the secrets to good work nights—food, orgasms, and sleep."

"I will need all of those when I get home, and the best part is, I can enjoy all three with you." He hooked Bowie in with one arm and kissed him, loving the hell out of the second of surprise.

Bowie grinned at him, his lover looking at him like he was the center of the earth. "Have a good day, Bear. I'll bring your bike home."

"I'm shooting for an eight. At least a seven. Thank you, babe, I'll see you in twelve." He grabbed his bag and headed out into the pre-rush-hour morning.

It was hot and sticky and just plain gross out. Sunny, but gross. and it wasn't even eight yet. So today would be heatstroke, little old ladies wanting a few minutes of air conditioning, kids with sliced-open palms and whatever else from opening fire hydrants, all kinds of craziness. So his job was to hydrate and keep his cool.

Ha. Nelson better be off today.

He did have one mission, however, and he pulled out his phone as he walked, leaving Daddy Mike a text he figured the guy wouldn't see until noon.

Hey, man. Need some specialty equipment. You still have a guy? I can't just walk in anywhere.

He dropped his phone back into his pocket and opened his travel mug. Yeah, he was the idiot who liked hot coffee on a hot day.

If they were at the beach, he'd be trying to talk Bowie into patos. Mmm. Bacon and egg and cheese.

The more bacon, the better.

He arrived at the firehouse and was greeted by a slew of smiles and some compliments on his tan, and one or two people, including Skip, even asked about his bike.

Nelson was there, leaning against a truck, arms crossed and watching him.

Skip leaned close to him. "Chief says he wants to see you two before we go out."

He shook his head, but he wasn't shocked. He headed for the Chief's office, Nelson following.

"So here's how this works," Chief said as soon as he'd closed the door. "You're going to have a discussion, fix the problem, and get to work. And this isn't going to happen again. Am I clear?"

"Yes, Chief." They both said at the same time.

Fuck.

"Fine." Chief left the office, closing the door behind him.

They stared at each other for a long minute. Finally, Nelson took a step toward him. He raised an eyebrow and took a step closer as well, squaring his shoulders. Nelson squinted his eyes, and he squinted back.

This wasn't looking good.

"Okay, so here's the deal. You're a fucking asshole who had better not touch my bike again if you want to keep your hands. And I already know there isn't a damn thing I can do to make you like me. But, we both need our jobs. So we're gonna walk out of here all smiles, shake hands where everyone can see it, and stay the fuck out of each other's way from now on. Deal?"

"Works for me."

"Fine." He crossed his arms over his chest. "And you're going to offer to pay for the damage to my bike."

Nelson bristled at that. "Like fuck I am."

"You are. Or I'll send your wife a picture of the blonde that picks you up every Thursday night after shift."

Nelson coughed. "Five hundred. Not a dime more."

"Works for me."

And that was how it went down. They left the room smiling and shaking hands.

He nodded. "Right on, man. Go save some lives."

"You too. Oh, and hey. I'm gonna pay for your bike, just send me the bill."

He was impressed Nelson got that out without choking on it. 'That's straight up of you. Thanks, man."

"Have a good day."

He walked away, headed for his truck.

Casey slapped him on the shoulder as they got in. "That was total bullshit, wasn't it?"

"Yeah, but I was right about the blonde." He gave her a big grin.

27

B urgers. Fries. Shakes.
Bowie felt good—the bike was home, he'd made some money, he was looking into some new properties, and *Chopped* was on the TV.

All he needed was his bear.

Gabe made it home a few minutes late but looked to be in a decent mood as well. "Somebody got Shake Shack!" Gabe dumped his bag and gave Bowie a grin. "Smells great in here."

"Shakes are in the freezer. How goes?" He was spread out on the sofa with his laptop, all showered and cool.

"Well, the day was about a seven, but I'm going to say that this makes it at least a nine." Gabe slapped a handful of cash down on the coffee table. "Nelson is paying for the repairs to my bike."

"Fucking A. Did you have to rip off his dick?" That was handy as hell. "I've worked all but two hundred off."

"I didn't. But his wife would if she knew about his Thursday night booty calls." Gabe grinned at him. "Did you say you were working off my bike? That's yours, then. I pay my debts. Zeke knows I'm good for it."

"I just knew I was there. I wasn't worried." He figured it was just easier. "Thursday booty calls, eh? That's problematic."

"It is for him, when people who think he's an asshole notice." Gabe sank into the couch next to him. "I should shower."

"Have your food first. I'll grab the shakes." He leaned over and took a quick kiss. He put his laptop on the coffee table and levered himself up off the sofa. The shakes were in good shape, and he handed one over.

Gabe took a sip and grinned at him. "Straight-up vanilla. Thank you. How was your day?"

"Good. Worked. Showered. Did some research. It's been a fine day." Bowie felt...just fine.

"What are you researching?" Gabe hauled off the couch and headed for the table.

"Houses. There are four or five that look interesting and affordable, if we put in work. Or for the same money, we can buy one in decent shape." He was less interested in that.

They set out the food. "You were serious about that, huh?"

"Well, we're taking our house off the market, so I'd like to see what our options are, you know?" He wasn't going to force Gabe to flip houses with him, but he knew that it was one of the things he was good at. A good way to make money.

Gabe nodded, chewing a big bite of burger, looking like a man that was thinking hard. Gabe wasn't really the thinking-hard kind and tended to get anxious. "I sure wouldn't miss three twelves in a row."

"There's no hurry. There's no stress. We have a ton of

options, but I'd love to work on a place or two with you. I think we'd have a fucking ball."

"We would. For sure, we would." Gabe smiled at him and munched on a french fry. "I have a ton of vacation time saved up, you know. A few months' worth, actually."

"Yeah? We could go out, spend a month, see what's what." He had to admit, he'd been happy down south—he loved the beach, the sand, the Gulf. He liked the work. "Maybe plan to go in October or something?"

"That'd work. Give me time to warn the chief, so he can get me covered. I liked Galveston. I really enjoyed...the beach. And everything. The house. You." Gabe swallowed a sip of his shake.

"Yeah. Yeah, I liked having you there in our house." Talking about changing things. Watching the storm. Being free.

"I felt like I fit in. That was cool too. I don't fit everywhere."

"I get that. I mean, it's a big thing, but we can give it a try. In October, it'll be quiet, barring hurricane season."

Gabe laughed. "The storm was exciting. I can't imagine what a hurricane would do to you."

Bowie's cheeks went red-hot because he'd been desperate, needy. They had done some...fucking hot shit on their week.

"So it's a plan, then. I'll take October off. I've got some money saved if you're buying. Set up whatever you want. I'm in."

"We'll pick a couple three places, have Rick go look at them, get back to us. He's trustworthy. What's your thought? A couple cheap fixers or a single in better shape?" He knew what he'd rather, but this was a "them" thing.

Gabe put his burger down. "I'd go cheap. We're doing

the work, so they'll turn more profit on a flip, right? Plus it just sounds like more fun."

"That's my thoughts on it too. The work's half the fun, and we get to decide all of it." He found the work satisfying, engrossing. Working with his hands made him happy. "We'll have to draw up agreements, you and me."

Gabe raised an eyebrow. "Agreements?"

"Ownership of the houses. In case something happens to one of us." That was fair, wasn't it? Reasonable. They weren't roommates.

"Oh. I guess. I don't know how that works. You give me something to sign, and I'll sign it." It really sounded like Gabe might not even look at whatever he did put together.

"I'll find a lawyer." He was a fair man. He wouldn't fuck Gabe over.

"That sounds so formal." Gabe grinned at him. "You mean the new houses, right? Can't we just get both of our names on them? Or doesn't it work like that? I've never owned anything."

"We'll find out. Rick'll know. He's a realtor." He wanted to reach out and squeeze Gabe's hand, comfort his bear, but it seemed weird, so he didn't.

"Rick is your management guy?" Gabe took a big swig of his shake. "That's cool. If you trust him, then I do. Hey, thanks for dinner. It hit the spot." Gabe got up and started shuttling dishes to the kitchen.

"Yeah. We were in together. He grew up in Galveston. He's the one that talked me into the first house." They'd known each other for years now. Rick had pulled his tour and scrambled home with his wife and his babies.

"That was a good call." Gabe stopped behind his chair and leaned over, hugging his shoulders. "I want *all* of this.

You just roll way faster than I do. I'm still stuck at staring at you and wondering how this is even possible."

"No worries." He had nothing to lose and nothing but time. "You want that shower now, Bear?"

Gabe kissed his neck. "Yeah. I do. You joining me?"

"Surely." He could scrub that fine body, and the water always felt good.

His phone and Gabe's went off at the same time, and he rolled his eyes. "Tommy and Sammy."

"What the heck?" Gabe answered, looking concerned. "Hello?"

What do you want, bubba?

U home? Want a beer?

He rolled his eyes. No. *Maybe tomorrow. Gabe's working a 3*

"Yeah. Got home yesterday." Gabe grinned at him. "That sounds great but I'm on shift for—Friday will work.... Sounds good....It was fantastic, we had perfect weather."

Friday? Sammy asked.

Sure. Mikes. 9? Bowie headed to the bathroom to start the water running.

"No, it was my first trip. Bowie has...yeah. Well, he has one that wasn't rented. It's was nice. Right by the beach. Hey, man, I gotta hop, early morning and all....Yes. Thanks for calling. See you Friday." Gabe hung up the phone and followed him into the bathroom. "Fuckin' A."

"Like they had to tag-team us." He looked over his shoulder at Gabe and grinned. Of course, that was his people—Sammy, Tommy, Momma and Daddy.

Tag-team galore.

"Friday. Tommy said dinner, and then I guess Sammy said drinks, so we're doing steaks and then Mike's, sounds like. Tommy wanted to chat—a.k.a. ask questions. I played the tired card." Gabe started undressing, dumping everything in the hamper. "Hard to tell if they're looking out or being nosy. Probably both."

"Probably. You know how Sammy is." He muscled Gabe into the tub. Food, check. Shower, next. Then orgasm and bed. "We like steak and beer."

Gabe was grinning at him and backing into the spray. "They're going to be very disappointed when all we talk about is the weather, the house, and the food."

"They'll learn to live with the disappointment." Bowie figured their private life was just that. Theirs.

"So serious." Gabe kissed him.

Was he? He smiled into the kiss, his hands running along his bear's slick skin.

"I kind of like how you get growly and protective of us, our privacy. It's...sexy."

"I'm not ashamed, but I trust you to know me, to know what I need, just like I know how to give you what you need. This is ours." Precious and not for public consumption.

"Completely ours. I hope to have a surprise for you on Saturday." Gabe leaned away and reached for the shampoo. "Something even hotter than the night we trimmed and conditioned your beard."

That had been something. How Bear turned something so simple into something sensual and erotic.

"Huh. I look forward to it. Hotter than the storm?" He took the shampoo and began washing Gabe's hair, fingertips pressing in, massaging.

"Ooh. Hm. I think it'll be kind of like if you took all that storm energy, bottled it up, and let it out real slow." Gabe drew out the last two words on a low breath.

That was intriguing. "You have my attention."

He kept on washing, pondering the type of release his

bear would ask for—hand or mouth, rub off against his belly, his ass. He was easy.

"Good." Gabe didn't offer him any more details. Just a sly grin. "Did I tell you everyone was impressed with my tan? I got a bunch of attaboys."

"Yeah? It suits you. Did you brag about your time in the salt and the sand?"

"Of course. To everyone that would listen. I told them I had incredible food, a great view, stayed in bed late, and drank beer." That was how he knew Bear really had enjoyed the beach. That smile, and that Gabe had bragged to his work buddies.

"It was the best time I've ever had there." It had been the first time he'd known he wanted to go back and stay one day.

"I can't imagine one better." Gabe finished rinsing and shut the water off. "I think we'd be okay there. I think we could be good."

He didn't have anything to say. He'd hooked his wagon to Gabe's, whether or not Gabe understood that. They were good. He handed Gabe a towel, and they headed for the bedroom.

"I've been thinking about you and my mojo all day, man. No lie."

"Mmm..." It was good to have a plan. He sat on the edge of the bed and brought himself eye to eye with the finest cock in history.

"Hello, there."

Bear groaned for him, and without even being touched, that cock stretched long. He got a thrill knowing he could do that, that Gabe wanted him that much. He cupped that sweet sac and licked a long line up his lover's shaft with the tip of his tongue.

Gabe hissed, fingers diving into his hair. "Damn, babe. There is nothing like your mouth."

He dragged the flat of his tongue over Gabe's slit, taking a taste and giving Gabe that rush, that hint of sting.

He felt Gabe's eyes on him, watching, locked on his every move. Gabe wasn't shy with sounds and moaned, encouraging him. Bowie let himself relax and work on making Gabe feel everything so that busy mind could sleep and rest. He played the slit until Gabe leaked steadily, then he went down, humming all the way.

"Fuck." Gabe sighed and rocked forward, and he knew his bear was going there, out of that head, focusing on what felt good. It was simple, the way Gabe just gave him that need. He opened and took all that Gabe needed him to, swallowing hard every time his bear eased in, offered him a low cry.

As usual on nights when Bear was working and tired, things ramped up quickly. Gabe was strong and single-minded by the end, deep thrusts became more shallow and quick until the last, when Bear drove into him and shot hard, a rough shout echoing through the room.

Bowie cleaned Gabe's prick with his tongue and eased him into bed before climbing up into his bear's arms.

Gabe sighed, and those arms wrapped right around him —protective, possessive—and fingers tangled in his hair. "I really appreciated the coffee this morning," his bear said sleepily. It sounded like a random remark, but he knew better.

He settled, kissed Gabe's jaw. *Yeah. Anytime. Also, I love you too.* "Night, Bear."

28

"So I looked it up. This steak place is kind of...steep. And I think we need to dress a little." Gabe stared into his closet, lips twisting. That could be Tommy wanting to bust his chops, or maybe Sammy wanting to dress Tommy up like a cowboy, but he had a feeling it wasn't about his friends at all. "They're fucking with us, aren't they?"

"Uh-huh. I'm not wearing a tie." Bowie looked a little belligerent about it.

He looked over at Bowie, head tilting as he imagined his lover in a tie. No way. "You'd look ridiculous in a tie, babe. You got a jacket?"

"Uh. I got a shirt with snaps." Bowie pulled out a dove-gray shirt in a dry-cleaning bag.

"Hey, that'll work. What about pants? I mean, I could call and ask for a different place but..." But he felt like they'd thrown down the gauntlet, and the only good response was to pick the damn thing up. And maybe wrap it around Tommy's neck.

"Sammy won't go anywhere they won't let you wear

jeans." Bowie sounded absolutely sure. "I'll wear my good jeans and boots."

Bowie was probably right; he'd never seen Sammy in anything but jeans. Or leather. "Sounds good. Great, even." He'd never seen Bowie dressed either, he was kind of looking forward to it now.

He reached into his closet and pulled out a black dress shirt and his black sports jacket. "I've got leather or black denim. You tell me."

"Will you sweat to death in the leather? It's hot out there, and if we're paying a zillion dollars for a steak, I think you ought to enjoy it."

He laughed. "You're so fucking right. Denim it is. Maybe I'll skip the jacket too. Fancy steakhouse in the summer. Get serious." He was looking forward to it though, the steak and the company. "Is your shirt good to go? You need the iron?"

"I had everything cleaned when I got here." Bowie pulled on a pair of dark jeans, then pulled on his fancy-assed cowboy boots.

"Mmm. Nice boots." He dressed easily, sharp-black denim and his black dress shirt. It had been a while since he'd worn it, but he did like the shirt; it was stretchy cotton, tight in all the right places. He looked at his feet and decided on his one pair of dress shoes. His boots were all heavy and chunky and didn't dress up all that well.

"Thanks. I got them for my high school graduation. I've worn them a handful of times." Bowie tugged on his shirt and snapped up, tucked in. The belt buckle had a grim reaper on it.

"That's a statement." He pointed to the buckle, then reached out and pulled Bowie in by it, giving him a quick kiss. "You clean up good, Sarge."

"Thank you, sir. Hair down or up? Up is probably nicer."

He ran his fingers through the thick waves before he answered, just because he could. Because he loved it. It was even better now that Bowie had figured out how to condition and care for it. His lover looked like a god. Like a fucking son of Poseidon or something, some god of the beach and thunderstorms that rolled in off the ocean.

Bowie was staring at him. God only knew what Mister Perceptive got from that train of thought.

"Uh. Sorry. Probably should wear it up, I guess. But I do like it down."

"If you like it, it works for me." Bowie grinned at him, all bright-eyed and happy.

He took another kiss. "I love it."

Bowie nodded like that pretty much settled that, and pride settled in, right into his balls.

He stepped into his shoes, combed his hair and his beard, and watched Bowie move around the apartment as he arranged an Uber on his phone. They were going to knock the tops of Tommy and Sammy's heads off, they looked so good.

"Why don't you have any ink, man?" Given his lover's look, it seemed like he ought to.

"Just never have found what I wanted to look at every day until I died, I guess."

"That's one way to look at it." That seemed too simple though, even for Bowie. He was pretty sure there was more there. When you don't know if you have a tomorrow, you make decisions for today.

"I think it's about the things I want to remember. The things that shaped me. And some stupid shit I just like." He grinned. "Tommy and Sammy used a guy we know from Mike's not too long ago. They said it was an amazing experience." Amazing was what Sammy said but the cowboy's eyes had said "fucking hottest thing ever."

"Yeah, he said. He said it was the best, and he'd been into that one guy in Austin, bad."

"That's some story, right? That guy, that experience." He grabbed his keys and held the door for Bowie. "I never get tired of it."

"It's a little weird, because brothers, but yeah. I paid for a big chunk of the ink. He needed something good." Bowie was the most generous man in all these random ways.

"I bet that made it that much more meaningful, that you cared enough to do that for him. That you understood what it meant. Ink is a big deal, and that injury, and those scars are no joke."

He noted that Bowie didn't bring the crutch again. He'd only really been paying attention recently, but it seemed like Bowie was managing without it more often than not lately. Still, he held back the elevator gate and squeezed in, grinning. It would be okay with him if his lover just decided never to use the stairs.

"It was no big thing." Bowie balanced himself on Gabe's hip, staying closer than he had to. "Rick emailed about those properties. We can look at the info tomorrow. There's a three-story one that we can make into three rentals."

"Can't wait to see them."

Things were moving fast, right? Like really fast. He was used to being the dipshit that jumped into things two-footed without looking, and damn the consequences. But Bowie was in some other category altogether. Bowie didn't seem to care that it was risky...or maybe Bowie didn't even know.

It made him feel a little unsettled, but not because it was a bad thing, just because it was a weird thing. It wasn't normal to want all of this so fast, was it? To...know what he knew, feel the way he felt this fast? To be this happy?

Man, he wasn't good at this figuring-out shit. He was better off just letting life happen. Stuff like steak and beer.

Bowie's hand slid down his spine, the touch sure and strong. *Be easy*, that touch said. *I got you.*

He smiled. Yeah. That he knew.

He backed out of the elevator, and they hopped into their mercifully air-conditioned Uber. "Okay, bets. Will Tommy be in all black or Wranglers?" He looked at Bowie. "Sammy loves to dress him up."

"Hmm..." God, he loved that, the way Bowie thought about things. The man could solve puzzles in seconds. "Sammy does love to see him in cowboy get-up. I'm betting Western wear tonight so that Tommy gets to have Sammy wear something wild tomorrow night."

"I like how you think." He bumped shoulders with Bowie.

One thing was for sure, he knew as soon as they walked in that this was their kind of place. Dark walls, leather seats, a long bar, and it smelled amazing.

"Oh, now this smells good." Bowie actually moaned. That was adorable.

"Hungry, babe?"

"Are you with the Ward party?" A tall man in a black suit approached them.

"Yes?" *The Ward party?* He blinked, surprised. "Uh. Yes."

"Follow me, please."

He gestured for Bowie to go first, and they were shown to a table along one side of the restaurant, where Tommy and Sammy were waiting for them.

Just as Bowie had predicted, Tommy and Sammy were in full-Western, both of them looking clean-cut and adorable.

Oh, he really wanted a Sammy hug all of a sudden.

Tommy stood up as they got to the table and offered them a smile and a handshake. "Gentlemen."

"Hey, Tommy. Love the shirt."

Tommy laughed. "You both look healthy and wonderful. Sun is good for you, Gabriel."

Don't do it. He did his best not to roll his eyes at the only person he knew that used his full name. "Thanks."

Sammy grinned at him, then launched into his arms, hugging him hard. "Angel. You look amazing. I've missed you. I want to hear everything."

He hugged back, giving his friend an extra squeeze. Sammy's greetings made his day every single damn time. Filled his bucket right up. "We had such a good time."

He pulled out a chair for Bowie and took a seat himself just as a server came over to take drink orders.

Sammy and Tommy ordered wine, they ordered beers, and they all sat to chat. There was an ease here, a true sense of family, and his Bowie seemed genuinely happy to see not only his brother, but Tommy too.

"So first of all, Bowie's houses are great. The one we stayed in has this incredible view, a hot tub, and an amazing kitchen. We cooked and grilled a ton. The other properties are nearby too. Have you ever seen them, Sammy?"

"I haven't. You closemouthed bastard. I would have come to help work on the houses."

"I've had them forever." Bowie shrugged and grinned. "I needed a spot to put things together."

"He did amazing work. These places were sold after a hurricane, and he fixed them all up. I was so impressed." He patted Bowie's knee under the table, feeling proud of his resourceful boy.

Tommy looked at Bowie, eyes focused with interest. "I

assume you didn't put the man to work while you were down there; surely you had some fun?"

"We had a ball. We didn't work a bit. Planned some, though. We're replacing the tub for sure, putting in a better security system, a surround sound." Bowie looked completely happy, to be planning, to be working.

"Bigger grill." He nodded. "And we need a better coffeemaker." He picked up his beer and took a sip, almost missing the look that passed between Tommy and Sammy. But not quite.

"God, yes. And a smoker."

Tommy put a hand on Sammy's arm and smiled at Bowie. "So, am I hearing that you've taken that property off the market?"

"Yeah, that's our house now. We have a great view, the hot tub." Bowie stroked his thigh, the touch unconscious. "And we might get a beer cooler."

He looked over at Bowie. "Yeah? A beer cooler? That's a fantastic idea, babe."

One of Thomas's eyebrows went up. "Well. Sammy and I are very happy for you both." Thomas let go of Sammy's arm carefully, like he might be letting the dogs loose.

"That rocks, man. I can't wait to see the house. What part of Galveston—right on the sea wall?" Sammy leaned closer. "Are you moving home, Bowie? Like to Texas?"

"We haven't decided anything one hundred percent except that we're keeping the house ours. Gabe and me, we're going to see what is what, together."

Sammy looked at Gabe, shaking his head. "You can't just leave forever and not say good-bye, okay?"

"Jesus, Sammy." He swallowed, quieting the weird twinge in his chest. "That would be impossible to do, since I would miss your stupid little redneck ass." A lot.

"Air travel is still a viable option," Tommy teased, winking at Sam.

"Yeah, and I'll have a place to rent, hmm?" Sammy teased.

"If it's not occupied..." Bowie could give right back.

"Have you told the folks? They're going to want to meet Angel, you know."

Bowie shook his head. "Nope."

"Nope." No parents.

Thomas laughed. "Chicken shit."

"Damn right I am." Gabe laughed, grinning broadly. "I'm not parent material." It seemed like eventually there would have to be a polite handshake, but that was going to be up to Bowie, and no way was he sleeping under their roof. Not after Bowie's nine days from hell.

"They're going to want to meet you, Angel, especially if you're close enough to drive to see. They're good people, honest."

"Drop it, Sam." Bowie fastened Sammy with a look that was cold as ice, stopping the conversation in its tracks.

Tommy reached over and took Sammy's hand, but the Dom's eyes were on Bowie. "Would you like another beer, Bowie?"

Gabe squinted at Tommy and opened his menu. "What are they known for here? I'm starved."

"I like their filet. It's like butter. You can almost cut it with a fork." Tommy ordered another round for them, although Gabe didn't think Little Sammy had touched his wine yet.

"Sounds perfect." Gabe leaned close to Bowie, sharing his menu. "What do you think? You want to try that too? Or were you thinking one of these others?"

"I'm going to get the strip. It sounds good and I'm

hungry." Bowie's voice was still all growly and low. "You want some potatoes?"

"Yeah. I'm in. Looks like sides are a family style thing." He looked at Sammy, who didn't look interested in dinner at all, then at Tommy. "You guys want to pick a side too?"

Man, this was going sideways. He could feel it.

Tommy set his menu down slowly and looked Bowie in the eye. "I don't think Sam deserved that outburst, Bowie."

One of Bowie's eyebrows lifted. "Fairly sure you need more than two words for an outburst."

"Oh, for chrissake. I'm fine." Sammy shut his menu. "You don't want to meet the family, Angel, don't. You don't want complications, Bowie, don't. It's none of mine. Let's order so we have something to do with our mouths that's not talking."

It wasn't that he didn't ever want to meet the parents, it was that Bowie didn't want it, at least not right now, and he had every intention of respecting that. Especially since he didn't do the polite company thing so well.

Tommy and Bowie didn't quite break their stare, and he had to laugh after he and Sammy reached over and gave them each a sock in the arm.

Spell broken, Tommy looked over at Sammy and shrugged. "The roasted brussels sprouts?"

"I like those." Sammy gave Tommy a half smile. "The best part is the bread though, right?"

"And the honey butter. Outstanding. You two will love it."

"Bring it on."

A big basket appeared as soon as they'd ordered, and while they waited for their meal, he put an arm across the back of Bowie's chair and let his thumb just graze over his lover's spine.

He'd tell Bowie to breathe if he could. He'd say family was hard. He'd remind Bowie that Sammy was different. Instead he just sipped his beer.

Gabe felt Bowie relax as he and Tommy chatted about work and ink and bikes. Normal shit. And everyone's mood improved as the steaks arrived.

"Look at this." His mouth was watering just looking at his filet. "It smells so good." He waited impatiently for everyone else's steaks to be set down.

"Almost as good as the ones we made, hmm?" That was just for his ears, Bowie's words soft as butter.

He bent an elbow just enough to make contact with his lover. "Almost. Hard to beat those." He picked up the bowl of potatoes and gave them each a big spoonful.

Tommy looked up from his steak. "Do you think you two might be interested in dropping by the club tomorrow night?"

He shook his head. "No, I don't think so. We have plans." Well, he'd made plans for them—he hadn't actually told Bowie yet.

"Ah. Too bad. Sam's going to look amazing."

He swore he could hear Bowie gagging in his head.

"Sorry, Sammy." He grinned over and winked. "I know we'll be missing a sight, but this has been on the calendar all week."

"Oh? Are y'all doing something wonderful?" Sammy asked.

"We are." That was all he planned to say about it, so he put a piece of steak in his mouth. "Mmm." It was pretty damn good. "How's your book coming?"

"Fine. I got into the PhD program on the weight of what I have." Sammy offered the information over, so casually, and Tommy's eyes went wide.

"What?" Tommy put his fork down and turned to Sammy. "When did you find out? Why didn't you tell me? Are you serious?" Tommy looked way more excited than annoyed.

"I found out right before you got home. I thought it would be a nice surprise to share."

"Congrats, Sammy! Way to go. You really do have something then, huh? Awesome." He reached across the table and gave Sammy a high five.

Sammy looked to Bowie, who nodded. "Not surprised a bit. You deserve it."

That was genuine. Understated, but that was Bowie, right?

With most things. He let himself grin.

"I'm so proud of you." Tommy put an arm around Sammy's shoulders and pulled the boy in for a hug. "So, we're celebrating then, gentlemen."

"Does that mean we get cake?" He was only sort of kidding; he really liked cake.

"Banana splits. Those are his favorite." Bowie winked over at Tommy.

"My Sam has a weakness for ice cream in general." Tommy was visibly happy for Sammy and firmly in Sammy's corner. He knew Tommy would have stood up to Bowie, or anyone, if it was really necessary, and he was glad Sammy had someone like that.

He was more glad that he didn't have to start taking sides himself. That had been a big part of his worry about getting involved with Sammy's brother to start with. And after the exchange tonight, he knew he and Sammy needed to talk.

Not that Bowie seemed to need him to take sides on anything. Bowie's heart was where it was. It was really more about Sammy; they'd already had the loyalty talk once, and he wanted to make sure they were on the same page.

By the time they'd finished their steaks, Bowie was showing pictures from the beach, and the brothers were head-to-head, discussing the pros and cons of property.

Tommy leaned toward him. "So, things are good?"

"Yeah. Really good."

"Are you really thinking about moving?"

"We're…really thinking about *thinking about* moving." He grinned. "We're going to spend October down there and see."

"The whole month?"

"Yeah. I got a ton of vacation."

Tommy nodded and finally asked what Gabe knew his fellow Dom wanted to know. "And you're both getting what you need?"

He understood that it was asked out of concern for a friend and not just curiosity, but the details were private. "We're good." That was a fair answer, right?

"But not coming to the club." Tommy raised an eyebrow.

"I gotta tell you, man. I don't think we'll visit the club. That's just not how we roll. I'm still on call for Clint though, and you can find us at Mike's."

"People miss you, Gabe. You two should come by for a drink sometime at least."

"We'll see, okay? Everything is still new."

Tommy nodded. "Understood. I respect that."

"Thanks, man. I knew you would." With any luck, that would be the end of that. He picked up his beer. "I am stuffed."

Bowie grinned over at him. "That was some good shit, wasn't it? Even the brussels sprouts."

"Even the vegetables. Wow." He smiled back, eyes

looking Bowie over again. The dress shirt thing kind of raised Bowie's level of handsome to eleven. "Are you still up for Mike's?" He had a box waiting for him in Mike's office he was going to need for tomorrow.

"Totally. Y'all?"

Sammy nodded to Bowie. "I think that sounds fun, and I can show Mister off. Isn't he gorgeous?"

Bowie looked Thomas up and down. "He cowboys up pretty good."

"It's all the O'Reillys I've known. Good-looking bunch."

Gabe laughed hooking a thumb at Bowie. "You can't have this one."

"He's too damn big anyway." Tommy pushed away from the table.

"For you, maybe, twiglet." Tommy wasn't that small, but he was fun to tease.

Tommy grinned. "Gorilla."

"No, not a bit." Bowie didn't explain, but Gabe knew what his lover was thinking. He was Bowie's bear.

"Mister has his O'Reilly. We're all good."

Bowie grinned at Sammy, the look wicked, almost naughty. "Are you going to make him call you Dr. Boy?"

"Ha!" He laughed so hard he almost fell back into his chair.

Tommy's eyebrow arched, but the grin followed, and full-out laughter after that. "Careful how you answer that, boy."

Sammy rolled his eyes, but grinned. "I think this is a 'just so long as you call me' thing."

"Coward." He winked at Sammy. "Come on boys, let's get a cab."

The four of them leaving the restaurant together must have been quite a sight. Loud and laughing, they got plenty of looks as they made their way out to the street. They weren't two feet clear of the front doors when he took Bowie's hand. Sammy beamed at him, and that felt good. He had nothing to worry about on that score at least.

They grabbed a cab and he stole a kiss as they pushed in together, making Bowie and Sammy both laugh.

"I'll get in front, shall I?" Tommy opened the passenger door and started up a conversation with the driver.

They goofed off in the back seat all the way to Mike's, except for when Tommy told them all to shut up.

That lasted about thirty seconds.

"Good thing that was a quick trip, I think we might have squashed Little Sammy." He reached in and hauled Sammy out of the cab with a big grin. "You good?"

"I am. You make him look happy. I like that. He's nice to you?"

"More than nice." He gave Sammy a wink. "It's good. We're really good." And how sweet was it that Sammy was looking out for him?

"Rock on. I love that three-story place. Y'all could rent three whole places. I love the idea of you two as beach landlords."

"It suits Bowie so well. I'm just hoping it suits me too. I think it will. I like working with my hands, I loved the beach air and the water. I think...between Galveston and Bowie...I think I really found something." He knew he had. He just needed that month in October to prove it to himself. To get that stupid little voice in his head to leave him alone.

"Wow. How cool is that? Seriously. We will be visiting y'all, if you move." Sammy leaned against him. "Bowie loves to come and go and see. You'll go see a ton of shit."

Tommy and Bowie were already chatting at the bar, and

he and Sammy were slowly bringing up the rear. "It isn't weird me being with your brother? It won't be...a problem?"

"Why? You two obviously are into each other. Bowie needs someone to care about. He took care of all those soldiers, and...man, they said he'd never walk again, and he doesn't have a cane right now!" Sammy grinned at him and hooked one arm in his. "I've never seen him smile so much."

"He has a great smile, doesn't he?"

He knew Bowie was happy, and he figured it was his job to keep his lover that way. He knew they would run into issues neither of them was expecting now and then, physical and emotional, but he wasn't in this to fix anyone. They'd just tackle those things as they came along.

"He hardly uses the cane. Mostly just long days, or if he gets a really super bad weather ache. You should have seen him on the beach!"

"That's amazing exercise for his leg, I bet. I know that it took a day or two for me to get used to how unstable it is." Sammy grinned. "So, you're going to stay for the Lone Star Rally?"

"We haven't talked about it officially, but if it's up to me, hell yes." He laughed. The huge bike rally was right in town; why not? "The ride down The Strand sounded cool, and they have some charity runs and stuff. Bike shows. I think Bowie should have a bike." They could have a blast riding together.

"I think that would be something. He can relearn. He'll just be a little unbalanced."

"He can do it." No question.

"Angel! Little Sammy!" Darla waved and a couple of beers got handed over heads to them.

"Thank you, beautiful!" Sammy raised a glass to him,

and they drank. "Are there gay-friendly bars in Galveston, Angel? Are y'all going to have to be in the closet?"

"Well, there are some gay bars. We didn't go in any, but there are more than a handful. And a bunch of the regular bars are supposed to be friendly, but we don't...I mean, a regular bar is really fine. We'll feel it out a little more when we're there." Assuming they went out.

"Cool. Bowie's a low-key guy, even if he is a bossy turd."

This was fun, hanging out with Sammy, letting their guys do their thing for a while. "Low-key is an understatement. He's also really perceptive. I can't get away with anything." He winked.

"He was a damn explosives expert, man. His job was to see everything. Everything." Sam shook his head. "I can't imagine how fucking hard that was, for all those years."

"Mmm. I'm starting to get it. Not what it felt like, obviously, but what it did to him. He doesn't have reference points for a lot of things. He doesn't have perspective like you and I do. He's very present. It's nothing bad, just different. Really different."

"Yeah. He was always fixin' to die or kill someone, and now he's fixing motorcycles and cooking fried chicken."

"His fried chicken is out of this world." He sipped his beer. "I figure at some point he'll look around and realize he has a future. A pretty long future. We'll figure it out."

"I'm glad. For both of you." And didn't that feel good?

"How are you and Tommy? He looks proud as hell of you."

"Good. Good. Things are...exciting." Sammy gave him a surprised little glance. "Now that we're not worrying all the time, there's time to...explore."

"Nice. It's good not to be worrying *about* you too." He

winked at Sammy. "You look great. When do you start the PhD thing?"

"September. After Italy. It's...it's going to be a brand-new life."

He held up his beer. "Well, here's to new adventures."

"Yes. For all of us." Sammy clinked their glasses together. "Love you, man."

"Love you back." He sipped his beer, wondering why that was easy with Sam, but words were harder with Bowie. Not that they meant the same thing exactly but...oh, hell. Didn't matter. "I gotta go pick up a package from Mike's office before I forget. I'll meet you guys back at the bar, okay?"

He watched Sammy head over and grinned at the way Tommy just pulled the boy right in. Bowie glanced over and he gave a "be right back" wave. He pushed his way through the crowd without much trouble, being big was sometimes a good thing.

In Mike's office he found the box waiting for him with two business cards, one of Mike's with a note on the back that said "Let me know if you have any problems with the order," and one from the guy he'd placed the order with. What a crazy shop that was. Cases and cases of toys and tools for all kinds of play.

It had been an enlightening couple of hours, and he'd chosen everything specifically with Bowie in mind. Saturday was one sleep away. He couldn't wait to use their new toys.

29

Man, Bowie wasn't sure what Gabe was planning, but the energy crackled in the air, had been buzzing all day.

He didn't mind at all, to be honest. He'd made biscuits and gravy, he'd taken a long shower, and he was fixing one of the speakers from behind the sofa. It felt like electricity was crawling along the floor.

It looked like they were going to invest in two properties —that three-story and a tiny little saltbox that was going for next to nothing. Two properties and a little less than sixty thousand dollars, and they'd have four rentals out of it once the work was done.

Bowie was eager to get to work, to take Gabe to the beach and start making something ruined good and right again.

Gabe walked over, cell phone in hand. "Okay, that transfer will go through on Tuesday to your account. Any luck?"

"They're ours. Rick says it's a go. They'll courier shit up in a week, we'll sign, Rick will take possession." Easy-peasy.

"Awesome. Is it October yet?" Gabe laughed. "I'm ready to go back."

"You and me both, Bear. You and me both. I like our bed here, though. We might have to get one for our place."

"That's easy enough, I'd like that too. I researched this one, comfort is important. Elbow room is also important. And room enough to play." Gabe was hovering, watching him work.

He looked up, meeting Gabe's gaze. "You're excited."

He was too, and he didn't even know why.

Gabe smiled, and those dark eyes flashed. "I am. I'm looking forward to our evening. To something new that I think you're going to enjoy."

New.

New.

How fucking exciting was that? He didn't ask what it was, because the anticipation was delicious.

"Did you and Tommy have a good chat last night? I enjoyed catching up with Sammy."

"Yeah. He's a decent man, and I couldn't have picked a better person for Sammy." He shot Gabe a glance. "I don't understand how someone so good for Sammy could have been with James."

Gabe shrugged. "Tommy...evolved to be with Sammy. The Tommy that was with James was...well, I don't know how much you want to know about your brother's kinks, but James was a very 'by the book' sub and Tommy had always been a 'by the book' Dom. I think he fell for Sammy and didn't have much choice but to toss the book."

"James was a by the book man, all over. He was like our mom. Me and Sammy are more like our father." They were just who they were.

"Tommy and Sammy put the work in for sure. They both

wanted it, and somehow they figured out their balance and their own rules. And that shit with James's murderer really just made them tighter, all said and done."

His fingers curled into fists at the thought of the asshole who'd robbed them of James.

"Yeah." Bowie stood up and moved right into Gabe's space needing connection. "I want you. I want to take you home to the beach and drink beer in our hot tub."

"I want to sit on the deck and grill more steaks and watch the sunset with you." Gabe's arm tightened around his back.

God, his whole body was lit, buzzing with a warm anticipation. "Storms, Bear. I want all the storms with you."

"Soon, boy." Gabe tipped his chin up and kissed him, and that buzz, that lightning arced between them.

Fuck, yes. He could stay right here, just right fucking here for an eternity or until they got bored.

Gabe's kiss took a more intense turn, and his lover released him. "We'll make some thunder again today."

He swayed a second, just the littlest bit lightheaded. Oh, he did like this. "Boom?" he teased.

Bear's low chuckle made the little hairs on his arms stand up. "Yeah. Boom. You want to get started a little early?"

"I can handle that." He was fascinated by this—that Gabe had planned something, that there was this secret his bear intended to share.

"Come on, I'll need you to tell me it's okay, we can talk a minute." Gabe took his hand and led him to the bedroom. "Sit on the bed, please."

He sat, still more curious than concerned.

Gabe pulled a fancy wooden box off the dresser and put it in his lap. "I'm leaving it up to you, boy. I picked that out for you myself, and I think you'll get off on it. It's new to me, and I'm assuming it's new to you too. You can open the box and we'll talk about what's inside, or you can hand it back to me, and we'll figure it out together." Gabe gave him a grin. "Your pick, no rush."

Bowie zipped through the options, filtering through what he knew—that Gabe had planned, was excited, had chosen and researched and worried. Was still worried, but not scared. Talking seemed anticlimactic really, given that neither of them was much on discussion. You did things or you didn't, simple as that, and no matter what was in the box, it wouldn't hurt him. The weight and smell were wrong for danger, and that was his specialty, not Gabe's. Gabe put people together; he blew them apart.

He handed the box to Gabe without a second's hesitation.

He couldn't have known how meaningful that gesture would be, but he knew it now. Gabe's smile said more than any discussion would have.

Gabe took the box and kissed him. "Thank you."

"You got my back, Bear." Simple as that.

"Mmm. I do. And your front." Gabe winked at him, straightened up, and headed for the bathroom. "Undress please? And then just lie back and breathe. I need to get a few things."

He stripped while Bear wandered off, and once he was naked, he settled into the sheets and closed his eyes, listening to the air move.

Gabe sat on the bed and took a second, gently encouraging him into a position that suited whatever his lover was up to; then Gabe quickly snapped a simple, black cock ring on him without warning. "I have others if that one isn't comfortable."

His eyes flew open, and he looked down, the ring

making his package look obscene and pretty damn impressive.

Gabe chuckled. "Like that? Used one before?"

"Once. A metal one. This one's not as cold."

"I think it fits pretty well; make sure you let me know if there is an issue. It looks great." Gabe cradled his shaft in one hand and ran a thumb over the head. "You'll want to watch...you can prop up on the pillows if you like."

He grabbed the pillows, shoving them under his neck and head, even as he spread his legs. The little buzz Gabe was drawing up in him was just fine.

"Mmm. Good boy." Gabe smiled and started moving again, spreading out a small towel on the bed, laying out lube and little packets of alcohol, setting the box down and sitting on the bed again, very close to his hip.

Gabe's hands were steady and moving carefully as his lover opened the box, folded back the lid, and lifted a single, silver rod out, holding it up to show him. "Have you used one of these before? Seen one?" Gabe held it out for him to see.

His cock throbbed once, a drop appearing at the tip, and Bowie found himself swallowing as he tried to wet his tongue. "Seen one, yeah. Saw a scene with one."

"Oh, nice. It's called a sound." Gabe opened an alcohol pad, held the sound at the end and cleaned it, slowly running the pad over every part that could possibly touch him. His lover was moving so slow, focused, making sure he could see everything. When it was clean, Gabe picked up the bottle of lube. "Good surprise?"

"Never expected it." He couldn't stop staring. "You ever done this?"

Gabe smiled at him. "No. But I know anatomy pretty well, right? And someone I trust taught me what I need to know. It's pretty straightforward, and we'll go very slow. I'm learning, too. Learning *you*."

Gabe dropped lube on the end of the sound and a couple of drops right on the tip of his cock, then slid gentle fingers up his shaft until they caught under the flared part of the head, holding it upright and steady.

Bowie stared as the tip of the metal rod touched the slit of his cock, and he wasn't sure whether to jerk away or arch closer, so he stayed perfectly still. The visual and the way the nerves in his cock burned as the sound slipped in an inch didn't quite match up. He closed his eyes, trying to understand what the fuck he was feeling.

"Breathe." Gabe stopped there, adding another drop or two of lube, pulling up on it gently and letting it slide down again under its own weight, but not allowing it any deeper. "It looks fucking hot. You good?"

He nodded, and suddenly his eyes were open again, watching this. "Feels fucking big."

He knew it wasn't. He knew the little rod was tiny, but it felt like it was touching him everywhere, sliding along the most secret parts of him.

"I believe it. I'm not going to talk now; I want you to just...feel it. I'm going to do this real slow, and unless you tell me to hold up, I'm going to assume you're good. So speak up." Gabe was focused, hands steady, handling him like he was fragile and precious.

Bowie watched, the slim sound stopping about halfway down his prick. He had a moment of panic, his heart fluttering, and then Gabe gently moved his cock, and the fucking thing just slid in. Then he did gasp, his eyes so wide, they pulled at the corner.

"Good?" Gabe's voice was soft and low, a little rough,

fingers playing lightly along his length, adding layers of sensation.

"Jesus. Jesus, Bear." He couldn't fucking breathe, the sensations in his cock near unbearable, but so, so fine.

"I've got you." Gabe's thumb massaged the head of his cock, cutting in along the stem of the sound, putting a little pressure on it and easing off again.

He sobbed once, sensation flooding him, his teeth clenched as he fought to figure this. *Focus. Focus. Fuck, you asshole. Do this!*

"Relax, boy. I've got you. Just feel." Gabe's tone was confident and reassuring. "Let go. Belong."

Gabe cupped his balls with one burning hand, and the other touched and nudged, the tiniest motions gigantic inside him. He arched, his ass clenching tight enough that he shook. "Bear."

Let go. God. He was going to howl.

"Boy." The word was part growl and part groan, and he knew Bear was right in this moment with him. The rest of Gabe's words were soothing and washed over him like cool air. 'I'm listening. I'm watching. Just say enough if I don't pick it up on my own."

Everything went still for just a moment, letting him get a breath, but it didn't last long. Gabe's fingers slid back behind his balls, tapping his hole, matching the rhythm of the touches to the metal wand filling his cock.

Lights sparked all along his skin, his body pure sensation, and all he could do was feel it, drown in it.

He floated just like that...every little touch to the device, every word Gabe said, the fingers stroking sensitive skin, all together made him lose time, made him have to use Gabe as his compass.

"Fuck, babe." Hot hands landed flat on his chest, and

Gabe's kiss was almost foreign at first, unreal. Then the world snapped into place and he cried out, Gabe's mouth the center of his world. It was an intense connection, as needy and hungry as it was comforting. Their tongues slid together, lips locking and releasing, everything more sensitive than normal. Even Gabe was ramped.

"I think that's enough for now, babe." Gabe's voice was barely a whisper. "You're drenched."

"I'm aching, Bear. I need." He needed to come; he needed Gabe to help him. Hell, he was so far gone, he had to trust Gabe would help him.

"I know, boy. I know. Just another minute." Gabe's hands were on him again, gingerly removing the sound, taking care not to move too quickly. The slow release of pressure was maddening and only made him more desperate. He felt Gabe's fingers just above his balls, playing with the ring, then a sharp tug and all that pressure and restriction was gone in a rush and his cock disappeared down Gabe's throat.

He bellowed, the roar hurting his throat as his balls emptied in a rush. His body burned in the best way, his prick throbbing, and the world just dissolved away.

Gabe gentled him through it with an attentive tongue and knowing fingers, and his bear climbed up beside him and pulled him in, kissed his face, stroked his hair.

He stared, feeling like he was glass, like it would take nothing to shatter him.

Thank God Gabe had him.

"That was...you are the most amazing and beautiful thing I've ever seen, babe. We can talk, you can close your eyes and sleep, you can just breathe with me. I'm here, I'm not going anywhere. Anything you need."

He reached out, grabbed Gabe's hand, and held on tight. "Bear. Love. Damn near broke me."

His bear tightened the arm around his shoulders a little and squeezed his fingers. "Won't break you. Love you."

"Thank God for that." Bowie turned his head and took another kiss, letting Gabe have him, letting Gabe in.

"Mmm." Gabe took everything he offered, but mildly, keeping the kiss easy and the tension down. His lover had to be aching; he could feel the firm bulge against his hip, but Bear didn't seem too concerned about it.

He would help, but he wasn't put back together, not yet. Soon. Not yet.

"That was way more intense than I'd expected. You should rest. We can get our heads around it later, maybe. Hm? Let me hold you and nap a little first."

He nodded, his eyelids getting heavy. He held on to Gabe's hand and as soon as Gabe's free hand slid into his hair, he was asleep.

30

When Gabe blinked his eyes open again, the apartment was dark, he was thirsty as hell, and he had to pee. He'd fallen asleep fast—he didn't know for how long—but he still felt a little wiped out. That kind of concentration and patience took a lot more energy than he'd realized.

But fuck, it was worth it. That kinky little wand, with a bit of his help, had taken Bowie to the moon. He'd never had firsthand experience with anything like that. He'd never had a sub, or a lover, just totally dissolve that way. Amazing. Hot. Bowie had loved it. Fucking loved it.

God, he needed water, but Bowie was everywhere, still holding on to him, and he really didn't want to wake his lover up. He started to free himself, gently slipping his hand from Bowie's, unfolding a leg Bowie had thrown over his, and suddenly Bowie grumbled and rolled over.

That made him grin. He leaned in and kissed a strong bare shoulder before he got out of bed. His cock was still a little happy, which made peeing a chore, but he managed it.

Then he went and got himself a bottle of water and grabbed one for Bowie too, not bothering to turn on lights, the little bit coming in from the street enough to get him to the fridge.

Hm. His stomach growled. They could do delivery tonight.

He buzzed all the way to the bedroom, feeling about ten feet tall, and sipped his water while he watched his lover sleep.

He could do that again, for sure. He couldn't wait to show Bowie the plug he'd bought too. That was going to blow the man's mind.

He finished his water and climbed into bed, spooning right in behind Bowie and tucking an arm up over those amazing abs.

"Mmm. Bear. I slept."

The husky words made him grin.

"Mhm. I wore your butt out." He nuzzled into Bowie's hair and inhaled. "Smell good." His boy was still half-asleep, heavy in the pillows.

"You blew my mind. Never happened to me like that."

"I haven't ever...sent anyone where you went. I've seen it done, but...wow." He rubbed his hand over Bowie's chest in slow circles and dropped a kiss here and there on that broad back.

"I...damn, Bear. I thought the world had stopped. It was..." Bowie shook his head.

The world had stopped. Was that Bowie's version of subspace? "Yeah. It was..." There really weren't words for it. "Intense?"

"Yeah. That's close." Bowie took one of his hands, squeezed it. "Never been touched like that."

He shrugged. "Neither have I, frankly."

Bowie took a deep breath and leaned against him. Hard. "No one but you."

His breath caught for a second at the emotion in his lover's voice, and he hugged Bowie tight to his chest. "It's ours, Bowie. I promise. I've got you."

"I know." And God, didn't those two words just satisfy things inside him. No hesitation, no doubt, just...*I know*.

"Good. Hey." He scooched back a bit and rolled Bowie flat, grinning. "It was good, right? It was fun? You want to do it again?"

"It was good. Fun doesn't begin to cover it. And fuck, yes."

"All right. See? It doesn't have to be so heavy. Just some wicked fun. Yes?" He took a quick kiss. "It was hot as fuck, Bowie. I swear. What a thing to see."

Bowie pinked, but that grin was wide, well-satisfied. "Shit, man. You fucked my cock."

"Right? And I could go like"—he just barely tapped the end of Bowie's nose—"and you would just howl. Jesus. Talk about feeling powerful."

"Shit, Bear. You touch it for a week, and I might hit my knees." No shame. Fuck, he loved that.

He laughed. "Oh, yeah? That'll be something to see too, man. Wait. Check this out." He reached over and pulled the plug he'd bought out of the box that was still open on the bedside table and dangled it over Bowie's head. The plug wasn't terribly long but long enough, it stepped up from fairly narrow to a good width, and had a ring that tucked under the glans. It was hollow, making it part function, part jewelry. "Look."

"What the hell is that?"

Oh, fucking hell, this was fun.

"This is a plug, babe." He demonstrated with his fingers

as he explained. "It goes in and stays in. This ring tucks right under your ridge to keep in place. Get it? And this bead here? This tucks right into your slit so...for you, that means a couple of taps will make your eyes cross." He gave Bowie a wink.

"Oh, you are a wonderful, evil motherfucker." Bowie stared at it like it was some amazing bug. "That...that's just...whoa."

Bowie grabbed Gabe's cock and started rubbing, nice and slow.

"Mmm. Right? You gotta watch me when I get a good idea." He bent a knee to give Bowie more room.

"Uh-huh. Jesus. Love your mind." Bowie knew him, knew exactly how to touch him, how to build his need up nice and steady. He set the plug aside and looked between them, watching for a minute, watching the way Bowie's fingers moved over him. He looked up again, right into pale green eyes, brushed his fingers over Bowie's beard, and leaned in for a kiss.

Bowie gave it, his boy focused on him, one hand cupping the back of his head and keeping him right there.

"Love how you touch me," he whispered against Bowie's lips. "Love how you're...right here. Always right here."

"Always." Bowie held his gaze, that hand moving just a little faster, thumb nudging the tip on every upstroke.

Bowie's obsession with details was a huge asset in bed, that was for sure. His lover knew that spot at the base that made his toes curl and that ridge down the right side that shot electricity into his balls if you pressed on it just so.

He sighed and slumped back in the pillows. "Fuck, yeah."

Bowie grinned at him, eyes crinkling at the corners. So smug.

He knew how that felt, and just the thought made his cock stretch farther and his balls ache. He moaned, already breathing faster. *Jesus.* It was fucking jacking off. How did such a simple fucking thing feel so much better when Bowie did it for him?

Bowie leaned down, bit his earlobe just a bit, fingers playing him like a master, hitting one hot spot after another. "My bear."

"Uh-huh." He reached up and flattened a hand against the headboard, the other tangling into that thick mane as he pressed up into Bowie's fist, wanting more. Bowie squeezed harder, giving him friction, a delicious burn, and that little bite came again, sharper this time.

He liked that. The pinch, the sound of Bowie's breath in his ear. He hissed, hips rolling. "Good. It's...yeah." He didn't give a thought to whether he looked too needy, what that sounded like. This was Bowie.

Bowie twisted the hand around his shaft and he gasped, his shoulders curled up off the bed. "Fuck!" When the hell had his lover figured that out? Jesus, he'd gone from a nice hum to single-minded just like that.

"Later. You can fuck me with the plug in. I'll ride you so you can feel what you do to me all around your prick." Bowie twisted once, twice, his boy's low growl tearing into him.

He shorted out, the image, the words, the look he imagined on Bowie's face doing him right in. He bucked through his lover's fingers until he shot, everything narrowing down to pale green eyes.

Oh, fuck. His Bowie was altogether too fucking good at that, and he was a lucky, lucky son of a bitch.

"Good boy." He croaked, grinning despite the aftershocks Bowie was teasing out of him.

"Mmhmm." Bowie chuckled against his shoulder. "Jesus, I'm starving. You?"

"Chicken parm?"

"*Uhn*. Garlic bread too?"

"Lemme find my phone." *God*. That meant he had to move. "In like a minute."

"Maybe two." Bowie chuckled for him, the sound satisfied as all get out.

"Yeah. Maybe two." Or ten. He tugged Bowie closer. Just a quick catnap.

31

"You are a million miles away, O'Reilly."

Bowie looked over at Zeke and nodded. He was. He was ready to be back at the beach, working on the houses. He didn't want to be here anymore. He had their plane tickets for next week. He was ready. "Sorry, man. I got stuff on my mind."

"Anything I can do? You and Angel need help, I'm here." Zeke set a cup of black coffee down on the toolbox next to him.

"Oh, I'm just ready to get to the beach, you know? We're going to get those two places into the dry, come back right after the big rally. You know how it is. You get a plan and that's where you are."

"Right. I get it. Chomping at the bit. You let me know when you're home, I'll have something for you to do." Zeke pulled a wad of cash out of his pocket and started counting out bills. "Angel at the beach. I gotta say, I don't see it. But then, he's a 'go with the flow' guy, I guess. And any place that welcomes bikers is probably a good place for him."

"Well, we're giving it a shot, right? It's just a month, and he'll be home." He'd bet they'd do the here and there thing for a while, but he was flexible enough.

"That's what it's about. I hope it's great for you guys." Zeke folded the stack and handed it over.

"Thanks, man. Seriously. I'll holler when I'm back in town, and we'll get to work." He grinned at Zeke. "And you know you're welcome down. I have great places for vacation."

Zeke grinned. "Who wouldn't want to get out of the city for warmer climates in November?"

"Sure. There's a great rally first week of November."

"You said. I'm interested, I'll be in touch." Zeke gave him a pat on the shoulder and headed for the office. "Safe travels."

His phone started to ring before he'd even left the building. He didn't recognize the number, but it was local, so he picked it up.

"Hello?"

"Hello. Is this Jim O'Reilly?"

He frowned. No one called him that. No one. "It is. Who the hell is this?"

"Mr. O'Reilly, this is Chief Derringer with the NYFD EMS. Gabriel Rogers has you down as his emergency contact. Have I got the right person?"

"Yes." He began to look for a taxi. "Where is he?"

"He's been taken to Mount Sinai. He and his team were in an accident. I don't have much information yet, except that he was conscious enough to ask me to call you. I'm headed there now myself."

"All right. I'll be there." He grabbed a cab, texted Sam, and waited for the cabbie to get him where he needed to go. There was a white noise that covered everything, a deep silence that allowed him to do all he needed to without complications.

The ER was a busy place, and he paused just inside the doors to get a look around. Lots of people coming and going, a half-full waiting area to his left, and a line a couple-three people deep at the triage desk to his right. But off to one side behind the desk were a few EMTs and a handful of uniformed firefighters talking, so he wasn't going to waste his time at the desk—he knew how to find Gabe.

He marched over and held his hand out like he was meant to be there. "Bowie O'Reilly. Chief Derringer contacted me. I'm here for Rogers."

The whole group went silent, watching him, and watching their lieutenant step toward him. "Mr. O'Reilly, good to meet you. I'm Lieutenant Jacques. Joe. Come on back."

Joe led him right through the crowd, and nobody got in their way. "Chief Derringer is with one of Gabe's teammates."

"Excellent. I'm glad he made it down here so quickly." *Where is my bear?*

"Right in here." Joe pulled open a curtain, and everything went into slow motion for a second as he took in the monitors and the nurse by the bed taking vitals, and Gabe in a hospital gown, staring at the ceiling, jaw twitching.

"Joe, you better tell your man here that I can't get decent vitals if he doesn't breathe."

"Can I get up now, please?"

"Gabe." He met Gabe's gaze, and his bear was in there— pissed and grumpy, but in there. That worked. That was the important part. The slightly glassy eyes would be temporary.

The look he got was complicated, but he read it all—relieved to see him, frustrated, really worried. "Hey, man."

The nurse glanced over at him. "Never mind, Joe, BP's better."

"Good. Gabe, I've got to watch the front. Send someone out if you need me."

"Wait. Joe. How's Casey?"

Joe did an excellent job of keeping cool and not really answering that question, but Bowie could feel the tension. "Derringer is with her right now, but I'll get you an update ASAP."

"Is she awake?"

"I don't know. Let's see what Derringer says, okay?"

"Yeah. Thanks."

The nurse waved him in, "Come on in, sir. I'll be done in a second."

"Afternoon."

There were bruises, a few cuts, but Gabe looked basically whole. There was a little plastic chair, and he took it and sat. "Hey. You gonna make it?"

Gabe frowned at him. "Casey's in bad shape."

"Sounds like it, yeah. What happened?" What? He was supposed to bullshit Gabe? The man was a fucking EMT.

"I'm not entirely sure. Head's still fuzzy. We were out on a call, we'd just picked up a guy, we headed into an intersection. Skip was driving, I was in the passenger seat, Casey was in the back. Something big hit us. An SUV or something, on the side. Then it's kind of a blank until Joe showed with another team and I kind of woke up doing CPR on Casey…"

Gabe looked at him a little horrified and just stopped talking.

He nodded. He got that. Bodies and brains weren't always in sync. You did shit you didn't know.

"They took Skip to surgery; they're putting pins in his leg or something. His hip? Something. They told me but I don't remember." Gabe tried to sit up and the nurse pushed him down. Impressive since she was about half his size. Gabe growled at her.

"Don't make me strap you in there."

"Goddammit, I'm fine." He looked at Bowie. "I need to see Casey."

"You know as well as I do, that's not how this works. If they restrain you, it gets worse." He met the nurse's eyes, offered her a partial smile. "Can you find anything out for him, ma'am? Please? He's a big boy. He can deal."

"You know I'm a New Yorker and I'm not supposed to fall for your Texas charm, right? But I will see what I can find out since you asked so nicely." She winked at him before she left the room, so obviously falling for his "Texas charm."

Gabe sighed and dropped his head down. "She wasn't belted in, she got tossed around in the rear of the bus."

"That sucks. I hope they get the bastard that hit you and boil him in oil." He wasn't required by law to be a nice man.

"She came in with us." Gabe looked at him. "She looked pretty bad too."

He didn't suppose saying "Good" would work. Honestly, he just didn't give a fuck about the asshole that hit the bus. He cared about Gabe. "Are you hurt anywhere?"

Gabe sighed. "Bruises. Two fractured ribs. Mild concussion making me feel stupid. The headache sucks. I'm not complaining."

"Ribs suck. That'll take some healing. The headache will be gone in the morning."

"You know what's funny? I can tell you how to treat

many different kinds of rib injuries. I know how to get someone transported so broken ribs don't do damage. I know pain levels and warning signs and all kinds of shit, but I never see anyone long enough to have any idea how long people take to get better." Gabe started to laugh, his wince making it look like it was a bad idea.

"Six to eight weeks. Compression breaks are worse." Bowie smiled over. This shit he knew. "Just relax and we'll keep them taped up."

"Six to eight nothing. I don't have time for that nonsense. I'm sure you know how to get me on my feet faster."

The nurse came back, bad news all over her face. She and Gabe had a quick conversation about Casey, the upshot of which was that she was beat-up bad, the docs weren't happy with the brain scan, and otherwise they didn't know much yet. Casey hadn't regained consciousness, and no, nobody could see her.

She also brought paperwork and told Bowie to take Gabe home.

He helped Gabe sit up, his lover looking pale. "Are the guys out there?"

"Yes. They were. Here. I'll help on the parts where you'd have to bend over. That bit sucks." He got Gabe's pants over his ankles, then the boots on.

Gabe didn't argue with him, letting him help and keeping steady with a hand on his shoulder. "Shit. Okay. I mean good that they're here for Casey and her family, but..." Gabe straightened up and hid the wince. "Okay. Get me out of here."

"Let's go. We'll get us a car and get home. Then you can lay on the sofa like a lump."

He headed out and let Gabe follow, making a path and

running some interference. Gabe shook hands with a lot of the guys, and Derringer said to expect a call.

"I'll get a nap and come back and join you guys later."

Derringer raised an eyebrow. "No, you won't. I will call you when I get word she is awake, all right? You get some rest."

Gabe sighed but didn't argue. "Call me."

"Take him home, Mister O'Reilly."

"On it." It was never going to be right, not being Sergeant O'Reilly. Weird.

He got them outside and finagled them a car, answering a series of fifty-seven some-odd texts from Sammy and Tommy both.

"The boys are worried about you. I told them you were mostly fine."

Gabe slumped against him in the car. "Mostly fine. Man, I kind of hurt, though. Did she leave me some meds? A scrip? Shit, I didn't even think to look."

"I have them. I'll get you settled and deal with it." He had enough pain pills to last his whole life. He could give Gabe one to get him through the next few hours.

Gabe took his hand, holding on. "That was scary, babe. Nothing fucking scares me, but that was scary."

He held on tight, because he got it, all the way to the bone. "I hear you. You didn't even get warning."

Gabe sighed. "Fuck, no. One minute Skip and I are talking about getting a burger for lunch and the next, he's bleeding and Casey...wasn't breathing."

"They do amazing shit. Amazing." At least he hoped for her people's sake that she was going to be okay rather than just...a vegetable. Brain injuries sucked.

"You walked in at just the right time. I'd've gotten myself strapped down I think. I don't know. It wouldn't have been pretty." Gabe kissed his fingers. "Thank you for coming."

"Anytime. I was there as soon as they called." He wanted to undress Gabe, right here, make sure Gabe was whole. A cab wasn't the place, though. Not at all.

The ancient, tight elevator wasn't any better, but at least they were close, at least he had an excuse to hold on. Gabe was shaking a little by the time they got into the apartment. "Should I...sit? I'm thirsty."

"Why don't you go lay on the bed. I'll get you a glass of water and get you all set up." He muscled Gabe into the bedroom so he could sit.

Gabe didn't pitch a bitch, letting him help with getting settled. Gabe's eyes were on him, watching him, paying attention. "You'll be right back. Yeah?"

"Let me bring you water. That's the first bit, then we can make a plan for your meds and food and all." The apartment wasn't all that big. Where would he go?

Gabe nodded. "Yeah, okay. Thanks. I'm not hungry, though." Gabe settled down, groaning a little before he relaxed.

"No. Maybe some toast after a bit, but water first. Then a Coke. It'll make shit easier." He leaned forward and kissed Gabe. "You're home."

Gabe nodded. "I am. I wish my team was. But I am, and I'll help them get home too."

"Right now, they're in good hands. So are you." That was the best any of them could do.

"I know. I know, thank you." Gabe sighed. "Sorry for this, I don't mean to be a big baby. I'll be better tomorrow."

"You were in an accident. You're allowed to relax in bed, man. I know how weird it feels, to be down. It's so fucking helpless."

Gabe gave him a nod and relaxed even more. "Right. Yeah. Of course you do. It is weird. I fix other people."

"You do. You're good at it." He grabbed water and brought it over. "Drink, Bear, and I'll grab you something fizzy next."

Gabe drank half the bottle in one gulp, took a careful breath, and finished it off. "That felt good."

Bowie nodded, pleased. "Good deal. You look better already."

A banging came to the front door. They both frowned for a second, then they both rolled their eyes.

"Sammy."

"I probably should have known a text wasn't going to cut it." Gabe started to get up and winced. "Dammit."

"Sit. Stay. I mean it." He gave Gabe his best bark before he headed to the door, finding Sammy and Tommy with food and soda.

"Hello, Bowie. Sam pointed out that you were always hungry." Tommy shook his hand.

Sammy shoved the food at Bowie and ducked around him. "Where is he? Bedroom?"

"He is. Be gentle. Broken ribs." Now he could run out and get Gabe's meds. Excellent. "Beer's in the fridge, buddy."

"Thanks, I'm good. Some Valium for Sam might be in order, though." Tommy winked at him. "How is he?"

"Sore. Wigged. He came out best of all of them on the bus. One gal is bad hurt."

Tommy gave his shoulder a squeeze. "Are you okay?"

"I'm good. Glad he's okay. While y'all are here, I'll run and grab his pills."

"Sure, we'll stay with him, not a problem." Tommy put the drinks on the kitchen counter. "We brought Chinese—soups, rice, chicken, vegetables, things that go down easy.

Are you hungry? Or do you want to wait until you get back?"

"Let me go first, if you don't mind." He popped his head in the bedroom door. "I'm going to go get your pills. Sammy, stay with him."

His brother was snuggled up close and didn't look like he was intending to move.

Sammy nodded. "On it."

"Thanks, babe." Gabe grinned at him. "I think I've got company for a while."

"I think you might. Take care of him. I'll be right back." He nodded to Tommy. "I won't be long, friend."

"We're here." Tommy gave him a meaningful look. "Unless you want company."

He gave that a second's thought. "Sure. I'd love some. Thanks."

He wasn't sure he needed company, but he liked Tommy and didn't want to listen to himself think.

Tommy gave him a nod, ducked into the bedroom to let Sam know, and followed him out the door. "Is Gabe a good patient? He doesn't strike me as the 'lie down and relax' type."

"He's going to be rough. He'll be at the hospital in the morning." He knew it.

"It's difficult, not knowing if someone you love is all right, and when you finally do see them, knowing that they're hurt. Even a couple of broken ribs." They made their way out onto the sidewalk and he headed for the pharmacy up the block. "You feel a little helpless. Sometimes completely helpless."

He grunted. Completely helpless wasn't really his thing, but Gabe had a couple busted ribs. Sammy'd been unconscious for days.

"I'm not suggesting this is quite comparable, just that I know how you must feel. Worrying."

He nodded to Tommy. "I haven't gotten there yet."

He reckoned Tommy understood that. Tommy had been there in Germany with him, and he got how slow Bowie could move in his heart.

"I hear you." Tommy rested a hand on his spine for just a second as they arrived. "I'll wait out here for you while you get that filled."

"I'll be two shakes." Two shakes, twenty minutes—whathaveyou. By the time the scripts were filled, he was growling, ready to get back to his bear.

"You look like you need food and a beer." Tommy fell in step with him. "I texted Sam and didn't get an answer, so I'm wondering if the pups fell asleep."

"They might have." Pups. His Gabe. That was cute. "He'll need his meds, one way or the other, in an hour or so."

They rode up in the elevator together, Tommy taking up much less room than his bear did.

They didn't have a lot of chatting; they just went in and checked on the guys—Sammy was sound asleep with Gabe, both of them snoring softly. Good lord and butter.

He chuckled and shook his head, then drew Tommy into the kitchen to grab a beer.

"You know, I'm happy to listen if you ever want to vent, but I'm not planning on snuggling with you. I just thought I'd make that clear." Tommy grinned at him.

"I'm not a snuggler, friend." He handed a beer over and gave Tommy a grin.

And if Gabe was with him, well, that was between him, his bear, and the bedpost. Just as it was meant to be.

32

G abe got home about four to find suitcases in the living room. They had plane tickets bright and early tomorrow morning for Texas and a little over a month at the beach. He'd had to take the month off as vacation time, but now he was on medical leave, so they weren't dinging his vacation after all. Not for a couple of weeks yet.

"Hey," he called and headed for the fridge and a beer. It had been a long afternoon at the hospital with Casey, but a good one. The best one since the accident.

"Hey, you. How goes?" Bowie was in the kitchen, head in the fridge, so his voice echoed.

"Casey woke up. Grab me a beer?"

"Yeah? Excellent. How's she doing?" Bowie wandered out, two beers in hand. He leaned in and took a quick kiss, then pushed the bottle in his hand.

He hooked a hand around Bowie's neck and pulled him back for another kiss, taking a long taste before letting him go again. "We don't know yet. But she moved her fingers. She obviously had a lot of questions she wasn't really able to ask yet. She recognized me, I could see that in her eyes."

"Good deal. I know you've been willing her to wake up. Poor baby." Bowie shook his head, sighed. "I've cleaned out the fridge for us, so we don't come home to nasty surprises. I hate that."

"Babe." He took a breath. Bowie would get it, wouldn't he? "I think now that she's awake that I should be here for a few more days...a week at the most. I'm her team leader, you know? She should know I'm here for her."

Bowie's head tilted once, but that was the entirety of the response he got. "Oh. Well, the tickets weren't refundable. Let me cancel yours and see if I can't get a voucher for later."

Then Bowie was up, earpiece in, dialing the phone. The suitcases were taken back into the bedroom, two at a time.

He watched that, watched Bowie on the phone, not sure what to make of it all. They didn't even have time to talk about it before Bowie was rearranging plans. He hung out in the bedroom doorway while Bowie finished the call, trying to figure out what his lover was feeling. Obviously Bowie had figured him out in half a second as usual; he just wasn't that quick. Especially not with someone as complicated as his lover.

Bowie rearranged clothes quickly, emptying two and putting one in the closet, still packed. It was efficient and sure. It never ceased to amaze him, how fast the big man was. "The one in the closet is stuff for the rally and all. What you want for supper?"

What the hell was that? He stared at his lover, clenched his teeth together to keep his jaw from dropping. "Are you okay?"

"Yeah. I had upgraded us because I know those ribs hurt, so I wanted to make sure we didn't lose all the money from it. You just tell me when you can come, and I'll make it happen."

Damn, Bowie was so thoughtful. And good with details. Okay, he needed to get them grounded here. He moved into his lover's space and cupped a fuzzy cheek. "I'm not doing this lightly, Bowie. You know that, don't you? I have been looking forward to the beach. To our house, our work."

"I know. This is important. The houses will be there. No worries." Bowie kissed him. "I'm sorry she's hurt, but she's awake now, and you'll be here to help."

"Well, that's just it. Now that she is awake, I feel like I should be here for her for a bit. Let her know I've got her back." Things changed. When she was still out, there wasn't much he could do.

"I hear you. You'll have to go grocery shopping, but there's beer and shit in the freezer."

"Are you saying I can't live on beer?" He grinned and kissed Bowie too. "Thank you for getting it. I know you must be disappointed."

"I'm a big boy." Bowie chuckled softly. "I'll head down and get to work, and you'll be there when you can. Are you heading back out tonight or are you home? That'll pick whether we go out or order in."

He grinned, giving Bowie's hair a little tug. "Oh, I'm home. I intend to send you off tired, so you sleep well on the plane."

Bowie snorted and kissed him hard. "So you say. First you're going to have to feed me. I'm hungry. You want pizza?"

"Sure. Loaded. Are we ordering in or going out?"

"I'll order in, spend our night together."

"Good. I'd like that. And that means you can wear your plug for me while we wait for delivery." He pressed a hand into Bowie's crotch. If he was going to have to sleep alone tomorrow night, he was going to enjoy the hell out of having his lover tonight.

33

Bowie grabbed the bag out of his truck, along with his drink. Everything was reminding him that he wasn't twenty anymore—from the cut on his cheek to the gash on his knee to each screaming muscle. Lord have mercy.

He made his way up the stairs and headed straight to the deck to eat and rest his bones.

He checked his texts—couple from Sammy, one from his momma, one from Rick. One from Gabe saying hi.

He judged the importance of them and answered Rick. *What you need?*

Got a vet new in town. Young. Needs work. You want help?

Sure. Send him 2morrow

Bowie could use another set of hands. It was supposed to start raining by the weekend, and he needed to get two roofs on.

Will do. Name's Colton Underhill. From here.

Good deal. He leaned back and inhaled his burger, then texted Gabe. *Good day?*

Yeah they put me on dispatch today. Light duty. You?

He read the text, that dull little emptiness inside him

just sucking it up. It had been weeks since he left New York. Gabe wasn't coming down. *Not much. Toodled around...*

He hadn't toodled. He'd been busy as hell.

He'd carried shingles. Climbed the ladder eighty times. Fell off the roof. Normal shit. It didn't matter.

I'd really like not to feel so useless. You were right about the ribs. Hurts to f-ing put on socks still

The temptation to answer that if Gabe was here, he could wear flip-flops was huge, but who wanted to text that much? *Sucks. :(Keep em wrapped up*

He checked Momma's text—yes, he wanted granddaddy's bedroom suite, he'd come get it in a few days —and Sammy's, which were just bullshit emojis saying hi.

Will do He got back after a short pause, and a second later, *Are you having good weather? Are you working? I got the paperwork you sent today.*

fixin to rain soon. Trying to get the roof on the houses. He hated this stilted shit. It was like talking to someone on deployment. It was easier to just remember when it felt good.

They're still short-handed, lots of juggling in the dept. they want me in early. I should go to bed. I miss you

Sleep good. Miss u. Night. He turned off his phone and stared up at the sky. Maybe he'd sleep here tonight. He wasn't up to moving, and nobody'd bother him but the mosquitos.

It wasn't shower, food, and an orgasm, but it would do for an old soldier.

———

IF IT WEREN'T FOR CASEY, THERE'D HAVE BEEN NO WAY GABE would have allowed them to put him behind a desk. He'd have been long gone, living in Texas with Bowie, toes in the sand.

But his team was still broken. Skip's rehab was going great, and the man had lots of support. Casey had her husband, but they also had two young kids, and the guy was stretched thin.

So he spent every weekday morning at the hospital, working with her. Flash cards, conversation, listening to her worry about what was next since her legs weren't going to work ever again. He spotted her in her upper body rehab and played memory games; he'd tickle her toes when she'd stubbornly insist she felt something, but she never really did.

Fabian would show up with the kids after school, and he'd go to work for six hours. He'd text Bowie on his way to work, knowing Bowie wouldn't respond, then again after work.

This was his new normal. Casey was getting sharper, and Bowie was getting blurry.

Just got home

Bowie never texted him first, never checked in during the day, never asked him any questions except to ask about his day. So he already knew what Bowie's response would be; he just waited for it.

Good day?

He wondered what Bowie would say if he said no.

Yeah. Got out of a chair without groaning today.

Small victories. He'd like to celebrate them anyway, but nobody liked a party for one.

Claps. Excellent. Then, *Ru heading 2 bed?*

Not yet. Off tomorrow

Gabe stared at his phone.

Tell me you want to have an actual phone call, Gabe

thought, willing his phone to ring. *Tell me you want to hear my voice. Tell me you need me down there...remind me I'm important.*

Hell, if all of that was asking too much, he'd take anything more meaningful than a weather report.

His phone rang, Bowie's name coming up.

Yes. Thank you. He took a deep breath and answered. "Hey, you."

"Hey, stranger. How goes?" Bowie sounded just like always—growly and inscrutable. Even harder to read than in person. Still hot, though.

"Long week but not a bad one. You?"

"Been doing my thing. Me and Colton got the roofs on in time for the rain. How's Casey?"

Colton. Right, the young guy. Probably a lot more help than he could be right now. "She's coming back. Still has a slur, but the words are coming easier. She gave the wheelchair a shot yesterday."

"Good for her. I know it's a long row to hoe. She's lucky to have y'all."

"She's family. We've been partners for six years." It wasn't luck, Bowie knew that. "They're talking about sending her home."

"Yeah? What does that mean for you? Sammy says they've invited you to do Halloween with them?"

Gabe heard a can open, heard Bowie grunt softly.

"I've been seeing them a bunch on the weekends. Sammy wants me to do the masquerade thing at the club with them." *What do you want it to mean for me?*

"Yeah, he's excited about dressing up."

He laughed. "Excited is putting it mildly. Did he tell you Tommy threatened to paint me green?"

"Green? What the fuck for?"

"He thinks I should go as The Hulk."

Bowie laughed for him, the sound making him smile. "Well, take pictures. That would be a sight to see."

"What? I'm not going as The Hulk. No way. I'm thinking werewolf." Scruff out his beard, get some fake teeth, spike his hair. Totally a werewolf.

"I can see that. Totally. It'll be a full moon too."

"What are you and Colton doing? Any good parties down there?"

"Me and..." There was the barest hiccup; then Bowie chuckled. "I just have some candy for the trick or treaters, going to watch the houses and make sure no one eggs them. I want pictures of your costume."

"If I go, I'll send some. I might just go to Mike's. It's a madhouse on Halloween." He could get some bruises to make him feel something different. Something other than achy ribs and the sick dread in the pit of his stomach.

The conversation went on, neither of them saying anything. Finally Bowie just sighed. "Love you, Bear. Have a good day off. Talk at you later, huh?"

"I love you too." He didn't mean for that to come out as bewildered sounding as it had, but then again, he was confused, so maybe it was right.

"It will be all right. Get some sleep. Night, Bear. Good dreams." Bowie hung up, the sound somehow gentle.

It will be all right? Maybe Bowie knew something he didn't know.

34

"Sarge! Jesus fucking Christ! Look at you, man." Colton stared at him, eyes wide. "You look fucking great."

"Shut up, kid." Bowie rubbed his hand over his head, the stubble weird and familiar all at once. The kid had been right. He'd looked at himself last night, and he did look like a homeless asshole. Now he looked like what he was—a retired vet with more years on him than he'd like.

"No, seriously. You look like a stud—not an ounce of fat, muscles from here to there. It's hot."

"How's the tile looking?" He didn't give a shit whether Colton thought he looked good. He cared that Gabe didn't mind that Colton thought he did. He cared that Gabe wanted to stay in New York enough that he wouldn't even talk about coming down for a weekend. He cared that Gabe's fucking work partner was family, and his parents weren't worth a handshake. He cared that he had pushed himself into Sam's life, and thereby Gabe's life, and he hadn't been supposed to be there. Maybe he'd been the summer's Casey, the hard-case.

Maybe he had been, but he wasn't now. He was

struggling because it wasn't easy to make himself move, to climb and do, but he'd thrown the crutch away. He'd said he would, so he did.

His phone rang, Sammy's number popping up. "Hey."

"Hey. What's up?"

"Working. What do you need?"

"Well, I had lunch with Angel. So, I figured I should check in and see how you are." That was the tone of someone not minding his own business.

"Been working. I'm laying tile today. Went up and got Granddaddy's bedroom furniture couple days ago."

"How are the houses looking? You hired help?"

"Yeah. Kid that just got out. Good guy. I can't do it on my own anymore." Sammy knew that. "How's Gabe? Taking care of those ribs?"

"His ribs are fine. He's been offered a promotion, did he tell you? He's thinking about taking it."

God, he was tired. All the way down to his bones.

"Oh. No. Tell him congratulations. That's great." He thought, as soon as the houses were done, it was time to go take a trip. Colorado for the winter, maybe. Or Montana. Somewhere off the grid.

"That's what you want me to tell him, huh? Congratulations? Okay. I'll do that. You want to tell me about this kid?"

"Uh. He's a baby. Got shot in his first round. Came home. Uh. Really, that's all I got. Dad's a general contractor outside of San Antone. Follows orders well enough, I guess. I pay him for twenty hours a week right now." Who gave a fuck about Colton? He was a decent kid with a good work ethic that knew which end of a screwdriver was which.

"Are you and Angel broken up?"

"He hasn't said so yet." But Bowie thought he would.

"But I know he doesn't care to be here. I sank a lot of money into these houses, so..."

"He told me he invested half in those houses too. He told you that? He doesn't want to be down there? Did you ask him?"

"I wouldn't screw him. Not out of a dime." He waved at Colton and headed outside into the rain. "Look, Sammy. I had a first-class ticket for him. I told him, anytime he wanted, I would bring him. I waited. All of October. Halloween. The Rally. Now Thanksgiving is coming in a couple three weeks. He's got a life—a family—up there. Y'all. His work people." And old vets were a dime a dozen. "One day he'll be ready to come visit his investment. It'll look great. It'll make him money."

Have a booty call, if he was in town.

"Jesus, Bowie."

"Yeah."

"Sometimes you just have to force the issue, you know? Thomas..."

Bowie chuckled softly. "Love you, Sammy. I have to go. I'll call." He hung up his phone and stood for a second. A promotion. Good for Gabe.

"You okay, Sarge?" Colton opened the door, peered out. "You totally don't look okay. You want to go get fucked up? I'll buy."

"No, kid." No, he didn't want to get drunk. He wanted to... "I-I want to go get a tattoo. You said you knew people?"

Colton's eyes lit up. "Fuck, yeah. I'll make some calls. I got a good friend, he did my chest piece. You're a virgin, right? This is going to rock so hard!"

"I am. Only thing left I haven't done, kiddo. I'll lock up."

———

"Hello, Gabriel."

"Thomas." He finished off his beer and waved at Darla for another. "Happy Saturday."

"You look like you've been sitting here a while."

What the hell did sitting here a while look like? "Couple hours. You and Sammy headed downstairs?"

"Yes, Sam was detained by someone when we walked in the door, as usual."

"Drink?"

Tommy shook his head. "No. Sam's still a little floaty, I'll have a Perrier. Sam says you've been offered a promotion?"

"Yeah." Offered. And when he hesitated, they made the offer better. When he said he needed a few days to think about it, they added more vacation. They wanted him. "They're not going to put me back on a bus. They've got enough younger guys now."

"What happened to Texas?" Tommy sipped his fizzy water.

"Nothing, right? Nothing at all."

"Coward." Sammy's voice shocked him. "At least you can tell him good-bye, tell him you never intended to go down to see him."

Coward? He spun around on his stool and stared at Sammy. "What the fuck are you talking about? What do you know about my intentions?"

"I know he has a ticket for you. I know he's fucking killing himself. I know that he loves you, and I know you're sitting here with all this vacation time and you are making him believe he's not worth your attention." Sammy stepped close, dropped his voice. "That's mean, Angel. Especially with people like us. To make him feel like he's not worth your attention."

He let everything Sammy spat at him sink in and settle next to actual reality.

"Sam." Tommy put a hand on Sammy's arm.

"I got this, Tommy." He looked at Sammy long and hard, so ready to defend himself. But he realized who he was talking to. This was Bowie's brother. In the end he just smiled at Sammy. "You know a lot, huh? It is mean. Not feeling wanted sucks. Not feeling like you matter sucks." He tossed a tip for Darla on the bar. "You guys have a good night."

"Wait. Wait, Angel. Look at this. Please." Sammy held up his phone, and there was a picture of some half-naked old man on a roof. Some frowning dude with a crewcut and a scarred-up face, lean and broad-shouldered, with a huge bear tattoo covering one side of his chest. "My folks took it in Galveston. They were bringing more furniture."

"Your folks." He took the phone from Sammy and leaned against the bar, studying the picture and trying to remember how to breathe. He handed it back to Sammy when his eyes got too cloudy to see it anyway. "Are you blaming me?"

"No." The words were immediate, sure. "I'm begging you. He needs you. I know that y'all...he would never say, and neither will you, but you're his Dom. I'm not stupid. I see things. He's down there believing that he wasn't worth flying out to see, even for a weekend. If he's not worth it, please just...I don't know. How can he not be worth it? Did you ask him to come home and he said no?"

Breathe. He didn't want to tear into Sammy for loving a brother. But he wasn't going to be made into an ogre either.

"I didn't. But I made every overture. I texted first, I asked questions, I waited for him to tell me even once that he needed me there. Instead, he hired someone. The more time went by, the less he was willing to talk about anything more important than the weather. I did intend to go. I haven't taken that promotion because I was still trying to figure out if he even wanted me. I won't be called a coward, Sammy, when your brother doesn't even question my being here still. He let go."

"He let go." Sammy shook his head, put his phone away. "You don't understand him at all, do you? I'm sorry I said anything. Okay. Cool. Mister, I have a headache. I want to go home. Now."

"Is it too much to ask for even one of you to try to understand *me*? You're a fantastic brother, Sammy. You're a lousy fucking friend." He pushed off the bar and turned his back as he headed out. "Hope your head feels better soon."

Sam grabbed his arm, green eyes flashing with fury. "Fuck you, asshole. I am a glorious motherfucking friend. I love you both enough to tell you the truth. I love y'all enough to say when you're both dumb as fuck. You want to be all noble and shit, and he's just lost. You think he's all that. You think he's this brilliant bastard and he's lost! He had the Army, and he had you. Now he's just...shit, I'm a good man. A good motherfucking friend. A good brother. I had to fucking mourn one all on my own when I got here. Sue me for not wanting to mourn a second."

Jesus, Sam could scream.

He turned his head but didn't quite look over his shoulder. Sam didn't need to see the hurt in his eyes to know it was there. "Fine. I'll book a flight. Don't you fucking tell him I'm coming." He didn't know if he'd stay. He didn't know what was next. But he knew if nothing else, Sammy deserved that much.

35

B owie sat on the edge of the bed, looked at the new shower in the bathroom, and felt a little like dying. He sent a picture to Gabe, because he'd paid for it. It looked good. He'd done it by himself. It had taken all week.

His text just said, *All finished.*

Colton had gone to San Antone to be with his dad over the holidays, so he was working on his own, and he was... making shit right.

He wasn't even sure how he'd fucked up so bad.

He heard a pounding downstairs, three raps. Then a pause, and three more. Someone was knocking. *Damn.* He still needed to fix the doorbell.

"Hold your horses! I'm coming." Was that a song? He chuckled at himself. He was a dork and a half.

Whoever it was must have heard him, because the knocking stopped, and he made his way to the front door without feeling like he had to rush. As he opened it, he thought to apologize for the doorbell, but the man standing there already knew damn well it didn't work.

Gabe was carrying a backpack over one shoulder and

looked about the same, except a little thinner and with tired, dark circles under dark eyes.

"Hey. The new shower looks fantastic."

"Bear."

Sweet Jesus. He reached out for his lover, needing to touch more than he needed to breathe. He wasn't sure why Gabe was here, but that didn't matter. His bear was here.

Gabe pulled him in close, same strong arms he knew going around him and holding him tight.

"Oh, God. I missed you." He leaned in, inhaling deep. He'd forgotten the smell of his lover, how it soothed him deep inside.

Gabe didn't show signs of letting him go anytime soon. "I missed you too. I missed you so much. I hate that city without you in it."

He took a kiss, not demanding or anything, just saying hello and I love you and I was starting to lose hope and Christ I need you so much.

Gabe answered him with all that and a little more, herding him into the house and kicking the front door closed behind them. Bear's hands moved to his face and dark eyes stared at him, going deep. "I'm here. There's more to say but right now I just...I'm here."

"Thank you." He held on and let Gabe look. It was like being able to breathe again, like knowing the sun was coming out. "I need you."

"Oh." Bear's forehead pinched and his lover looked away, like there was something in those eyes Bear didn't want him to see.

Oh. Right. Okay. He straightened up, standing on his own two legs. He wasn't a mooch. He had this. "You want a beer or a Coke or something?"

He couldn't offer Gabe food, because he hadn't been cooking all that much.

"No. Nonono don't do that." Gabe swiped at his eyes with the heels of his hands and looked at him again. "I'm sorry. Come back, I'm sorry."

"I don't want to fuck up again." He was so tired—not just in his heart, but in his body, in his soul. He was worn out.

"Me neither. And you didn't, at all. That was just exactly what I needed to hear. I really...I can't explain how much." Gabe curled fingers around his neck and pulled him into another kiss.

Bowie didn't fight it—not because he was tired, but because he didn't want to. He opened up, the way Gabe tasted him, explored him easing a thousand little aches.

Bear dumped the backpack on the floor and stepped into him, guiding him gently backward into the foyer wall. One hand splayed out on his chest right on top of his ink. "This."

"My bear. My heart." It was his way of keeping the faith.

"I love you. I didn't keep my promise. It was too hard that far away."

"It was hard. It was a long way to hurt." He held on like Gabe was his buoy. "It was...I need you, Gabriel. You."

He shut himself up with a kiss, losing himself in it.

Gabe's hands started moving, roaming over his skin, finding and remembering ridges and scars, and places that made him ache. "Yeah. I need this. Close. I'm no good at that...distance. We're no good like that."

"Uh-huh." He worked Gabe's buttons open, shivering as his bear found a new scar on his arm, the new skin whole, but so sensitive. "From the fall."

Gabe stopped him, grabbing at his fingers. "Fall?"

"Uh-huh. I fell off the roof at the big house. Banged myself up."

"And you didn't tell me? Nobody told me."

"You were busy, worried. I didn't tell anybody. I'm a tough old bird. I just came home and slept on the deck for a few hours."

Bear clucked at him. "We could both use a little less tough old bird. Next time...never mind. Next time I'll be here." Gabe let his fingers go and went back to exploring that new scar.

"Next time we let the fearless twenty-two-year-old baby do it while we do something more fun." He'd learned his lesson. "Together."

His eyelids were getting heavy, the sensations buzzing through him in steady, wonderful waves.

"It's a plan." Gabe let him slip the shirt off over broad shoulders while Bear's fingers found the button of his cutoffs and popped it open.

He couldn't stop smiling. He was fucking high, soaring, and every inch of his bear that he touched made it better.

Gabe shoved his pants over his hips, and they slid right to the floor. Then he pushed a hand under his balls and bent to pinch a nipple between dangerously careful teeth.

His moan slipped out, that little bite offering him a thousand perfect promises. He wanted—everything. He wanted to suck. He wanted Gabe to fuck him through the mattress. He wanted to wear every one of Gabe's marks.

Gabe's answering growl made him shiver. "Upstairs."

"Our bed." He was all in. He'd gotten that mattress Gabe loved. Good sheets. Bowie grabbed Gabe's hand and led him upstairs. It was raining, chilly, and gloomy, but Bowie couldn't think of a better time to make love.

Gabe didn't so much follow as lead from behind,

bumping up against him, touching and kissing bare skin, warm breath on his shoulders. They stumbled into the bedroom, where Gabe kicked out of worn sneakers and shoved ancient denim jeans off like they were offensive.

He reached out, running his hands down Gabe's hip, lips parting at the heat of Gabe's cock along his wrist.

Gabe followed suit, fingers gliding over his abs, down his flank, and wrapping gently around his shaft. He held his breath, anticipating, and he wasn't disappointed. Bear's thick thumb rolled around the head of his cock and without hesitation, slipped into his damp slit.

He grunted, his thighs beginning to shake at the glorious sensation—part burn, part ache, completely entwined with Gabe.

Bear gathered their cocks together in one big hand and squeezed, gliding that thumb over them both. "I need you, babe."

"Yes." What other answer was there? "Please, Bear."

Gabe smiled at him and nodded, led him over to their bed and coaxed him back on it. Moving him slowly just by crawling over him and shifting a knee this way or that. Gabe's eyes were fixed on his, even as they ground their hips together, even as they shared a moan.

All the words in the world didn't mean anything, so Bowie let his hands talk, and let himself feel. Surely his Gabe saw.

"Mmm." Gabe ducked suddenly, teeth clamping down on his chest above his nipple, sucking up a mark right through his ink.

He cried out, his hand sliding into Gabe's hair and holding his bear right there. *Yes. God, yes.*

Gabe grunted finally, easing up on the bite, backing off

on the pressure, and eventually sliding free of his hand. "Mine."

The throb in his chest matched the one in his prick. "Yours, Bear."

There was no one else. No one that could come close.

That seemed to satisfy his bear, his Dom, and his lover all at once, and Gabe kissed him, a deep, claiming kiss he had no hope of fighting if he'd wanted to. When neither of them had breath left, Gabe reached over him and gloved up, the bottle of lube landing beside him on the bed.

Bear wasn't subtle, pressing slippery fingers inside him with purpose, twisting them enough to make him squirm. He rode the touch, his lips open, his whole body waiting impatiently to take his lover, to feel Gabe, deep inside.

The switch was quick, fingers gliding away and the head of Gabe's cock pushing in, stretching him. Gabe lifted his knees, baring him more, stealing his leverage. "Fuck, yes. Need you."

"Yes." He let Gabe hold him, trusting that his bear would balance him, give him what he needed. "Please, Bear."

"Right here." Gabe started to move, long, slow strokes that could only be meant to make them both impatient, drive them both mad. There was a grin tugging at the corner of his lover's lips, and Gabe's eyes held a little mischief, a little dare in them.

He reached up and touched the corner of Gabe's lips. Then he squeezed, as tight as he could, ramping them up and offering his bear a challenge.

"Jesus." He watched as Gabe's eyes crossed and his lover made a strangled sound. "Fuck, I missed you." Bear let his legs down and reached for his shoulder, driving inside him, using him for leverage at the same time.

"Yes. Not losing you." Not ever again.

"Never." Gabe took him, over and over, connected, needing. "I'm yours."

Yes. That was it. That was all he needed. They worked together, finding a solid rhythm guaranteed to send them over the edge.

"I've got you." Gabe gripped his shaft, working it through hot fingers, teasing at what they both knew he wanted, but holding it back.

He waited, damn near holding his breath for that touch, that burn.

Gabe shuddered. "Close. Fuck." That thumb dove in, sweeping through his most sensitive spot, plunging, pressing deep several times over.

Bowie shot, eyes wide and unfocused, pleasure flooding him and pouring out of him. He felt Gabe come right behind him, that short but wild moment where his lover disappeared into sensation.

Bear hung over him, kissing his jaw between heavy breaths, and what sounded like short bursts of laughter. When he could focus again, he found Gabe grinning down at him, eyes twinkling.

"Hey stranger," he murmured. "I know you."

Bear nodded. "You do. I won't be one again. I'm so fucking relieved you let me in."

Oh, he would always—always—let his bear in. "It was never a question. It was the best surprise."

"I was hoping, but I really didn't know what *was* a question anymore. We should talk when we're fed and rested, okay? Try to?"

"Yes. We should. Weird as it is. I love you. I need to be with you." Those should be the important parts.

"Me too. It will be a pretty easy talk then, right?" Gabe

shifted and ditched the rubber before stretching out alongside him.

"Yes." He moved to his spot, his head on Gabe's chest.

"Mmm. I do like how we fit." Gabe only hesitated for a second, and the hand that would have tangled in his hair rubbed over his head and settled at the back of his neck instead.

"The boys said I looked homeless," he admitted.

"You...let it go, I guess? Do you like it better this way?"

He knew what his bear liked. "No. It feels like an old costume."

Gabe kissed his head, squeezed him. "It will grow. It's only one beautiful piece of you; there are many more."

Beautiful. Him. *Ha*. Still. "Thanks, Bear. Nap and then I'll feed you."

He felt Gabe relax into the mattress, ready to sleep. "Can I please have bacon?"

"Anything you want, Bear. I promise."

36

Gabe opened his eyes and looked around the bedroom. He was a little confused at first, but he figured out fast enough where he was, even if the bed felt like New York. Bowie must have bought a new mattress like they'd talked about. He may have woken up by himself in bed, but he knew he wasn't alone; he could smell coffee and hear Bowie's music playing in the kitchen.

That by itself would have been enough to set his world right. But he had more.

People talked about being frozen by fear or worry—he'd never felt that until one second before he knocked on the front door. That one second turned into two, then ten, then maybe a full minute before he realized that even with the door closed, even just standing on the front stoop, he already felt like he'd come home. Whatever happened once the door opened, he'd have dealt with. They'd have dealt with it. Fixing things had been the only possible option.

Bowie's greeting was everything he wanted. They didn't need fixing. They just needed each other.

He pulled on the jeans he'd dumped on the floor, took a

second to admire the new shower in person, and made his way downstairs.

Bowie was singing.

Singing.

He peered around the stairs into the kitchen, where bacon and eggs waited to be started. Bowie was at the kitchen table, coffee and a dog-eared copy of *The DaVinci Code* in his hand, just singing with CCR.

He'd smiled more in the last twelve hours than he had in the last twelve weeks. He leaned in the doorway, watching and listening, admiring. "Hey, you."

"Hey. You get some good sleep?" Bowie put his book on the table and stood, the old camo pants barely holding on to those hips.

"The best." Bowie needed some bacon too. Everything would be okay now. He'd been an idiot, Bowie too, but it wouldn't take long to get his lover healthy. He moved in close tugging on Bowie's waistband to make a point. "Skinny."

"Been living on sunshine."

Gabe looked out at the pouring down rain, and Bowie cackled.

"Well, it's November."

"It is, and Thanksgiving is next week, so you can start living on food again." He kissed Bowie, his mood shifting. He didn't fight it—there wasn't a good moment for conversations like this; you just had them. "You didn't think I was coming at all, did you?"

"I thought you'd come, maybe not until the summer when you had time, but I thought you'd come."

When he had time. He sighed, looking Bowie over. "I thought about you every day. All the time. I had a reason to stay behind for a little while but...we need to find a way to talk to each other. We can't always hold out hope the other one gets it, right? That's what got us here."

"I didn't think any of this would take so long, you know." Bowie sighed, the expression in those eyes odd, disturbing, and gone.

He nodded. He understood from his argument with Sam that Bowie didn't know how to handle things. And knowing how was only one of several steps his lover was missing. He didn't know how this was going to go, but he knew he had to be honest. "It didn't have to, but the time went by and I...you didn't seem to need me here."

Bowie sighed softly and headed for the kitchen door, looking out. "I tried not to. Not in my heart, that needs all the time, but in the rest of me."

He waited, giving Bowie space to breathe, reading the tension in those tired shoulders. But they'd had enough space; what they had to do now was close it. He walked over and slid his hands along Bowie's hips. "Why?"

"Because I should be able to do this." Bowie's muscles were trembling under his hands.

That was hard for Bowie to say, he knew. But there was more that needed out before they were done, before he understood everything his lover needed, everything his boy needed. He hugged Bowie to his chest and rested his forehead against his lover's closely shaved head. "To do what, babe?"

"All of it, Bear. I didn't expect it to be so hard, the work. I didn't expect it to hurt so bad. I thought I could do it and come back to you. Convince you to try again, and I couldn't."

He lifted his head and swallowed around the ache in his chest. He'd expected Bowie to say something about not wanting to admit to needing him, but not all of that. Not anything like that. He'd had no idea.

He wasn't sure what to do with it either. There was a tough line there between wanting to help and making sure Bowie felt supported, not humiliated.

"We were supposed to do this together. You were never meant to do it alone; you might not have taken on the project if I hadn't been in it with you, right?"

"Yeah. I wanted you here. I know it was selfish, so I didn't say it, but you belonged here with me."

"Hey." He turned Bowie around to face him and made sure he got hold of those pale green eyes. "It wasn't selfish, babe, it was love. It was a promise I didn't keep. You just said it yourself, I belonged here. But I needed to know you still felt that way. I started to feel like maybe you didn't."

"I'm sorry. I didn't know what to do. I've never been in love before."

Those three sentences were the world—so simple, so honest, so raw, and Bowie gave them to him.

"I'm sorry too. I have, but not like this. I still got it wrong." He took a kiss, sliding his hands over Bowie's head, enjoying that feeling under his fingers.

Bowie leaned into him, heavy hand on the small of his back. "What happens now? Any ideas?"

He jumped on that, what happened next was what this was about. "Yeah. For starters, I turn down that promotion, and I move here."

Bowie searched his eyes, reading him so fast, and then that smile broke out. "Okay. I'll come and help you pack."

How he ever let himself live without that smile, he'd never know. "That would be great. Your brother will be happy to see you." His grin answered Bowie's. "He thinks we're a couple of dipshits."

"He might be right. Sam's pretty good at figuring shit out."

272 | JODI PAYNE & BA TORTUGA

"He is. Right, I mean. We deserve each other." He laughed. "And bacon. I deserve bacon."

"It's ready to cook. You want to go out to see the houses after? I was thinking fajitas for supper and hot tubbing in the rain."

Oh. Oh, hell yes. "Yes. Yes to all of it. Yes to anything you want." He felt a hundred times lighter all of a sudden, and he couldn't have hidden his grin if he wanted to.

The Allman Brothers came on the radio and he tugged Bowie into the kitchen, both of them singing at the top of their lungs as they started breakfast.

37

B owie found that there was nothing on earth more fun than walking with Gabe on the seawall, the rain barely falling, planning their Thanksgiving supper.

"I've never cooked a turkey, but we're pretty smart. We could put it on the smoker."

"I have cooked an entire Thanksgiving dinner, including the turkey, but I didn't smoke it, and that sounds better. We can make dressing in the oven instead."

"I like the snacky parts too—I was thinking stuffed jalapeños, maybe ranch dip and chips?"

"Stuffed jalapeños get my vote for sure. Butternut squash turnovers? Bacon-wrapped roasted chestnuts?" Gabe was having as much fun as he was and sounded ready to cook for a nonexistent crowd.

"I'm not sure we can find chestnuts. Butternut squash, yes." Bowie made a mental note. "We're buying pies?"

Gabe stopped and looked at him. "What? You can't make a pie?"

"Never tried. You?"

"Sure. Apple, blueberry, pumpkin. Never made pecan...

what did you want? I mean, we should be able to figure it out, right?"

"Fancy. I like pecan best, but we can have two." Sure. Like pie crust was just easy.

"How do you make your dressing? Are you the celery and onion type? The bits of sausage type?"

"Cornbread, celery, onion, bread, but I'm flexible. No oysters, please. I can't go there."

"Ooh. I've never had cornbread dressing. Let's make yours." Gabe poked him with an elbow and gave him a sidelong smile. "This is fun. Planning this. It sure beats going to a Halloween party alone."

"You aren't going to miss the big party that Sammy and Tommy are going to?" He was tickled shitless. They could goof off, watch football, eat. It sounded like heaven to him.

"Well, let me put it this way. I've been going to that potluck for five or six years. The first year, I went with my lover at the time. The last bunch I've gone alone. Going to a holiday party stag is a step above spending the holiday alone, but it still sucks. This year is going to be better than any of those."

"Yes. This year we will cook, drink beer, watch the ball games, laugh, and you might get a blowjob."

"Might, boy?" Gabe laughed. "No worries, I'm not opposed to strong-arming you into it."

Bowie snorted. Like Gabe had ever had to do that. Sucking his bear was one of his joys in life. He could totally play along, though. "I'd like to see you try."

"Oh, don't start that with me out here where I can't...you know. Oh, speaking of...because that made me think of our awesome beat-up couch...do you think I should get out of my lease? Or do we want to keep the apartment?"

"I don't know. I mean, I guess we need to figure out how

much time we're going to spend up there versus the cost of the apartment. It's just like buying houses—we've got options." They just needed to crunch numbers, figure out what they wanted, and weigh their options.

"Factor in whether we'll hurt Sammy's feelings if we don't stay with them when we're up there...because...no."

"Right." Apparently Sammy had thrown a bit of a temper tantrum all over Gabe at Mike's. Big enough that Sammy had called to apologize, even. "Well, are we talking about running up for a few weeks a year or a few months? Half a year?"

"Do you think we need more than a few weeks? I mean, we'll invite them here too, right? I don't have any attachment to the city, just the people in it."

"If we're talking a few weeks a year, then we need to let the apartment go. That's a huge amount of money that we can free up to travel, invest, do improvements, whathaveyou. We'll have the rentals available by Christmas, which is good, because we're booked in the other three. In fact, the original houses are booked from now until the end of summer, for the most part." Bowie waited to see Gabe's response; as far as he was concerned, they were a "we" now. All the way.

"Jesus. I'm definitely making that pie. I gotta start pulling my weight around here." He got a quick grin. "You want a smoking jacket and a cigar too, moneybanks?"

"I'm going to put you to work tomorrow. We've got to finish painting and start putting the furniture together. We have three floors of IKEA furniture in boxes."

"Jesus Christ. You mean I have to think? Where's your boy toy when we need him?"

He swatted Gabe's butt. "He'll be back mid-January hunting a job. He's a baby. You'll love him. You're into twinks, right?"

Gabe's eyes dragged over him from his toes up to his eyes. "Not anymore."

"No?" He couldn't have stopped his grin from growing, or his cock.

"Nope. I'm into searing hot retired Army Rangers with a knack for blowing shit up."

"I like it when you're in me, Bear."

Gabe looked at him, completely shameless. "I can get pretty lost there, babe. You feel like nothing I've ever known."

He reached out and squeezed Gabe's hand. "You ready to go home? Get dry and warm?"

"Yeah. I'm ready. You have an idea for dinner?"

"I haven't thought of it. You have a thought?"

"Rainy day food maybe. Soup? Tater tots?" Gabe grinned at him. "You for dessert. Or maybe an appetizer."

"Soup sounds good." Soup and tater tots even better. "We can take a shower first."

Gabe pulled him around to the deck once they got home. "My mom always made us take wet stuff off outside. Something about her floors."

"Did she?" His favorite part about this deck was the privacy. "We can put things right into the washer on our way in after."

"That's what I remember, yeah." Gabe pulled a damp T-shirt off and slipped out of a pair of long gym shorts.

Bowie stripped down, his eyes trailing over Gabe's strong body, the strong muscles, the heavy cock. "So fine," he muttered.

"Come on inside." Gabe picked up their clothing and dumped it into the washing machine as they went by. "I want to remind you how gorgeous you are."

He grabbed Gabe's ass, squeezed. "Damn, man. I love this—us in our house, naked."

"Yeah? We can just ban clothes in the house, then." Gabe laughed and headed upstairs giving him an even better view of that naked ass.

That was a better sight than squeezing together in the elevator. Score.

"I still can't believe I have a house. I can't believe it's on the beach. I'd have a hard time believing you actually existed if you didn't regularly remind me how solid you are."

"We have a house on the beach. You and me." He caught Gabe on the landing, gasping as their chilled bodies met.

"Mmm. Chilly?" Gabe fondled him, grinning. "I can warm you up."

"I bet you can." He opened his arms wide. "I'm willing and able, Bear, and I'm all yours."

"Yeah?" Gabe looked thoughtful and impish. "Where in the bedroom did you put the little box I got you? Why don't you pull that out?"

Bowie felt his body heat up. He'd been surprised to find the box in Gabe's backpack. More than surprised.

Stunned.

Excited and fucking over the moon, because that meant something—something that was uniquely theirs.

"I put it on the chest of drawers. It's a pretty box." And he liked to see it, waiting for them.

"It is, isn't it?" Gabe kissed him, steering him into the bedroom by the shoulders. "Gonna get out the fancy one."

A shudder went through him and goose bumps covered his arms. "Yeah?"

Gabe nodded. "And we'll get in that great big shower. Lie down, babe." Gabe gently guided him to the bed, then pulled the box off the dresser and other supplies from the nightstand. Bowie's body responded like there was a button and all Gabe had to do was touch it.

"God, look at you." Gabe sat beside him, watching him, silent for a long moment as he lay there, exposed, skin tingling. "When I left New York, I didn't know for sure how things would go between us, but I was hoping, you know? And I packed this box in my bag first, the very first thing, because I knew if things went the way I wanted them to—I knew we'd need it."

Gabe was touching him everywhere, speaking quietly from the heart. "Sammy reminded me of my responsibility to you as your Dom. I think that was my biggest mistake, not remembering that sooner. It was easy to make though, right? Because it's subtle with us, the line blurs all the time for me. Does it do that for you too?"

"I don't think there are lines. We're more than that. There's not a wire we can cut to disarm what we have. We're our own system. We have what we need." And he needed Gabe.

It took Gabe a second to decode that; he saw the wheels turning behind those dark eyes, but Bowie got the most amazing smile. "You're so right." He caught a flash of a cock ring as Gabe picked it up. "You don't really need this for the plug, I just like it. I like what it does to you."

"I do too. I like what you do to me." He loved that Gabe pushed him, that Gabe made him feel touched and taken. Hell, he got hard, thinking about Gabe's eyes as Gabe fucked his slit.

"I like this. This is ours. That's why I knew we'd need it, this trust. It's important." He felt the first few drops of cool lube on his prick, then Gabe lifted his plug out of the box and held it where he could get a good look at it.

Bowie bit his bottom lip, muffling his groan, and Gabe's smile widened, became wicked.

He watched as his bear ran the bottle of lube along the metal toy, slicking it for him. "Watch all you like, but don't forget to breathe, boy." That was said with a wink like a man who knew damn well he'd forget. The tip of the plug was cold as Gabe slowly ran it across his slit several times, warming the toy for him. "Tell me when you're ready."

"Oh, fuck…" He realized his hands were fisted, his teeth clenched in anticipation. He forced himself to open up, to relax. Breathe. God, he wanted. "Ready, Bear."

"Damn, I wish I could bottle this moment." Gabe took a breath, and there was a second of stillness as the room went quiet. Then Gabe gingerly pressed the very tip of the plug inside him, working it gently and letting him adjust.

"Please…it's so good." He felt Gabe in his fucking soul.

Gabe didn't give an answer—he didn't expect one. As a rule, his bear was quiet for this, listening and concentrating. But the plug slipped deeper under its own weight, stretching a little, and a little more as it went. His lips parted as his slit did, like it would help make room.

Bowie sucked in a deep breath and let it out with a raw groan.

As the toy sank deeper, Gabe carefully worked the head of his cock through the glans ring at the end and seated the arm that held the ring in place right where he could feel that too. Bear hummed low, fingers testing the fit and admiring.

He pushed up on his elbows, his abs tightening as he fucked Bear's fingers. He cried out as the touch disappeared.

"Pushy pushy," Gabe teased.

His bear closed the box and stood up to put it back on the dresser, then moved slowly around the room, putting things away, leaving him lying there to wait, to watch. Gabe's cock was full and heavy looking, and his lover wasn't shy about cradling it in thick fingers, stroking idly.

He groaned, tracing the ring that circled his cockhead, jostling the plug the barest bit.

"So beautiful." Gabe leaned over him, bracing one arm on the mattress, and kissed him, tongue gliding past his lips and along his tongue. Bowie sighed and let the kiss take him, melt him deep inside.

He felt Gabe's fingers lace into his along the stiff length of his cock and gently pulled them away, flattening his hand out on his thigh. "I said you could look. No touching," Gabe whispered against his lips.

"Bear..." Bowie whimpered, a jolt of excitement hitting him. He didn't think about it; he let himself get off on Gabe, on bowing to his bear's will.

"Good boy." Gabe took his hand again. "Come on. Shower."

They moved together into the bathroom, and Gabe turned the water on while he found fresh towels. Gabe steered him into the new walk-in shower first, following very close behind. Close enough he could feel Gabe's wood on the skin of his ass.

He hummed low and pressed back, rocking along Gabe nice and easy.

"Naughty boy," Gabe purred in his ear but did nothing to stop him moving. One hand reached around his hip and gave the top of his plug a nudge.

"Bear. Damn." He dropped his head against Gabe, his hips still moving. He felt that everywhere; it was a buzz he couldn't escape and one he didn't want to.

"Mmm. You." Gabe kissed his neck, ran a hot tongue over his shoulder, and shifted him away and under the shower spray. "So tomorrow I guess we'll go shopping for Thursday, hm? Get everything in the fridge so we can make a few things ahead and have time for football."

Was Gabe talking about shopping? What, now?

"Whatever you want." They had to go to the houses and make furniture and shit, but they could do that too. Later. Now they needed to focus.

"Please tell me you have an Allen wrench attachment for your drill, because those little IKEA L-shaped fuckers hurt my fat fingers. Plus, I drop them all the damn time." Gabe scrubbed shampoo into his scalp.

"You know I do." He leaned into Gabe's fingers, reaching to find Gabe's cock and pet it.

His bear laughed softly and shifted away. "Didn't I say look but don't touch, boy?"

"You didn't say anything about touching you, Bear."

"True. But I'm making us wait." Gabe rinsed the shampoo out of his hair and started washing his back, his shoulders, his ass.

"Our shower is perfect." No worries about falling, plenty of room.

"I love it. It is perfect, and it looks amazing too. You did such a good job and every time I look at it, I think about how you did it for me. For us. I can't wait to get to work tomorrow, I really want to help. I want to be involved, make up for lost time." Gabe turned him around and scrubbed his chest scratching fingers through the patch of hair there.

He stretched up tall, giving Gabe access to all of him. "I can't wait to show you, have you there with me."

"Wow, this is maybe the only way you really look taller than me." Gabe grinned at him. "I'm pretty sure you're taller, you just don't look it to me." Gabe scrubbed pits and hips and abs; then a hand moved behind his balls. He didn't think that was washing, though. Gabe pinched the skin, gently. "You ever thought about a ring here, boy?"

Bowie chuckled, hoping that it didn't sound too shocked. "No, but I'm not letting a stranger down there. You'd have to do it."

Gabe's dark eyes flashed like lightning over the ocean. "After Thanksgiving. We'll pick something out together. And I want some ink to go with yours. Where did you get this done?" Gabe leaned in and tasted his inked skin.

"There's a place here. His name is Skye. I told him about you. About how you're my bear." Gabe was going to love Skye—the man looked like a sprite or something. Someone fierce and spiritual and weird and wonderful.

"Yeah?" Gabe smiled and stroked him, slid a thumb over the length of metal plug nestled over his slit. "What did you tell him?"

"I—" He barked out a happy sound. "That I needed you. That you gave me so much." He'd been flying. He'd sat for eight hours and he'd been lost. Skye had listened without judgment.

Gabe kissed him, a warm, gentle kiss, then looked at him. "I love you. I'm going to try to say that more. When I should." Gabe smiled and traced the outline of his ink. "I want a storm. Rain and lightning, and waves crashing on the beach. What do you think?"

His prick jerked, just the slightest bit—not because of the storm, but because Gabe knew. "I think that would be... fucking magical."

"I think so too." Gabe traded places with him, ducking under the water. "Amazing how salty I feel just from walking on the sea wall. Does it rain a lot in winter here?"

"All the time." He found it comforting after all those years in the desert. "But we'll have good sunny days too."

Gabe shrugged. "I don't mind the rain. I'll take it over snow and ice any day." It didn't take long for Gabe to wash up, still not letting him touch, even to help.

He wasn't sure what Gabe's plan was, but he was trying to figure it out, follow along. He wasn't used to not knowing the plan. He always knew the plan.

Gabe hustled him out of the shower and he wrapped up in a towel, stomach growling. "Tater tots are definitely calling my name."

"Tater tots. Gabe?" What the hell did his bear want?

"To go with our soup?" Gabe grinned at him. "How does your ring feel? Is it too tight?" His lover reached over to test it for himself.

The heat and touch made him buck, and he rocked into Gabe's hand.

"Boy. I asked you a question." Gabe let him rock, his cock sliding against Gabe's palm. "I don't feel like we need safe words yet, but that means you have to tell me if something is wrong. How is that ring?"

"Good. Tight." His eyes crossed, but there was nothing he wouldn't give Gabe. "I like it."

"Me too. You're such a sight in it. But tell me if gets...too restrictive." Gabe's hand fell away, and his lover finished drying off, headed for the bedroom, and pulled on a loose pair of shorts. "You want to watch a movie?"

"I thought you were hungry?" He was beginning to growl a little, confused. He didn't do confused.

"We can't watch a movie and eat at the same time?" Gabe moved close and kissed him again. "It's okay, boy. I've got you. Put on some shorts if you want to. Or not."

"I'm not going to cook with my cock bobbing around like this." He stole another kiss, feeding his need.

His bear laughed, a full, pleased sound. "No, I guess that

would be weird." Gabe waited while he found something he could wear comfortably, but even loose sweats rubbed his prick just...well, right.

In the kitchen, Gabe got out a baking sheet for the tater tots. The man was actually serious.

He was going to growl, to bite Gabe and make him as crazy as he was. When Gabe bent to get the potatoes from the freezer, he bent and bit Gabe's butt.

Gabe yelped and jumped sideways. "What the...did you just...?" Bear leveled him with a look, just one twitch away from dissolving into giggles. "Boy. Bites count as touching."

"You have to be more clear about things, Bear." He managed not to crack a smile.

"Obviously." Gabe raised an eyebrow, and this time did grin. "Next time, you'll know. And you've just guaranteed yourself a next time."

"You think so, Bear?" He could just hump Gabe like a naughty puppy.

"I do." Gabe moved behind him, too close, brushing a hand over his ass. "Soup, hm? Get to work."

"I will bite you again." He hoped he left a mark.

"No, you won't. You're going to want to stay on my good side." Gabe was enjoying this way too much.

He grabbed two cans of tomato soup and started doctoring it so that it tasted good—hot sauce, cream, pepper.

Gabe stuck the tots in the oven and leaned against the counter, looking at him, then reached a hand out and stroked him through his sweats. "So how does the plug feel? Is it different when you move?"

"It's like...yes. It's different." That was easy enough.

He got a dark laugh. "Words are hard?" Bear didn't press, though, and let him leave it at that. "Beer?"

"No, thank you." He was high enough. "There's plenty in there for you, though."

"Are you trying to get me drunk so I'll be easy?" Gabe took a quick kiss and opened the fridge. "Might work."

"One beer won't even lube you up." He was lubed up, and the temptation to pump his cock was huge. He waited, though. He wanted to see how this played out. He wanted the explosion.

"And I can't have more than one, because my boy is in bondage." Gabe sipped his beer and gave him a smoldering look. "Of a kind."

"I want you." He knew it, Gabe knew it, but it seemed important to say it.

"Yeah." His bear reached for him and pulled him into a hard kiss with one heavy hand and let him go almost as quickly. "But you're going to have to wait."

He growled but stirred the soup before it stuck. Evil bastard. Wonderful evil bastard.

"That growl makes my balls ache. Just so you know." Gabe casually grabbed a hot pad and a spatula and stirred the tater tots around like they weren't playing this game at all. "How should I get my bike down here, do you think? Ride it? Ship it? Rent a truck? Maybe we should fly up and drive back."

"I've been thinking about that, Bear. We can drive up to the ranch and pick up my trailer and take a road trip, pick up the bike and the stuff in the apartment, then head home. I don't know if you need a truck of your own; we need to talk about that."

"Probably not if I have my bike." Gabe closed the oven. "What's the worst, I get a little wet sometimes? Maybe if gets really cold, but I can't imagine it's worse than...oh, but the wind off the water bites I bet, huh? Hm."

"My truck's in great shape, but you might need something that can haul shit." He shrugged; then he had a thought. "Or something cushy like that SUV we rented. That would make road-tripping easy, and we could haul a trailer."

That SUV had been nice on his hip.

Gabe grinned at him. "You know, I did like that beast of a thing. And if we found one we like off the lot, we could have it for this round trip we're about to make."

"I liked it too. A lot. Way more comfortable than my truck." He served up the soup, grabbing spoons.

"So...Black Friday car shopping?" Gabe plopped the tater tots in a bowl. "I'll call my landlord tomorrow and see about the lease. I'm sure it's too late to get out of December, but I bet I can break it for January."

"Sounds good." Bowie felt like crowing. Listen to them, having a life.

"I'm starved. No more skipping lunch for me. I burn too many damn calories lusting after you." Gabe winked at him and brought the bowl and his beer to the table.

"Uh-huh. You might have to have a cookie for the energy spent being a butthead."

Gabe snorted. "But a hot butthead."

Like he could argue with that. "Blistering." He paused and gave Gabe a long look. "And mine."

Gabe looked at him, everything that meant swirling behind those deep blue eyes, and gave him a slow nod without saying any of it. "Always."

He nodded. "Eat your soup, Bear. I'm dying over here."

Gabe grinned and picked up a spoon. "Are you? The whole thinking of ice cubes thing isn't working for you?"

"I thought it was baseball."

"Sno-cones?" Gabe picked up his beer and leaned a little closer. "Or maybe...thunder?"

"Hush." The rain was still coming down, and there was a chance for a boomer, wasn't there?

"Lightning? Wind?" Gabe sipped his beer.

"That would make me insane, Bear. Not even the ring could stop it."

"Oh, what are the chances?" Gabe looked out the window. "Probably slim, huh? Shame. If you're good, we'll make our own thunder. Like last time. Eventually." Gabe adjusted himself, grunting softly, and dug into his soup.

"Butthead." He ate, but only some. He wasn't hungry for soup.

Gabe ate his soup and popped tater tots and drank his beer, not in one bit of a hurry. His lover kept looking at him though, eyes roaming, smile just a little naughty.

Bowie finally gave up and put his food in the microwave for later and went to the deck. It was damn chilly out there, but the gulf looked amazing—rough and choppy and deep.

"Babe, it's freezing out here. Come back inside." Bear's arms slipped around his middle.

"It is." He surprised himself. "I was a million miles away."

"Watching the water?" Gabe slowly headed for the shelter of the house, pulling him along. "How do you feel?"

"I was getting growly, huh? But I'm ready to play again." He was ready to see where Gabe led him next.

"You're a big boy, Bowie; if you're not feeling it, you should tell me." Gabe kissed him behind his ear. That close, Bear's low tone was easy to hear, even with the sound of the waves trying to drown everything out. "I'm not the one with surgical steel in my cock."

"No, you're the one that put it in. I'm feeling it. I'm new

to this side of things, but I'm right here with you." And he wanted.

"Are you? Great. Give me a safe word." Gabe pulled him into the house and slid the door closed. "Let's find a boundary. See how you like it."

"Halt. I won't forget that. Ever." He couldn't. It was part of him.

"Halt. That's a good one. I won't hear that anywhere else these days for sure." Gabe kissed him lightly. "My worry is that ring. It shouldn't hurt, and it shouldn't get comfortable. Either one and you use that word, please."

"Fair enough. It doesn't hurt. It makes me want to jack off."

"Good. That's perfect. Now, grab a couple bottles of water and head upstairs, boy." Gabe gestured toward the stairs. "We'll clean up later."

He nodded, feeling off-balance, off-center, but curious and excited. Young. It made him feel young.

Gabe followed him up the stairs and took the water from him, setting the bottles on the dresser. "Let's try a couple of simple rules. First, let's see how you do addressing me as 'Sir.' " Gabe reached for him, hooking fingers in his waistband and dropping his sweats to the ground.

"I don't know, you and I worked for a living, Sir." He winked at Gabe, knowing his bear would get the joke.

"Smartasses get spanked." Gabe snorted and cupped a hand over one ass cheek. "I'm lifting the no-touching rule. The new rule is, you can't come without my permission. Be prepared for me to say no."

Thank God for the ring. "Yes, Sir."

He reached for Gabe the second his Bear's shorts came off, his hands desperate to touch even though it had only been an hour, two.

Gabe laughed and pulled him in. "Eager."

"Yes. God, yes." He laughed too and caught Gabe's lips in a kiss.

"No touching is the worst rule ever." Gabe stepped into him, backing him up, moving him toward the bed, grinning. "And that's God, yes, *Sir*."

"No touching sucks. And God, yes, Sir." He grabbed Gabe's ass and squeezed, hard.

"Watch it, I think I have a bruise where you bit me." Gabe reached out and gave him a strong shove, knocking him off-balance onto the bed and climbing right over him.

Bowie groaned at the sight of his lover covering him, and from the way his filled cock bounced against his belly. Lightning shot up his spine, and his balls drew up tight.

"Mine." Gabe kissed him, grunting and driving a stiff cock along his hip. "Want."

"Yours." He wrapped one hand around that perfect prick. "Tell me how you want me, Bear. I'm all yours."

Gabe's eyes narrowed. "Ride me."

"That would be my pleasure"—he paused for effect—"Sir."

"Oh, listen to you." Gabe rolled to the side and reached for the nightstand. "I'm going to make sure you take that seriously before we're done here."

"I do. I'm just playing with you."

"I know, boy. You'll be done playing in a bit." Gabe grinned at him and tossed him a rubber and the lube. "I'm looking forward to this."

"I am too." He rolled up and found his balance; then he leaned and sucked the tip of Gabe's cock, just because he could.

"Mmm." Gabe rolled flat on his back and stretched out like a cat in the sun. "Good boy."

He luxuriated in the suction, the flavor, letting Gabe have some love, some worship, before easing away to smooth the rubber on his bear. He got a long moan as his fingers slid along the length of Gabe's prick, and Gabe rolled up into his hand.

"Beautiful." Gabe made him ache, made him want to soar. This was insanity of the best kind.

"Thank you, boy. Let me see you, now." Gabe's eyes were half-lidded, and his breath already seemed shallow.

"Yes, Sir." He straddled Gabe's hips, rubbing his hole over the slick tip of his bear's cock.

"Oh, fuck." He could feel that Gabe's hips wanted to buck right up; everything tensed but his lover stayed in check, fingers desperately digging into his thighs hard enough to bruise.

He licked his lips, took the tip in, then stretched up to let Gabe pop free.

His bear gasped and curled up off the bed, fingers moving briefly to his hips where they fumbled and slipped on his skin. Gabe growled and grabbed his cock in a tight fist, thumb pressing on the plug.

"Bear!" He sank down, taking Gabe in a single, wild thrust. He could feel his muscles work Gabe's cock, but what he knew was that pressure at his prick.

Gabe shouted something he couldn't hear over his own cry, and collapsed into the pillows, eyes shut tight and taking hiccuping breaths. "Fuck, you're so—" Gabe moaned and rolled up under him.

Bowie braced himself on Gabe's chest, slamming back, riding that heavy prick like he was a rodeo man. He was going to drive his bear wild.

His lover managed to get the breathing under control but didn't get a grip on anything else. It was fun as hell to watch Bear try, though, big hands grasping, feet sliding in the sheets. Nothing was more beautiful, and he kept riding, keeping the rhythm up, grinding against his bear.

"Bowie." Gabe's voice sounded rough and dry, his name carried on a raspy breath. Then rough fingers found his cock again and circled gently around it, making him push through that fist as he moved.

"Yeah." He nodded, swallowing hard. "Yeah. Yeah, Bear. Beautiful motherfucker. Love you."

He was fucking babbling.

"Fucking close, babe. Jesus. So good." Gabe planted heels in the mattress and bucked, making him lose his leverage.

All Bowie could do was hold on and give Gabe what he needed. Gabe's hips fell back to the bed, and his bear shuddered and moaned, that long cock pulsing and jerking inside him.

Damn. Look at that fine bastard. He reached down, stroking Gabe's belly, nudging the tip of his filled cock, as he stole a kiss.

"You're gorgeous. You make me crazy. I love you," Gabe babbled at him between hard kisses and ragged breaths, hands running over his skin as if to make sure he was real.

This was how he could spend the rest of life. No problem.

"Damn." Gabe took a breath and smiled at him, snaking a hand between them, a hot palm searing the head of his cock.

He cried out, hips rolling forward as he fought to get more.

That made his bear's cock shift inside him and Gabe groaned, spent prick slipping free. That hand shifted to his shaft and started to stroke, a couple of good pumps and then a wide thumb slid over the plug again.

He bared his teeth, his eyes rolling at the rush of sensation.

"Good?" Gabe shifted, rolling him to the side, and got up to ditch the rubber, but came back quickly and stared at him, standing at the edge of the bed. "My beautiful boy."

That was wonderful and uncomfortable—all at the same time. He reached up, searching for a touch, and Bear took his hand, tangling their fingers.

Gabe sat on the bed, beside him, and the other hand reached out to grip him again. "What's the rule, boy?"

"Don't shoot without your word." He pushed up into those amazing fingers.

"Good boy." Gabe leaned over him and just like that, took the swollen head into his mouth.

His cry tangled in his chest, and all he could do was stare and feel, his legs drawing up in a wild rush.

Gabe was careful, easy on the suction, shifting the plug with a wicked tongue, fingers playing up and down his shaft.

Focus. Focus, man. Don't come.

He was in so much trouble.

Bear's fingers moved to the ring still in place around his balls and the base of his cock and jostled it. "Mmm. Oh, that's tight, boy."

"Mmhmm." *God, please. Touch me. It's all so fucking good.*

Gabe let it be and went back to stroking him, lazy and slow, but after a few strokes, that hand fell away. Instead, Gabe stretched out long beside him and went after his nipples, first with fingers and then with teeth, nibbling and pinching.

Bowie touched, but it wasn't soothing, not at all. In fact,

the more he touched Gabe, the more the ache in his balls made him want to beg.

"Irresistible." Gabe sat up on an elbow, leaned in and kissed him, cradling his head in one hand.

"Need you." He breathed into Gabe's mouth. "Please, Bear. Touch me."

"Please, *Sir*." Gabe traced his jaw with a thumb, lips still tasting him.

"Please, Sir. Please." He wasn't too proud to offer the honorific, just too caught up in wanting.

"Good boy." Bear hummed and reached out, petting him, following ridges and lines with one finger.

He spread, his balls trying to draw up, the ring pinching. He grabbed them, tugged, giving himself space.

"Not without my permission. You understand that means you can ask me for it? Though if you ask me just this moment, I'll say no." Bear closed his fingers around him and started to stroke, pumping slowly.

"Oh, sweet fuck." He flailed a second, then grabbed the headboard, the wood creaking. "I need you like breathing."

Gabe kissed him again. "You are my only reason, my love."

"Oh." He tackled Gabe, because that was the only way he knew to respond to something that made him feel so much.

"Whoa." Gabe laughed and held him, trading kisses. "Boy."

"Sir." He rubbed, losing himself in Gabe's mouth.

"How is that ring?" Bear traced it with a couple of fingers and arched, giving him more friction.

"Tight. Tight, but if you take it off, I'm gonna shoot."

"If I don't, you're going to hurt yourself. On your back,

boy." Gabe maneuvered him over. "You're going to have to dig deep for some self-control."

He groaned, but he didn't know. He ached, and Gabe was fucking crazy-making. "I'll try."

"That's all I can ask. Breathe. Breathe in, breathe out. I'll see if I can't ease the pressure off instead of opening the floodgates." Gabe winked and he felt the ring release. "Breathe."

He held Gabe's eyes and inhaled, filling his lungs and letting it center him. "I need to come, Sir."

He wasn't going to, but he needed to.

"Since that isn't a question, I assume you're good?" Gabe smiled at him, and he knew what that look was. Gabe was proud of him.

"Yes, Sir." For a bit. He hoped.

Gabe held the quick-release ring up where he could see it. "This was too tight. Don't let it get like that again." He got a kiss though, so Bear couldn't be that mad. "Now, I'm going to make you...not good."

Gabe went after the plug, adding pressure and releasing it. One leg drew up, and he cried out, warning Gabe that he was too close.

"Ask my permission or use your safe word." Gabe's voice was calm, but that touch didn't let up, Bear adding pressure and letting it release again. "One or the other, boy. Don't disappoint me. Ask or use your word."

God, he was confused. Totally. Which one did Gabe want? "Please. I need to come, Sir."

"Lovely. That was just perfect. But I'm going to say no." Gabe started stroking him. There was no way Bear didn't know how desperate he was.

He sat up halfway, gritting his teeth. He could feel his orgasm, right in the small of his back, too big to deny. If he asked again and Gabe said no, it wouldn't matter. "Halt, Bear. If you don't stop, I'm going to shoot."

He might shoot anyway.

Gabe smiled and kissed him. But didn't stop. "Good boy. Come for me."

Bowie blinked at his lover, making sure he heard what he heard.

"Oh, you are a good boy. Yes. You can shoot, babe. Let me see you. Right through that gorgeous plug." Gabe ran a thumb over the hollow metal, making it move inside him.

Bowie bit out a roar, his fucking bones rattling with his orgasm, the world tightening down to that sweet, deep burn.

"Fuck, yeah!" Gabe shouted with him, stroking him through it, kissing him between gulps of air.

The pleasure went on and on, everything in him just buzzing.

"Gorgeous. God, look at you. So beautiful." Gabe loved on him, touching and kissing him, right there, close where he could hold on.

"Love." That was the only word he had.

"Yeah, love you." Gabe pulled him in, tucked him against that broad chest. "I've got you, babe. Just rest. I'm right here."

"Right here." He moaned, his body melting as the sound escaped.

"That's right. We'll talk about how incredible this was when you wake up." Gabe's fingers slid over his head and settled on the back of his neck.

He nodded and let Gabe hold him, ease him into sleep.

38

It was obviously his turn to make breakfast, because despite all the work Bowie said they needed to get done today, it was after ten and his lover was still sleeping. Gabe wasn't shocked; Bowie woke up to pee in the middle of the night, and when Gabe took the opportunity to remove the plug, he accidentally started round two.

His own personal god of thunder was well used and worn out, and he was damn smug about it. He didn't care if Bowie slept all day long.

He made himself a cup of coffee, looking forward to moving his good coffeemaker from New York here, and watched the rain through the doors that led to the deck. It was a good thing what they needed to get done today was indoors, because it was really coming down.

They were talking about buying a car, which, okay, they'd bought two houses together already, sure. But they were really doing this. Here. Now. And he was looking forward to it.

Since he'd left the service, home for him had become

about the people he was with. Home really had been wherever his heart was happiest, and there was no question his heart was with Bowie now. He'd even say his heart was in the beach, and in their house too.

People were his only regret about the move. His team members were both still pretty broken, and he was actually a little worried about Sammy too, but he was only a text away, and it wasn't like Bowie would object to a visit to the city if he was needed.

Sammy had told him Bowie loved to go, loved to travel. It was going to be a whole new life.

One without shiftwork. One where he didn't have to save anyone, where the only emergency he had to deal with on a regular basis was running out of beer. And maybe once in a while his lover. He was pretty sure that was what people called living the dream.

He glanced up the stairs, wondering if maybe Bowie would be annoyed about not being woken up. They did have work to do, and as far as he was concerned, Bowie was the boss when it came to that work. He was quite capable, could take a project and run with it, but he was a much better worker bee than a foreman.

He decided he'd make a half-hearted effort to wake his lover, and if he ended up getting pulled back into bed instead, that would be just fine with him. He made a fresh cup of coffee for himself and one for Bowie, and headed upstairs.

Bowie's eyes cracked when he walked in. "Bear. Morning, you."

That smile broke like the sun through the clouds.

"Good morning. I brought you coffee." He set both mugs on the bedside table and bent to take a kiss.

"Good to me." Bowie drew him in and rasped him with his rapidly filling beard. "Want to head to the house today?"

The beard, the hair, Bowie's weight—his lover was looking healthier already, and he was determined to see that wild beachcomber of his again. He sat on the edge of the bed, grinning. "I do. IKEA furniture won't build itself."

"You know it. This is the last rush of busy before we start renting." Bowie rubbed one hand down along his arm, fingers digging in. "Then I'll take you to supper and we'll shop for turkey day."

"Sounds perfect." He lifted his arm and kissed the back of Bowie's hand. "I don't mind busy. I owe you some work, right?" Months of it.

"There's a sound system over there, man. We'll have tunes." Bowie turned his face and kissed him again. "I can't wait to show the house off."

He could trade kisses and laze around all day. He really could. "You better start by getting up. If you can move."

"Tell me about it. You make me ache like no one else. Ever." Bowie's grin was pure wicked joy. "My bear."

"Come on." He stood up, offering Bowie a hand. "Before I show you how much you make me want. Again."

"We'll have a whole long weekend to make each other hungry." Bowie grabbed his hand and stood, the motion not as smooth as it had been, but not bad.

He had some guilt about that, but he wasn't worried. Bowie needed rest, to be gentle to that leg for a bit, and he would make sure it happened. "I have an appointment with your artist, Skye, to get ink on Friday."

"You do?" Bowie blinked once, then tilted his head. "Can I come watch?"

"Yes," he answered immediately. No question. "When I

told him it was for you, he seemed to know what I needed. I'd love to have you there."

"I want to be there. I want you there if I have any more." Bowie began to dress, tugged on his old jeans.

He grinned. It had taken Bowie just the one huge tattoo with the right artist to get hooked. He had no doubt Bowie would go for more before long. He was looking forward to meeting Skye.

"Thank you for the coffee. You want to grab a half-dozen doughnuts on the way out?" Bowie tugged on a shirt that was literally held together by paint.

"Works for me." He shook his head, grinning at the outfit because it was so Bowie, and decided he could tear the shirt off his lover later, and they'd be rid of it.

"Car this weekend too?" He picked up his mug and took a big sip.

"Gonna be huge sales. Let's go for it. We can run into Houston, if we need to." Bowie grabbed him, kissed him hard enough to make his eyes cross. "Love you."

He blinked, feeling a little drunk on that kiss and the mood Bowie was in. "I love you too."

"Good. I'm glad. Come on, Bear. We got a great week in front of us. Huge."

"I'm in." He followed Bowie downstairs and stomped into his boots. His jeans were worn, but they weren't as beat-up or paint-splattered yet. He grinned. "I'm gonna have to try for that 'I work for a living' look."

"You mean your 'you don't work in a uniform' look."

"Yes. That." He drew a hand down Bowie's back. "Because I don't work in a uniform anymore, do I?"

"No, sir. Right now we're trying this together. Flipping houses, you and me." Bowie gave him a look that promised him the earth. "Come on. Get in the truck, and we'll get started."

Get in the truck. Yes, sir. He grinned and went right for the radio once he'd climbed in, finding something they could sing to on the drive.

39

They'd gone from Houston to Momma and Daddy's, where the parents had fawned over Gabe, and Momma had fed them biscuits and gravy while Daddy had helped hook up the trailer. Then Memphis, Nashville, Hershey. Gabe was a hell of a traveling buddy—Oreos, cherry Coke, Funyuns, and Slim Jims.

Hotel blowjobs.

Bowie thought, now that the apartment was emptied and the trailer parked in the garage at Tommy's, they could relax for a day before heading home, trekking another way, seeing different things.

Gabe had settled easily on the couch with Sammy like they lived there and was laid back in the cushions with an arm up, jeans pulled tight in all the right places. "Well, look at this."

"Oh, you thought one of these was for you? Well, all right." Tommy laughed, handing out beers to all, including Gabe.

"Ha!" Gabe's laugh rang against the high ceiling. "I appreciate your charity, sir."

Bowie sat on a dining room chair, searching for a comfortable place for his leg, feeling his muscles hum with a familiar burn.

Tommy looked at him, and a hand landed on his shoulder. "Can I get you some ice for the leg? Would that help?"

"I'm—" He started to say he was okay, but that ice would feel damn fine. "That would rock, brother. Thank you."

Tommy gave him a wink and headed off to the kitchen, returning with a couple of ice packs in a dish towel.

Gabe's dark eyes watched him. "Not much gets by Tommy."

"Not much." More than got by his bear. His bear watched him close.

"We were a little worried about you, Bowie, but you look good." Tommy pulled up a chair and sat with him.

"I'm fine. Solid." Happy as the proverbial pig in shit. Gabe made things right in a deep, satisfying way—from the sex to the work to their house to that storm tattoo that covered Gabe's skin.

Tommy nodded at him. "Solid. Good. Without a cane, I noticed, too. And if Gabe were any more smug, his chest would burst out of his shirt. I assume that's your doing?"

"Nope. That's the beach. It works for him." Of course, there was a helluva chance they'd see snow on the way home. That would be new.

"The beach." Gabe huffed and smiled at him. "Yeah, okay."

"Mmm. Salt air, hot sand. I'd believe it. Sam and I liked the beach. Didn't we, sweetheart?"

"We did. We might come in the spring to visit. We're going to stay in the city for the holidays and explore this year again. There's so much to see."

"You'd be welcome anytime. We haven't discussed the holidays yet. We did get an invitation from your parents..." Gabe gave Sammy a playfully horrified look.

Bowie chuckled, but he thought they'd stay home. Decorate their house, buy a tree, do all the silly area things. He had a ring for Gabe already. He liked the idea of a Christmas Eve proposal.

"Oh, how is Stephanie? How does Dan look? Sam's been wondering how honest she's been about him."

"They looked just fine to me. She stuffed me full of amazing food, and he told great stories. Aside from that godawful bed, it was a nice visit, don't you think, babe?"

"It was. Everything seemed normal. They're talking about taking a cruise after Christmas."

Sammy hooted. "I know! This is a great idea!"

"They seem convinced they won't have to save their money for grandkids, so they're gonna spend it up on themselves." Gabe grinned at Tommy. "Unless you're planning on having little Little Sammys."

"Right. I have my hands full with the one I've got, thanks. No bouncing baby Bowies for you?" Tommy shot right back, laughing.

"I raised all my kids in the service. No more." He'd lost all the family he was going to lose, dammit.

"You heard the man. We're good. And I have no interest in making the house baby proof." Gabe grinned at Thomas, then sent a wink in his direction. "Or PG."

"I hear you. You've done your time." Thomas gave his knee a pat. "So what changed your mind about visiting the parents? Last we talked about it, you both sounded completely uninterested."

"Yeah, that was a total miscommunication thing." Gabe looked at Sammy. "Honestly, the whole 'meet the parents' idea made me nervous at first, and Bowie is super sensitive to whatever I'm feeling, you know? So he got the vibe that I was worried about it, and he didn't want to push me on it."

Tommy shot Sammy a curious look. "Super sensitive?"

"He just knows." Gabe nodded, easily accepting that for what it was. "Instinct. Like...Spidey-sense. Anyway, we had to talk about it finally, because we needed to pick up the trailer, you know?" Gabe grinned at him. "Helps to actually talk sometimes, right?"

Bowie grinned over. "Possibly. We can take it on advisement."

Actually, working together had helped a lot with that. They both wanted to communicate, they wanted to make shit work, and they wanted each other, long-term.

"If you assholes haven't learned that lesson after our argument at Mike's—"

Gabe sat up abruptly, got Sammy in a headlock, and gave him a noogie on the head. "Shut up."

Bowie grabbed his phone and shot a picture. Someone would like that.

Sammy struggled, pushing on Gabe's arm. "Ow! Hey!"

"Gabriel." Tommy leaned forward in his chair, but the Dom wasn't upset, instead barely hiding a grin. "Let the boy go, please."

"Aw, man. You're no fun." Gabe let Sammy go. "You deserved that, turd."

"I had y'all's best interests at heart. Always."

Bowie didn't bother to argue. Sammy probably had. Didn't mean it was the little fucker's business.

"I know. I don't know about talking, but we sure learned we can't do the distance thing." Never again. They'd do whatever they had to do together. Gabe had worried and he'd gone wild. No more of that.

"I'm not fond of it myself. Sammy and I need to...well. We have needs." Tommy leaned back in his chair, draping one arm over the back and stretching out one leg. Had to be a show for Sammy. An invitation.

It must have worked, because Sammy untangled from Gabe and headed over. That freed up the couch next to his bear.

"Hop on over here, babe." Gabe watched him and held out a hand, but he knew Gabe wouldn't offer help in front of the boys. "When you guys visit, we'll show you the rentals. They're amazing."

"They are. They're booked for the holidays and March, though. Just so y'all know." And wasn't he proud of that? They'd lost one rental and gained four and a home.

"Think about us for April. That was a great time of year for a visit last time, right sweetheart?"

Gabe helped him settle into the couch just in time to see Sammy nod and kiss Tommy's chin.

"You tired after all that moving?" Gabe hooked an arm over his shoulders.

"Little sore."

Gabe settled the ice right where he needed it, and he groaned, his body tensing, before relaxing in a rush.

"Better. Tommy was going to take us to that steak place we like, but we could do Chinese or something and stay in if you want."

Sammy looked over at them. "Sure. We could stay in and watch a movie or something."

"It's up to you, man. Seriously. I know you want to go to Mike's and say good-bye, but we could go tomorrow." He would do whatever his bear needed. Then they were going home.

"I was thinking we should leave early tomorrow, you

know? Beat rush hour. Can you handle Mike's for a bit? We can cab over there."

He knew Bear was anxious to be home too. He could tell when they were packing, Gabe felt nothing for that apartment at all anymore. He remembered when he moved in, all the white walls, no furniture. Gabe had never really cared about that place to start with.

"Works for me. You have family there to say good-bye to." His family was here, and Bowie knew how to say good-bye to Sam.

"I do. And I am hoping to see my team too, they said they'd come by for a bit. Then I can be done with the city, right? It'll just be a place I visit after that. You guys still go to Mike's a lot?"

Tommy nodded. "We do. That lounge is truly ideal for us. Though we did have Thanksgiving with Clint at the club as usual."

He listened to his bear tell the boys all about their Thanksgiving weekend, Gabe sounding like a kid, all excited and proud. "Oh, and I got new ink!" Gabe hopped up off the couch to show it off, tugging that arm free of his T-shirt. "This artist is amazing, I know you have your own guy up by your folks, but you would love him, Sammy."

The ink still made him hard, just the sight of it. It was a huge storm rolling in off the ocean, the lightning splitting the sky, lighting up the clouds.

Tommy reached right out to touch it, physically turning Gabe a little for a better view and tracing one of the clouds with a curious finger. The tattoo covered one shoulder completely and continued in a sleeve down that arm to the elbow. "Just stunning, Gabe. Look at that, Sammy, the lightning."

"It's gorgeous. Seriously, Angel. It's exceptional work. Can I see yours, man? I haven't yet."

"Sure." Bowie tugged his shirt up, exposing his bear. It was fierce and wild and dark and all for them.

He heard the rumble in Gabe's chest, a little bit possessive, a little bit turned-on, totally unable to hide either. "It's so much better than in that picture, right?" Gabe was watching him. "Skye's gifted. It's great to have someone you trust so easy to get to."

"Yeah. Yeah, it was right, having him do our work." Skye was something special—wild and free and...connected. Bowie appreciated that.

Sammy took a closer look at his ink and gave him a smile and a nod before heading to Tommy. Gabe tugged his shirt back on and sank into the couch.

"That's your brother's first ink, you know that? All those years in the army and nothing. Pretty bold choice for a first dive."

Sammy grinned at him, chuckled. "I'd say I was surprised, but I'm not. Bowie is the king of bold choices. Did you do it in one sitting?"

Bowie dipped his chin. "I did."

"Stud."

Yeah. Yeah, he was. He'd needed something to hurt bad to begin to distract him from how his heart felt.

Gabe hooked fingers over his thigh and gave it a squeeze. "You ready to go get some dinner and a drink, stud?"

"I am. You think I need a clean shirt?" He was going to have a jacket on one way or the other.

"Yeah, I think we both do. I dropped our bag in the guest room." Gabe got up and offered him a hand.

"Good deal." He took Gabe's hand and hauled his ass up. "We'll be right back, y'all."

"Oh, no rush." Tommy's tone might have been a little dry, and Sammy chuckled.

"I don't know what they think we'd get up to in their guest room." Gabe followed him into the room and closed the door, snickering. "We do have a hotel room, right?"

"We do. The guys need their space, and we need a king bed." They were too big and liked to sprawl, even if they fell asleep with Gabe's hand in his hair, still.

"Cool." Gabe nodded, pulling shirts out of their duffel. "You were kind of hot showing off your ink, babe."

"Was I?" He chuckled softly, but that tickled the shit out of him. "It's a good piece of art."

It was his bear's art.

"I guess it was something you were doing more to get over me than for me. I love it, but I don't like to think about it that way." Gabe tugged his shirt down and kissed the back of his neck.

"No." He turned and met Gabe's eyes. "I got it because I needed to believe. I got the ink to remind me that I was yours and you were mine, no matter what."

Gabe swallowed and nodded. "Yeah. No matter what." His bear reached for him and pulled him into a tight hug. "Thank you."

He nuzzled in, daring to touch his lips to the mark on Gabe's throat, sucking a bit, deepening the color.

"Mmm. You're a naughty boy." He could feel Gabe grin, hear the play in that deep voice.

Yeah. That was him. Naughty. He chuckled and scraped his teeth over Gabe's skin, hard enough to sting. Gabe hissed, fingers digging into his spine.

"Okay. Okay." Bear guided him back a step, grinning like a fool and putting space between them. "Dinner. Mike's. Keep that thought for the hotel."

'Dinner. Mike's. Hot sex at the hotel. Got it." Best of all? Tomorrow they were heading home. Together.

For good.

How fucking glorious was that?

40

"Jingle Bells, Jingle Bells, jingle all the way!" Gabe sang his way through the kitchen, setting a Bloody Mary down on the counter next to Bowie. "Cocktail? God, that smells so good."

He was high on their week off and looking forward to the first Christmas Eve dinner he'd really cared about in years. And he really did care about this one. They'd spent half the day in the kitchen, cooking, and the other half singing and putting the last of the decorations on the tree, which he was just about to declare finished.

"Oh, that looks festive." Bowie looked happy and relaxed in his sweat shirt and shorts. His own personal beach bum. "You want to check that jalapeño popper dip? I think it's damn near done."

"Oh, yeah. On it." He grabbed a spoon and gave it a stir. "Tree looks good. I don't think there's a blank spot left between the ones we bought and the ones in that box your mother sent us."

"I sent a bunch to Sammy too. Goofy redneck shit from the Walmart."

Gabe had come to learn that Bowie's position on Christmas was *more* is more. The entire goddamn house could be seen from space. There were lights. Inflatable things, rocking things, singing things. There was an entire side of fence dedicated to the troops overseas, along with no fewer than three sleighs, an entire herd of reindeer, and a mailbox that told stories and promised to get letters to the North Pole.

It was all good. His lover was making up for lost time. Once Bowie enlisted, that was the end of traditional—and light-up, blinky, kitschy—Christmas. He was happy to have fun, happy to blind the neighbors and not be the least bit ashamed of it.

And he did like their inflatable half-naked Santa in the bathtub with the little rubber duckie. Something about the way Rudolph looked on and carried Santa's towel made the whole thing seem a little wicked.

"I bet Tommy loved the ornaments." He chuckled and sipped his drink, then tasted the dip for the poppers. It was totally done. He pulled the pot off, popped a top on it, and set it aside on a trivet.

"I think Sammy is teaching him a little about Christmas. James had issues." Bowie obviously did not approve of how James and Thomas had spent the holidays away from home.

"They sure enjoyed the last two." They used to invite him sometime that week for dinner, but they disappeared for the holiday itself. They were making their own traditions, just like he and Bowie were now. He'd spent his on his own for a bunch of years, but he had traditions too. He liked to haul out the movies on Christmas Day, and he was hoping Bowie would too.

"Good. That's the point. Fun. Joy. Hope. Love and shit.

We have to wear the Grinch pants Momma sent and take a picture at some point."

He actually didn't hate the Grinch pants, but he was shocked she found ones in their size. "Tomorrow. Tonight we're busy. Tomorrow we can wear them and watch the Grinch at the same time." He laughed. *Love and shit.* He really did love this guy.

"Works for me." Bowie wrapped one arm around his waist and held him, thumb drawing lazy circles.

"You like the holiday movies?" He leaned. "That's how I usually spend Christmas. *It's a Wonderful Life*, popcorn, and eggnog."

"I love them—*White Christmas*, *Scrooged*, *Elf*. You name it, I'll watch it."

"Oh, we are going to have a good day." He took a kiss. Movies, so they could snuggle and pretend for a bit that it was cold and snowy out despite their shorts and flip-flops. "I should whip the potatoes."

Time in the kitchen with Bowie would never ever get old.

"They can wait a second. Come out to the deck?"

"Sure. What's up? Do we have another board loose?"

"Nah. It's solid." Bowie led him outside, the back porch like a rainbow unicorn sneezed lights everywhere. "Come sit a second."

They plopped down on their chairs, Bowie bringing his around to face him instead of the ocean.

Whoa.

"Sit?" He started to ask what was wrong but hesitated before it actually came out of his mouth. He'd been watching his lover all day; they were fine. He was in a great mood, and Bowie was crazy happy. "Why am I sitting, babe?"

"Because I'm going to ask you to marry me, and I wanted to do it out here without you falling down."

He laughed and shook his head. "Yeah, okay. Because you're going to ask—"

Well...hang on.

That didn't look like a face that was making a joke.

Jesus Christ, he was glad he was sitting down.

"You to marry me." Bowie pulled a ring out of his pocket —the thing solid and gold and simple. "Will you marry me, Bear?"

He stared at the ring. Just *stared* at it. Not like it was going to bite him, or like he wasn't going to say yes—of course he was going to say yes—but because it was this magical, meaningful thing, and he wasn't sure it wouldn't disappear in a puff of purple smoke if he looked away.

The house, the beach, the ink, the car...the ring. This was a hell of a ride.

He did look away from it finally, to smile at his lover. What did it matter if it disappeared? It wouldn't change a damn thing. "I will. Yes, I will."

Then he felt his cheeks heat up and he clasped his hands together in his lap to stop them from shaking.

"Thank God." Bowie leaned forward and kissed him, lips so soft and gentle that it was almost too much. "Give me your hand, huh? I want you to wear my ring."

Those were words he'd never, ever even considered he would hear. Never. Not for one second. He put his hand in Bowie's, not worried that it was still trembling, Bowie would understand. But it actually got better as soon as Bowie gave it a squeeze. If he smiled any harder, he was going to hurt himself.

The ring went on like a dream, the metal already warm,

the fit perfect. Bowie's smile grew wider, those eyes just catching the Christmas lights. "It fits."

He held his hand between them where they could both see it. "It's just right. It's perfect. And look at you." That smile. He reached out and took Bowie's face in his hands. "This is a crazy surprise, babe. I love you."

"I love you, Bear."

He leaned closer and offered Bowie a kiss instead of taking it, giving his lover this moment.

Bowie's hand landed on his thigh; then their lips met, the kiss going deep, dizzying. *Oh.* Oh, that was...amazing.

Bowie was his; he loved to think about that, let it straighten out his spine. He didn't think all that often about how completely he belonged to Bowie, but he was right now. It was the truth.

He had a ring to prove it.

"Today is a ten," he whispered against Bowie's lips.

"Yes, Sir." Bowie winked. "And we haven't even had supper yet."

ENJOYED ANGEL AND BOWIE? COME MEET CYRUS AND DEX!

Interested in learning more about BA's cowboys and Jodi's gentlemen? Want free fiction and news? Join our newsletters!

What's Up with Jodi
http://bit.ly/whatsupjodi

Spurs and Shifters
https://lp.constantcontact.com/su/A9CRUzp/baandjulia

Hey, y'all!

We want to thank you for giving The Soldier and the Angel a try.

If you can spare a few minutes to post a review at the retail website where you made your purchase, we'd very much appreciate it!

Don't forget to "like" our Facebook pages and groups to keep up with all the news--new releases, sales announcements, giveaways, sneak peeks-- and of course the rodeo pictures, coffee memes and just general fun. We'd love to have all y'all!

Yeehaw and thanks for reading!

BA & Jodi

The Cowboy and the Dom Series

Book One: First Rodeo

Book Two: Razor's Edge

Book Three: No Ghosts

FIRST RODEO

When a killer strikes, Texan and former rodeo cowboy, Sam O'Reilly, loses his older brother. Unbeknownst to Sam, James was also the lover and sub of a sophisticated New York City Dom named Thomas Ward. Sam comes to the city determined to stay until he can bring the murderer to his own brand of justice, while Thomas' more ordered mind is hoping for a legal solution. Neither man expects their connection to the other, but having each lost someone irreplaceable, their hearts are crying out for comfort almost as loudly as their bodies are screaming for each other.

Some yearnings refuse to be ignored, but transcending their differences to explore the fragile connection between them will prove to be a steep a hill to climb--the first of many. As Sam and Thomas take the first tentative steps on the rocky path that might lead to a relationship, the killer steps out of the shadows...And this time, his sights are set on Sam.

Note to our readers: Each of the three books in The Cowboy and the Dom Series has a fully realized, romantic ending. However, the overarching suspense element will leave readers on a cliffhanger after books one and two, to be fully resolved in book three.

RAZOR'S EDGE

Razor blades left by a murderer continue to remind Sam and Thomas of James, the man they lost to violence... whose killer is still out there and seems to be watching them constantly, biding his time.

Meanwhile, their carefully built relationship also teeters on the edge of a knife. Sam's efforts to be the kind of full-time sub he thinks Thomas wants fail miserably, and Thomas must accept the fact that Sam is unique and his lover's needs don't lend themselves to the typical high protocol BDSM lifestyle. They contend with jealousy, confusion, arguments and stress, and when communication starts to break down, they struggle to reconcile their massive differences and learn what it means to be a them.

An emotional misunderstanding might be the last straw--or the opportunity the killer has been waiting for to take Sam out of Thomas's life once and for all.

Note to our readers: Each of the three books in The Cowboy and the Dom Series has a fully realized, romantic ending. However, the overarching suspense element will leave readers on a cliffhanger after books one and two, to be fully resolved in book three. Readers should begin the series with book one, First Rodeo.

NO GHOSTS

Months after James's brutal murder, Sam gets an opportunity to help Thomas find closure. That means leaving New York City to travel to the O'Reilly's Texas home, to meet Sam's parents and get a taste of how and where the O'Reilly brothers grew up.

Their vacation is also an opportunity for Thomas and Sam to

move beyond the past, drop their remaining baggage, and finally solidify their tumultuous relationship.

But that may be easier said than done given that Thomas has a secret he's been keeping from Sam, and Sam is sick and tired of everyone in his life knowing what's going on but him. It's the worst time for their trust to break down, because their final confrontation with James's killer looms, and if they're going to walk away, they'll have to do it together.

Note to our readers: Each of the three books in The Cowboy and the Dom Series has a fully realized, romantic ending. However, the overarching suspense element will leave readers on a cliffhanger after books one and two, to be fully resolved in book three (this book). Readers should begin the series with book one, First Rodeo.

ABOUT JODI

JODI takes herself way too seriously and has been known to randomly break out in song. Her men are imperfect but genuine, stubborn but likable, often kinky, and frequently their own worst enemies. They are characters you can't help but fall in love with while they stumble along the path to their happily ever after. For those looking to get on her good side, Jodi's addictions include nonfat lattes, Malbec and tequila any way you pour it.

Website: jodipayne.net
Newsletter: http://bit.ly/whatsupjodi
All Jodi's Social Links: linktr.ee/jodipayne

ABOUT BA

Texan to the bone and an unrepentant Daddy's Girl, BA Tortuga spends her days with her basset hounds, getting tattooed, texting her grandbabies, and eating Mexican food. When she's not doing that, she's writing. She spends her days off watching rodeo, knitting and surfing Pinterest in the name of research. BA's personal saviors include her wife, Julia Talbot, her best friends, and coffee. Lots of coffee. Really good coffee.

Having written everything from fist-fighting rednecks to hard-core cowboys to werewolves, BA does her damnedest to tell the stories of her heart, which was raised in Northeast Texas, but has heard the call of the high desert and lives in the Sandias. With books ranging from hard-hitting romance, to fiery ménages, to the most traditional of love stories, BA refuses to be pigeon-holed by anyone but the voices in her head, insisting her cowboys get their happily ever afters.

AVAILABLE FROM JODI & BA

The Collaborations Series

Refraction

Syncopation

East Meets Westerns

(single titles)

Heart of a Redneck

Wrecked

Land of Enchantment

Window Dressing

Flying Blind

Special Delivery, A Wrecked Holiday Novel

The Cowboy and the Dom Trilogy

First Rodeo, Book One

Razor's Edge, Book Two

No Ghosts, Book Three

The Soldier and the Angel

The Triskelion Series

Breaking the Rules

Les's Bar Series

Just Dex